Set in the dus‌ the 1960's, a group of friends finds themselves coming of age in a world spinning out of control. A nuclear standoff with the eastern world, an unpopular war in Asia, religious wars in the Middle East, racial tensions, and a growing chasm between ideologies created a generation ripe with the belief that change, to the point of social revolution, was imminent and necessary.

The quest for a more sane world becomes a journey unto itself, for better or for worse, traveling the less traveled roads to unforeseen adventures spiked by sex, psychedelics and the passionate desire for freedom.

Those who can handle liberation dance with those who cannot, and when fate tolls its bells for the world to hear, some hear Heaven, while others hear the slamming of a jailhouse door.

Reverb

AN ODYSSEY

Joe Ely

ISBN 978-0-9914648-4-5
Library of Congress 2014949504

Published in 2014 by LettersAt3amPress:
6923 Indiana Avenue #266
Lubbock, TX, 79413
E-address: editor@3amproductions.org

Publisher/Editors: Jazmin Aminian, Michael Ventura
Editor-at-Large: Rebekah J. Morton
Word Captain: Martha "Marty" McKenzie
Cover Art and text layout design: Joe Ely
Cover Design: Seth Teeters, Matthew Eskey

We gratefully acknowledge the support of
Deborah Milosevich and the late Elvira Bain.

LettersAt3amPress

"It started out like a ballad," Joe Ely told me. It
ended up as Reverb, a quest-novel in the tradition of
Knut Hamsun's Hunger and Henry Miller's Tropic
of Capricorn, the odyssey of a young artist who
may not yet know he's an artist and who sets out
to explore a dangerous world—a very dangerous
world—with no resource but his sense of wonder
as he searches for what? He doesn't know; his
desperate hope is that he'll know it if he finds it.

This young seeker is the son of "pioneers who came
seeking freedom and found so much of it that they
couldn't handle it." He lives in Lubbock, Texas, a
town that exists "in a normal state of static chaos."
It's the so-called "Summer of Love," and thousands
of people his age are being drafted to kill and die
in Viet Nam while thousands protest, get high, and
make fairly certain that, for better and worse,
the country will never be the same.

I know no novel that captures the underside of that
summer with the immediacy of Joe Ely's Reverb.

—Michael Ventura

Reverb

AN ODYSSEY

CHAPTER 1

Gene felt the tear of the tendon in his teeth. His jaw pressed harder against the ear. He shook his head like a dog trying to pull meat from a stubborn bone. He could feel Smallwood's tiny hand inching toward his gun. The whirling red lights pulsed like helicopter blades along the surface of the parking lot. The gravel dug into his elbow and cut channels into his flesh. He used his elbow as a fulcrum to hold Smallwood away from his weapon. The warmth of blood sprayed into his nose as he felt his knuckle pop against the jaw of Smallwood. He felt a strange guilt come over his body. He had never expected a physical confrontation to come between him and Smallwood. He rose from the parking lot like a drunk on a dance floor. His friends were standing in front of their cars shining their headlights on the scene. They raised their beers high and toasted Gene as he found Smallwood's gun and threw it into a dog-infested backyard on 35th Street. The adrenaline started in his forehead and rushed through his heart to his feet. He saw before his eyes no obstacles nor did his senses perceive any physical barriers between him and freedom. Red lights were now coming from all directions, flashing the walls of sleeping houses with sabers of quick color and the many sirens overlapped with howls like those of a pack of wolves. Gene bounced off of tin trashcans, over fences and through random yards, diving and ducking, feeling for a clue in the pitch-dark night for a safe haven that might shelter him until morning...

The morning wind at Earle's house banged the screen door against the weathered frame with a rhythm like that of a mad horse, kicking and twisting, going this way and that, as if unsure whether the passageway led to freedom or confinement. The TV in the front room was tuned to The Price Is Right with people laughing and making deals, while a radio played The Eve of Destruction in the back room. The swamp cooler shook the back wall with a rumble that added an element of doom to the everyday household soundtrack. In back of the house, the dust blew through the crooked trellis causing it to heave like a landlocked sail imprisoned in a godforsaken landscape.

Earle poured a glass of milk and, when he put it to his lips, old memories erupted from down deep and lodged in the back of his throat. Since his father had died a few years ago, he had taken refuge in sound. When certain situations set off poundings inside his chest, he could only put them to rest by scratching out some restless ode, transporting himself away from the mausoleum his home had become. He picked up a pencil from the table and, on the back of his mother's latest doctor's prescription, wrote:

Let the Dead Wake Up!
I Know they're sleeping
Trapped between Barrenness
And the green Prison moat

Let the Dead Wake Up!
And coffee come scorch their throat
Why turn away, O Dead One?
Is Life too Heavy to Float?

Let the Dead Wake Up!
Let the Dead Wake Up!
Let the Dead Wake Up!

And the Dying...
And the Dying...
And the Dying...

Maggie, Earle's mother, called out faintly for her
medicine from the far side of the house.

Earle had already left through the torn screen door,
letting the slam blend in with the TV and the
rattling of the rusty brackets that held the
swamp cooler in place. The Allstate 125 motorbike, dozing under the Sycamore, awoke with
a single crank, and rolled a tattoo between
the west wall of the add-on garage and the unknown neighbor's bedroom. It let go a screech
of burned rubber that chased it out into Boston
Avenue and lost it a block down.

Sergeant Ryan Baylock sat in the Hi-D-Ho parking
lot scanning his radio, sipping a cherry lime
and admiring, on the front seat of his squad car,
the powerful sheen of his blue .45.

Three blocks down, Chicken Box Jimmy opened the
back door of his restaurant, closed his eyes,
sighed, and said a prayer asking for strength.
His head pounded as he calculated his poker
losses from the night before at Ringo Tom's. He
dreaded the impending weekend rush but added
to his prayer that he make lots of money to pay
his debts so that he might play again tonight.

Gene Holiday awoke face down on a wooden floor in
a razor-thin shaft of sun with the taste of blood
in his mouth. He tried to reconstruct the particulars of each cut and bruise from the previous
night, but an alcoholic lack of detail left him
with nothing but an empty, bleeding head.

Ringo Tom counted his poker winnings by his Bar-
B-Q pit, pausing to glance across the street as
the employees arrived at Chicken Box Jimmy's
restaurant. He spoke and laughed, although no
one was in the room.

Dumb-ass, chicken dippin' bastard.

Maggie looked across her dusty kitchen windowsill
and, catching just a blur of Earle's red Allstate

125, confirmed to herself that her life was blowing away just like so much dust in the wind.

Sgt. Baylock started his Plymouth squad car and cruised slowly down the alley behind the Chicken Box hoping that any minute now Gene Holiday would show up for work.

Earle turned off of Boston and on to 34th Street daydreaming of the Spanish Fandango piece he was learning at Dunagan's School of Steel Guitar and how it reminded him of the opposite of his present condition.

Lance, the fearless, woke up at Betty and Bill's to Ray Charles singing Crying Time. He shuddered to remember it was the same song playing on the Christmas morning when his father shot himself in the back yard. The song had played again later that night when his mother hung herself in the bathroom while all the family had come over to their house drinking and mourning. He opened a beer and lit a smoke as Betty came in, hungover as all hell, and told him for the millionth time that Ray Charles was responsible for his parents' death.

Lance glared at her and told her to shut the fuck up, called her a dumb bitch and asked what the fuck did she know? He picked up the phone and called his girlfriend, KC, and spent fifteen minutes calling her a whore and a slut. As the conversation progressed he carefully turned it around, telling her how wrong he was and what a bastard he had been. Before long he was telling her how much he loved her and couldn't live without her and would she please come over and give him a ride to Pete's Pool Hall? And would she maybe spot him a few bucks to play with?

Sgt. Baylock's Plymouth squad car appeared when Earle turned into the alley behind the Chicken Box. There was no way to avoid the imminent confrontation. Baylock stopped his car, blocking the alley, and walked up to Earle in that slow, bowlegged, stiff arms-too-far-out-from-his-side, John Wayne sort of way. Earle half expected him to ask the same question that he always asked, about whether he had five dollars in his pocket, and, if he did not, did he know about the comprehensive vagrancy laws in the state of Texas? And, did he know that he, as a sanctioned officer of the law, could take a preacher out of a pulpit or a pilot out of a cockpit and book him on the charge of misdemeanor vagrancy? Earle braced and was ready to tell Mr. Baylock that, as a matter of fact, he had almost twelve dollars in his pocket, a consequence of having a steady part-time job at the Chicken Box, but, curiously, Sgt. Baylock did not ask his usual question.

I'm sure you heard what happened last night and I was just kinda wonderin' if you were a witness?

Earle shuffled gravel into two piles with his boots and spoke still looking down.

> No, sir, what is it that you're refer-ring to?

> Seems your co-conspirator Mr. Holi-day attacked Sergeant Smallwood in the Hi-D-Ho parking lot and bit off a piece of his ear. Your friends just stood and watched...

Earle looked up.

> What d'ya mean co-conspirator? I ain't got any co-conspirator. Me and Gene cook chicken together—

> Like I said.

> Mr. Baylock, you know exactly where I was. Playin' up on that flatbed. You were there too. You seen us.

> Earlier, yeah.

> Across the street.

> Where?

> The opening of the A&W. You were circling the parking lot.

> That was way earlier.

Earle knew where Baylock was going with his inter-
rogation but he had been across the street when
it all went down. He reminded Sgt. Baylock
with a laugh,

> What about when the owner got on
> the microphone, all drunked up, and
> cussed out all his customers? What
> about that? You were right there.
> What about when he told 'em all to
> leave his premises and to all go to
> hell?

> This was after that.

> Well, I suppose I was tearin' down
> and packin' up 'n stuff. I got stuff to
> do. Besides, I work for a livin'.

Earle had, in fact, arrived at the Hi-D-Ho parking
lot right after the fracas, while every one was
looking for the piece of Smallwood's ear. Gene's
friends had given the account of him hightail-
ing it toward Betty and Bill's with a swarm of
red flashing lights spinning around the parking lot looking for a direction to head.

> If there's something you're not tell-
> ing me, I guess you know tamperin'
> with evidence is a crime in the state
> of Texas?

> Yessir, Mr. Baylock. I ain't tamperin'.

What are you, just barely 18? You got
your whole life ahead 'a you. Don't be
a fool, Earle.

I ain't.

And one more thing.

What's that?

Get a haircut.

Baylock walked back to his squad car. He u-turned
and headed off in the direction of Pete's Pool
Hall, scattering gravel and dust. As the hard,
steady wind brought everything back to its normal state of static chaos, Earle exhaled a breath
of relief. Lately Baylock had used the vagrancy
clause to throw him in jail every other time he
had seen him.

Gene crawled to the door, opened it, crawled down
one step and dry-heaved for several minutes
before looking up and seeing Strictland's green
'55 Nomad in the backyard of his crash-place.
He realized for the first time where it was he'd
spent the night.

Damned idiot, he said to himself.

Maggie made her way to the kitchen and boiled some
coffee. While it was making she collected an

armful of pill bottles from the medicine cabinet and laid out her morning ration on the green Formica table.

Chicken Box Jimmy held four chicken legs upside down in each hand, one between each finger, first dipping them in flour, then batter, then flour, then, right before he dropped them in the scalding grease, he dropped four back in the flour so that he could reach for the batter-covered telephone.

> Gene. What? Gene. Damnit, Gene. They'll be a hun'rd people in here soon as church is out.

Gene got right to the point.

> I think I pulled a double-ought fuck up last night, and they ain't much I can do but sail outta Lubbock. I'll call Shears to fill in for me till I git it fixed up. If you see Smallwood or Baylock don't tell 'em I called or nothin'.

Jimmy shook his head.

> I seen Smallwood over at the vacuum cleaner shop early this mornin'. Had a bandage clean around his head. Now, Gene, you didn't have nothin' to do with that did you?

Gene avoided the question.

Tell Earle I had to hock his amplifier
to get gas money and it's downtown
at Huber's and the ticket's at his bass
players house, that guy named—oh
shit, I can't remember his name.
Just tell 'im I'll send some dough as
soon as I get some. I'm sorry, Jimmy,
guess I drank too much potato juice.

Damn, Gene, I'll swear. You do have
a knack. It ain't gonna do no good to
run, may as well face the music. I'll
help with your bail, just come on back
and I'll call my law—Gene, goddam-
nit, Gene, don't you dare hang up on
my ass, Gene, you son-of...

Earle walked in the back door just as Jimmy slammed
the phone, sending batter crackling in the hot
grease and yelling that he was going to kill him,
the sorry-assed son-of-a-bitch he'd helped too
many times get out of a fix, when he should've
let him rot in the county jail years ago, and
then he'd be in Huntsville now, out of his hair.

Must've been Gene, Earle said.

I'm gonna kill him. Boil the son-of-a-
bitch in oil.

Wasn't exactly Gene's fault. I heard
Smallwood's been harassin' him for
weeks. Somethin' was bound to give.

Son-of-a-bitch! Son-of-a-bitch! What'd
he do?

Bit off a chunk of Smallwood's ear.

Holy— !

Squad cars buzzin' the Hi-D-Ho like
mad hornets with Gene on foot. Gone.

This ain't too good.

Ain't good at all. I just seen Baylock
out back. He had that determined
look in his eye. The whole damned
infantry's on his trail.

Just what I need, Baylock buzzin'
this place while everybody's gettin'
outta Sunday school.

Ain't good.

Gene said to tell you that he hocked
your amp downtown at Huber's. Left
the pawn ticket over at your bass
player's.

Earle looked down into the pit of bobbing chicken
parts rolling in oil.

Shit, why'd he do that?

Gas money.

Gas money? Where's he goin', Cuba?

Jimmy changed the subject.

Why in tarnation did God make weekends follow weekdays? I need help.

Earle waited a breath or two.

Think I could draw some 'a what I got comin'? I need my amp, I got a gig tonight. Damn, that pisses me off.

Chicken Box Jimmy grudgingly went to the cash register and got two twenties for Earle. All his employees knew his heart was much bigger than the hard-ass front he portrayed to the public.

Gracias, said Earle.

I'm always paying someone's pawn ticket. Someday I'm gonna start a fuckin' pawnshop.

You'd for sure go broke—and that's a compliment.

Earle walked out through the tiny kitchen past Miguel slicing mounds of potatoes into French fry strips. He was glad that he had been able to cut down his hours since his band had gotten a steady gig at the KoKo. He tiptoed around the potato peelings and slid out the greasy back-door to his motor scooter. He wracked back on the starter crank and felt the winds of freedom come over his body when the engine came to life. He wheeled down the alley and across the Hi-D-Ho parking lot. He saw KC driving Lance around to the back of Pete's but decided not to get tangled up in that particular mess at the moment. Baylock was bound to head there next, and he had little desire to see Baylock again. Besides, he had to track down Gene's pawn ticket to get his amp out of hock. No telling where that was.

He sputtered down the alley to the parking lot of the Seahorse Swimming Pool where he parked his Allstate and found an A&W Root Beer flyer pinned to the fence by the wind. He wrote on the back:

> Let the Dead Wake Up!
> Walking and Talking
> In Slobber and Drool
> Talking and Walking
> The Wise Man with the Fool

Sgt. Baylock turned up the alley, creeping in the direction of the pool hall. When he saw Earle hunched over the gas tank of his scooter, writing, he slowed even more and watched until Earle looked up. He almost said something but looked away instead with a disgusted shrug and one of his I-know-what-you're-doing shakes of the head. Earle's heartbeat quickened as did the tempo of his writing.

World Brain Wrestlers
Freight train Trestlers
Car Hops and
Traffic Cops
With Faces contorted
In a Plea to the Dead
Set their Tattoos
Loose on the Highway
Give them Tongues
That Speak the Truth
Let the Dead Wake Up!

Let the Dead Wake Up!
And the Dying!
And the Dying!
And the Dying...

He looked around at the Lubbock landscape. The wind was blowing harder now, churning up the dust and turning the sky into sandpaper. As the dust chaffed the air, it created static electricity and he could feel it steal around his body like a snake, irritating him into a manic state. It made the hair on his body stand up and his eyes dry out and it made his skin feel as if there was something underneath that moved of its own will. He was writing like a madman trying to hold the paper against the gas tank with all his fingers outstretched except for the thumb and forefinger that held his pencil. The smell of chlorinated water from the Seahorse pool struck Earle as oddly surreal in this parched, Martian sandstorm. The wind was crashing through the sunbaked Chinese elm trees and sounded like what an avalanche might sound like if it were gaseous and pliant and able to swoosh around in many places at once. This nudged him to write.

In the Avalanche Journal
The words of the Dead
Tell of Events
That will never be Read

While Down Main
Walk the Bones of the Dead
Brittle from the Heat
Rattled by the Breath of the Dead

Let the Dead Wake Up!
And the Dying!
And the Dying!
And the Dying!

Lance walked into the back door of Pete's Pool Hall with a cocky swagger and stopped at the snooker table where Scotty Chanteaux and Lester, the poet hustler, were playing golf for five dollars a pocket.

You can't make jack-shit, Scotty, and
I got twenty that says so.

Beat it, lightweight, this is a man's
contest.

Then how come your girlfriend keeps
callin' me?

Fuck you, piss ant.

Scotty missed his shot in the corner pocket, leaving
Les an easy run, making the game—which had
taken an hour up till then—have an absurdly
quick ending.

Pete yelled out if Gene was there and someone said
that he was not.

Sgt. Baylock came in the front door with a hint of a
smirk on his face like he knew something that
everyone else knew but they didn't know that
he knew they knew.

Got a warrant, Baylock? said Pete.

Social visit.

Want a table?

Baylock ignored the question.

Seen Gene?

Don't expect to.

The sergeant barked across the room.

Lance!

Yessir, Mr. Baylock.

Where's Gene?

Swimmin' the Panama Canal, prob'ly.

A couple of muffled chuckles slipped out.

Dj'you know that by watchin' last
night made you an accessory?

We weren't watching, we was drinkin'.

More suppressed chuckles rumbled the dead air.

You're on pretty thin ice, smart-ass.
One more screw-up an' you're makin'
license plates.

You ain't got nothin' on none of us.

Baylock froze and gave Lance the snake-eye. He waited several seconds before he spoke.

More'n you could ever think. More'n
you could ever know.

Scotty cracked the balls on the back table after what
seemed like a week of silence. Everyone had
been glued to Baylock's words while pretending
to study the layout of the balls on the pool table.
Pete asked Baylock a question.

You gonna buy anything?

Baylock replied.

You're housin' a lousy bunch here.
Not a keeper in the pack.

Pete was quick.

'Least they paid.

Baylock, smiling arrogantly, looked at Pete then around the room ever so slowly. He then opened the door, stopped halfway, adjusted his gun belt, and dramatically spun away.

Earle's band, The TwiLites, were playing that night at the KoKo Club, a Polynesian-style private club next door to the KoKo Inn and in the basement of the KoKo Palace. Old alcoholic men roamed like vultures, dressed in country-club-meets-car-salesman garb, trying to pick up alcoholic widows who wore outfits from Dunlaps inspired by chain-smoking alcoholic divorcees. Earle preferred the Music Box and the Linger Longer where the college kids hung out. The KoKo paid halfway decent and it was better than washing dishes at the Chicken Box, but it made him want to leave this sad town to see if everywhere was as haywire as this.

Earle drove over to Gary Bass's house, where the band rehearsed, and was surprised to find the pawn ticket stuck in the screen door at the front entrance of Gary's house.

Gary's mother came to the door in a cloud of L&M smoke and asked who the guy was that came to the door all scabby and left the envelope in the screen.

Some guy I used to work with, how come?

She gave a quick glance up and down the street.

Just wonderin'.

Gary drove Earle down to Huber's Pawn and Gun Shop to un-hock his amp. The smell of new leather in Huber's sent him back in time to his father's side at the old used clothing store, the Disabled American Veterans Thrift Shop. Earle had worked each summer by his father's side selling clothes to the migrant workers. They came to Lubbock by the thousands in beat up old trucks to plant, chop, and pick the sea of cotton upon which West Texas floated. Every day at lunch Earle and his father would eat at Chandler's cafe and stop by Huber's to pay their regards. The walls of the pawn shop were covered with accordions and guitars and fresh-oiled cowboy boots and chaps from Monterey and Juarez. In the back were saddles, bridles and Mexican spurs in the shape of every star imaginable. In glass display cases nearby were rows of black and blue and chrome pistols and knives that gleamed like revenge under the blue fluorescent light. Serapes, holsters and boxes of bullets were stacked to the ceiling on an array of coffee tables, and the combined scene gave Huber's the aura of a weird cultural fortress, maybe even a museum, that reflected the hidden psyche of Lubbock much more than did the public museum at Texas Tech.

Earle gave Hernando the pawn ticket and the two
twenties he'd been advanced from Chicken Box
Jimmy. Hernando leaned over the counter and
looked around to make sure no one was within
earshot. He spoke to Earle.

Man, Gene looked bad, d'y'know
where he's at?

Earle knew that Baylock came to Huber's every morning looking for stolen goods and that Hernando,
while maintaining publicly that he couldn't
stand anyone with a badge, was fairly well
known as a double agent.

Cuba's what I heard, whispered Earle.

Hernando pulled Earle's Super Reverb amplifier out
from under the counter and chinged the cash
register, giving Earle one dollar and fifty cents
in change.

I keep everything muy confidential,
said Hernando.

Claro, vato, you bet.

They rattled away on patched brick streets down
Broadway and then out Avenue Q to the KoKo
Club. They descended the stairs into a progres-
sively twisted interpretation of what Polynesia
might look like in the mind of a truck mechanic
who'd never been out of metropolitan Muleshoe
and who was prone to migraine headaches.

Tiny, all 280 pounds of him, was setting up his drums by a plastic palm tree under a black light, whistling Fever and watching a drunk woman try to get up from her table that was covered with drink umbrellas that she had used to keep up with her bar tab.

The owner, Mr. Jim, came in dressed in a white shirt with a white silk tie and a blue blazer with gold buttons. He walked up to the bandstand, his suntanned skin looking burned and blue in the color-warped ultraviolet light that defined the stage area.

Gotta gig for you guys. Don't pay great but the publicity will be killer.

Not Jimmy Reed again, I hope, said Tiny.

Only two weeks before they had opened the show for Jimmy Reed until he got drunk and fell off his bus at the back door and was out cold the rest of the night.

Nope, Ace Cannon.

And what if he don't show, then what?

The band remembered that Mr. Jim, who promoted the show, had asked the TwiLites, in a panic, to play another set to cover for Jimmy Reed as the audience became more and more hostile, but, wisely, the band not only said no, but split out the dark kitchen door of the KoKo Palace without so much as a wave. Mr. Jim said,

Ace Cannon ain't Jimmy Reed.

Tiny replied.

Nobody is.

Nobody is what?

Nobody is.

Gene rode low in the driver's seat of Strictland's Nomad south down Avenue U to 82nd Street then west to the Slaton Highway and on to Farm Road 400 then north to the Idalou highway, circling the town to avoid the collective wrath of the Lubbock police force who, on this most perfect and gorgeous of Sunday mornings, were by now worked up into a froth usually reserved for bank robbers, serial killers or university students.

Thirty minutes later Gene descended down the Caprock past Crosbyton, driving by the roadside park at Silver Falls, remembering the day long ago when his family stopped for a picnic and saw the water moccasin sliver across the steps that led to the breaks under the highway bridge. He had wanted to chase the snake and kill it but his father said that, usually, killing snakes was not the best action to take because there would be more down the line and they could somehow sense a snake-killer in their midst. In a way he was now like that snake, being chased from all sides. He thought about his present condition—running from the law—his miserable hangover headache, and wondered, for a brief second, where it was he was going and what he was going to do when he got there. He decided that this decision was not totally up to him, though he couldn't really tell at the time who else would influence his future. The past is fiction and the future is dreams, he told himself, and let it go at that.

He drove and drove, letting the highway cleanse his thoughts, flashing now and again on sights and smells that tossed him ten or twenty years in a single instant: the smell of crude oil, an irrigated cotton field, a feed lot. He drove past the Four-Sixes Ranch and the shape of the white letters against the red barn set off a memory of his great-grandmother whom he had not seen since he was four. He remembered his family telling the tale of how the ranch was won in a poker game, four sixes beating a full house. As he drove, time began to vanish and a pleasurable feeling replaced his misery for a short while. For a moment he wondered how this windy end of the earth had been created and even thought briefly about his idea of God until he told himself he shouldn't be thinking about things that he didn't know anything about. An instant later a sparrow miscalculated and whonked against Gene's windshield, sending him brutally back into his personal, no-good present.

Lance led the pack of seven Allstate 125's into Charlie Dern's barren front yard. Charlie was on the concrete slab porch smoking and teasing his dog. The sun was setting behind the Frito truck that was parked in his driveway. Charlie had older cousins that worked with his dad at the Frito factory who would go to the Strip and buy beer for his friends. Charlie knew what Lance wanted.

Darrell ain't here.

Where's he at?

Baylock took him in.

What for?

Questionin'.

About Smallwood?

I reckon.

Charlie flicked his cigarette into the driveway and watched the wind carry it down the street. Lance went on.

Gene's gone.

Where to?

He's took Strickland's Nomad. Hocked Earle's amp.

Earle's amplifier?

Gatherin' resources.

He'll be gatherin' rocks if they find
his ass.

Ray Beetle's '55 Chevy pulled up to the curb and Beetle
leaned his head out and before he could yell over
the roar of his cam-crazed engine Charlie said,

Everybody's askin' the same thing
and no, we ain't.

He's got—

Yeah, Strictland's Nomad.

Chicken Box Jimmy wants to kill him.

Baylock want to chili powder his ass.

Dumb fucker.

The sun was setting in Gene's rearview mirror as he
saw the endless row of honky-tonks through the
jagged neon that framed each side of the Jacksboro highway. He pulled in to the Pig Stand and
sat in the rear booth facing the wall and ordered a Pig Hip, onion rings and two Falstaffs.

Earle's brother Mark came in late from summer
school and turned on the TV to Augie Doggie.

The gnarly sound of the dog's cartoon voice irritated Maggie to such a degree that she called
Doctor Black and set up an appointment for
next Monday.

Earle skidded his Allstate 125 all the way from the
sidewalk to the sycamore tree by the path to
the back door. He cut the engine and sat staring
in silence at the English ivy that grew, silent
and malicious, prying the brick and siding off
the front of his house a fingernail's thickness
at a time and wondered, in twenty years' time,
what would become of it all.

He thought of those who came when there was only
land and sky. He thought about the pioneers
who came seeking freedom and found so much
of it that they couldn't handle it. He thought
about his granddad Morgan who had arrived
on the high plains sixty years earlier and who
had probably thought the same thoughts while
watching the dust blow everything away that
was not nailed down. Of course old Jefferson
Napoleon had survived nine straight years
of drought during the Great Dust Bowl of the
'thirties, and seemed to have come away from it
with the absolute certainty that some day, somewhere, all the dust would settle back to earth.

Something about the way the juniper trees rubbed
against the ivy shifted his thoughts to his great-
grandfather Sullivan. His brutal Irish wit bewildered the adults and charmed the children.
He created havoc with his light-heartedness and
was the talk of family reunions from Dalhart to
Little Rock. He was known to sip from a flask
(*gasp!*) and sing Irish songs with the children

for hours at a time. Somehow he seemed to be immune from all things dreary and/or boring. He survived all the curses from each side of the family and lived to be 98 years old. He mocked self-righteousness and self-pity in any form or fashion. He had that eternal sparkle in his eyes that revealed to some his fully realized nature. To others, the sparkle was a mirror that reflected back to them their own wretched being.

Earle wondered what kind of blind faith would lead all those nameless pioneers to expose themselves and their loved ones to life in the vast West Texas uncertainty. He thought about how the eyes of the old people seemed to always be gazing over the edge of the horizon.

He wrote on the inside of a matchbook:

> Children bend to pick the flowers
> And so prepare for worlds to come
> Old men stand still and shield their eyes
> To the faint horizon and beyond...

Maggie yelled that the macaroni and cheese was getting cold.

Just as he was about to go inside, a new Buick pulled up to the curb and honked. It was Patricia Loney. Patricia was his clandestine girlfriend with whom he was madly in love, but he feared her Corvair-driving, Winston-smoking, crazy ex-boyfriend. He had told Earle in so many words that he would kill him if he ever saw him so much as glance at Patricia again. Up until then Earle had only experienced brief pleasures of infatuation, and had never been in a situation where love could cost him his life.

But there she was, parked at his curb, beautiful, sweet-smelling and seductive, a teenage siren calling him over to her new Buick with her sultry eyes and naughty grin. It took all of two seconds for Earle to reason that love was worth any price, even death, and so he parked his scooter and sauntered over to her car.

I've missed you, she whispered.

I've missed you, too.

I want to make you melt again.

Patricia, you can't keep stringing me and Dan on like this. He wants to kill me.

We've broken up. For good this time.

As of when?

As of yesterday.

Broken up how?

I'll never see him again.

You said that before.

This time it's forever.

Can I come by tonight after the KoKo?

Be super quiet.

I'll park down the block.

They looked long and deep into each other's eyes, as several eternities passed. Maggie yelled that his food was getting cold.

Coming!

Patricia whispered.

Earle?

Huh?

Believe me....

His knees were disappearing.

I do.

Earle watched her sparkling Buick drive off into the red sky as if this were a scene in a movie where the rich girl defied her family and society to venture into the shanty side of town driven by passion and justice. He watched until the last red of her taillight went behind the last lilac bush. Then, just in that second when she disappeared, he felt a strange sinking feeling as if he had entered into another world, unconnected to his own, where he didn't know the rules nor did he know anyone who did.

Maggie had the plates set on the coffee table in the living room where Bonanza was roaring out of the TV and filling the room with large tan cowboy people with operatic voices.

> Hoss is from Tahoka, said Maggie.
> He was born there.

> I've heard that somewhere before, said Earle.

He had had this conversation with his mother dozens of times before. He couldn't figure out if she actually didn't remember telling him that fact every week or if she was simply trying to glorify the town of Tahoka by reiterating that it had a mystical connection to TV land. On the other hand, maybe she was justifying Bonanza because it had the good sense to feature an upstanding West Texas actor and *that* in itself was merit enough not to miss a single episode.

The salmon croquettes were especially good that night, thought Earle. He liked the soft little bones that came packed in the cans of salmon. He liked tuna fish, as well. His uncle from California had once said that people in Lubbock thought all fish came in a can except for catfish, perch and carp. They came from under the dam at Buffalo Lake.

There was a huge bowl of Kraft Macaroni and Cheese that vanished into thin air after a couple of times around the table. A crown of cherry Jell-O encrusted with marshmallows did the same. Every Friday since his dad had died the dinner had been the same, a sort of desperate stab at a family tradition.

At least their family was back together. The first couple of years after Earle Sr. died, everything took a dive into chaos. The thrift store was in immediate jeopardy. Granddad Morgan came to Lubbock to try and keep it open. Bob the Turk worked as much as he could and some of the Mexican guys from Huber's came down whenever they could to help load bales of clothes onto the flatbed truck. Bill and Ruth, longtime employees, lent a part-time hand even though the chance of being paid was next to none. Earle and Mark had come down everyday after school to pitch in, but as Maggie slipped deeper into depression it was decided to let the store go and to put her in the sanitarium at Big Spring. Carthel volunteered to keep Mark in Amarillo and Granddad Morgan took Earle with him to Houston.

After Bonanza there was a news story about burning draft cards that got Earle's attention. The escalation of the war was getting everyone's attention. Some of his older friends had joined the Army and some had been drafted and shipped to Viet Nam.

Maggie had seen one of her brothers disappear in a submarine in World War II and now Carthel's son was missing in Viet Nam. She was openly verbal about the draft

> They'll have to send the whole platoon over here to take any son of mine, draft or no draft. My family gave enough in the last war. Besides this ain't even *our* war, this is *their* war.

Mother...

Well it ain't. Lyndon Johnson
politick'd his way into office and now
he thinks he can politick his way out
of this war. Them people over there
don't care. They don't just bluff like
they do here. They shoot to kill.

Mark ran to Earle and gave him a hug.

Don't go join the Army, or if you do,
join the Navy, like Daddy.

I ain't joinin' nothin', little brother,
until I figure out what's goin' on over
there.

Mark had barely known his daddy. Life ain't fair.
Earle wished he could be closer to Mark but
there was eight years difference in their ages.
Besides, trying to stay in school and keep his
afternoon job at the Chicken Box, as well as
playing all night at the joints, kept him working all the time. He was merely trying to keep
everyone's head above the water in a slowly
sinking ship.

Earle put on his band outfit, the pale blue, collarless
coat with the emblem of a black cat stitched
over the pocket; tied his skinny black satin tie
and strapped his Telecaster case over his shoulder. He then asked Maggie if he could take the
car so he wouldn't have to ride his scooter late

at night. She told him that the back seat had a 50 pound bag of carrots in it and would he bring it into the kitchen before he left?

Betty and Bill went on their nightly run to the Strip, stopping first at The Chicken Box to see if there was any news of Gene, and, since there was none, bought an extra case of beer. They went back to their house and did what they always did: they put on Ray Charles singing I Can't Stop Loving You and opened a round of beers.

When Lance and Glen and John Silo came over that night they found Bill crying in the living room and Betty crying in the kitchen surrounded by a platoon of empties. The phone rang and Bill asked Betty to pick it up.

Honey, get that.

Wha'smatter with *you*?

Just git it, damnit, honey...

Betty picked up the phone and let go a shriek.

Gene! Hey everybody, it's Gene! Turn that damn hi-fi down! Gene—

The phone was barely audible over the din. Betty tried to swap her beer hand with her phone hand and dropped the phone in the process. When she reached down to pick it up she lost her balance and slid to the floor, pulling the phone chord out of the wall but, miraculously, not spilling a drop of beer.

The rest of the house came running in the kitchen only to find Betty sprawled out on the floor tangled in telephone wires.

Gene, Gene—

Lemme talk to him—

Where's he at?

Gene....

Lance saw the frayed wires at the wall and told Betty she might as well give it up. This advice did not register in Betty's drunken state and she continued to yell for Gene to answer. Bill opened up the phone jack with a kitchen knife and wiggled it around in the tangle of colored wires. A fountain of sparks blew from the outlet and a hefty jolt of current sent him backwards into the kitchen table. The party watched as every beer rolled off the table in slow motion. As they hit the floor, they exploded around him like alcoholic mortar shells.

Lance called both of them dumbass son-of-a-bitches and turned over the table into the cupboard, adding dishes and silverware to the broken glass and debris piling up on the floor. He then kicked Bill in the ribs for spilling his beer. Bill curled up in a ball and begged him to stop. Betty was screaming at the top of her lungs for Lance to get the hell out of the kitchen. Lance

was breaking everything in sight, yelling how
she screwed up everything that she touched.
Ray Charles was now singing *Take these chains
from my heart and set me free.* Lance then went
for the hi-fi and tried to pull the record off the
spindle when around the corner came Betty
with wild, watery eyes, her housecoat wide
open, wielding a butcher knife raised above her
head and screaming in a drunken slur.

F'you s'much's'touch Ray Charles I'll
slice y'r ass up for ant bait.

Lance dropped the record and ran, pulling cushions
and knocking over chairs behind him. He and
John and Glen raced for the door and, with a
foot through the screen, ripped the hinges from
the flimsy door. They ran into the still, cool,
starlit Lubbock night and leaped into John's old
Ford. They fired up the engine and burned rubber all the way down 37th Street from Elgin to
Flint as lights turned on in their rearview mirror like sparks from a bottle rocket.

Gene chuckled to himself as he hung up the phone in
an outer-Fort Worth honky-tonk. Same ol' Betty and Bill he thought. He had a sudden longing
to be there with them, sharing a good ol' Nean-
derthal evening with his old friends. A shudder
of fear followed and ran through his body. He
knew Baylock was on his trail. But when the
waitress brought him a Southern Comfort on
the rocks he was distracted by her uptown cow-
girl cockiness and his fear receded quickly.

You look like you been shoveled over
into the ugly pile.

Thank you, sweetheart, for nurse'n
me up with this medicine.

Gene held the whiskey up to the light and looked
through the amber glass. The waitress acknowledged Gene's gratitude.

That's my job.

As the sweet whiskey warmed his throat he thought
to himself that he might get along pretty good
in this town, after all.

Back in Lubbock, Earle pulled up into the parking
lot at the KoKo Club, turned off his headlights,
turned on his dome light and tried to take up
were he'd left off this afternoon.

Let the Dead Wake Up
Snoozey Dead, Siesta Dead
Dead who—

A hard knock on his window drove his heart into his
throat. It was Tiny. Earle cracked his window.

We're on.

Damn, don't people even think, Earle thought to himself and folded up his flyer. Did everybody have
to put up with so many distractions? Of course

they did. Everyone driven by passion suffers from the attention that passion itself generates. His favorite guitar player, Don Bagget, had revealed this to him while showing him how to play two songs at the same time. He told him that he practiced playing the guitar by using the commotion that surrounded him.

The more the better, he said. Just listen for the rhythm, find the key, then jam along with it.

Mr. Jim was frowning and checking his watch when the band reached the stage and began the set with a rousing but safe version of Linda Lou. The dance floor quickly filled with people stepping all over each other. Earle recognized most of the people in the audience: Nicky, the gas station heiress widow; Pinkie, the bootlegger entrepreneur; Willard, his mother's insurance man; J.C., the owner of the Caravan Club, and dozens of familiar faces with no names. They played Summertime, Walk Don't Run, Nightlife, and Fever before taking a break. He saw Sgt. Baylock peek in between the palms apparently looking for Gene. Surely he didn't think Gene would be that stupid. Nicky, the gas station heiress, came over and sat in Earle's lap, her words smelling like a fuel spill.

D'y'all know Mishty?

Earle swaggered, mockingly.

What keysh'it in?

She gave Earle a dirty look and stared at him for several seconds till her eyes started to cross when suddenly she reached up and pulled one of her breasts out of her low-cut dress.

You wanna kish it?

Earle looked around, embarrassed, in a silent but desperate plea for help. Mr. Jim had been watching the situation from the beginning and was already there.

> You two-timin' me again, Nicky? he joked. I can't leave you alone for a second without you runnin' off with another man.

> I'm jusht makin' a requesht.

> These boys'll do whatever you want. You're our biggest customer.

He raised his eyebrows to Earle.

> 'Bout time y'all started up again, ain't it?

> Yeah, sh'bout time, slurred Nicky.

I'm sick of this crap, Earle thought to himself. Their band had been playing here twice a week for two months now and the novelty was gone. They had played Amarillo, Plainview and Clovis, so why the hell were they stuck in the KoKo week after week? He closed his eyes and saw every

event of his life that had lured him to this moment. It was better than washing dishes, but
not that much better. Surely Wally Bear and Jo
Don felt the same way. Earle decided then and
there to leave this town of sleepwalkers and to
go out into the world in search of a place where
people celebrated for other reasons than just
for getting drunk and tossing aside their dig-
nity. Why couldn't people intoxicate themselves
with ideas of beauty and meaning instead of
burying everything in some forgotten recess
of their guilt bin? What was the matter with
being drunk with love? Why escape from the
very thing you desire? If people never showed
their emotions in day-to-day life why was it so
easy for them to show their ugly ass after a few
drinks? Well, Earle thought, that's easy to say
right now but what about the times when your
friends had to pull you out of the trees? Aren't
you being a bit of a hypocrite?

The band must have had a break equally as bizarre
as Earle's. They walked onto the stage from
opposite ends of the club, strapped on their instruments and broke into a furious version of
Long Tall Sally. Everybody was playing with a
rage not normally witnessed within the sedat-
ed walls of the KoKo. Earle was singing with
a vengeance. Jo Don and Wally were wailing,
their guitars in sync with Gary's bass. Tiny was
beating the drums into oblivion. This is what
heaven is all about, thought Earle, and as he
looked around the bandstand all the guys were
smiling. The audience was staring from their
tables in horror and not a soul came on to the

dance floor. We must be doing something right, thought Earle, maybe we've found our deal...

Across town in the tiny back room of Ringo's Bar-B-Q, Chicken Box Jimmy bet his last fifteen dollars on two pair, jacks and eights. Ringo Tom easily beat him with three nines. Jimmy called him a lucky son-of-a-bitch and excused himself, saying he had a family to go to unlike some poor bastards he knew who slept on cases of whiskey bottles. Ringo Tom replied that with the money he made off of Jimmy that night he could buy a couple more cases of nice warm whiskey bottles. Jimmy went out the back door, slammed it and sprayed gravel around the parking lot, fishtailing away from the very weakness that he nourished so well.

Three hundred miles to the east, Gene was closing down the Bloody Bull, primed and ready. He followed the bartender and the cocky waitress to the Cellar Club and listened to the American Blues play a set. He bided his time, shooting the bull with the bartenders and bouncers before venturing to a ranch west of town. They stayed up till sunrise, laughing and drinking, all the while talking about drinking and laughing as if the world and its pleasures might last forever....

Lance and Glen and John were wobbling in the middle of a cottonfield, sharing a hot Coors and watching the final race between Ray Beetle and Mickey Schott. Mickey had just put a 348 in his '59 Chevy Hardtop and it sounded like a well-oiled, open-geared cotton gin. Of course Beetle never told anyone what he had in his car because he didn't figure it was anyone's business to know. It rumbled low and mean as if there was something inside its inanimate being that was evil, something troubling and wild, threatening anyone nearby. The kids, even the drunk ones, kept their distance from Beetle's '55 either out of respect or fear or both. No one was able to let their gaze linger on its ominous metal skin for more than a couple of seconds. It created an unspeakable emotion not guided by logic or reason. It was like a voodoo doll wrapped in a metal skin. The idea of an engine with such latent power created an anxiety full of fear and fervor. On this sparkling clear night the full moon was bleeding its milkiness over the chrome bumpers and grill lips, creating odd-shaped torches to reflect its flaws in the baby-sized hubcaps that floated in the center of Beetle's perfectly polished wheels.

In the first race, the ragtag bunch of onlookers unanimously raised the opinion that Mickey had jumped the gun. In the second race some idiot had spilled beer in the left lane. No one had said anything about it until Beetle hit the puddle and his rear wheels lost all traction. By the third race both machines and drivers were pissed off and ready to race.

98th Street was an old farm-to-market road that had been recently blacktopped. It had been discovered recently as an alternative road to the Strip from Ropesville and Levelland. It was perfectly suited to be a drag strip with its new asphalt and perfectly level surface. With nothing but cotton fields on all sides, it served as an unobstructed lookout zone where a lawman could be spotted from miles away. It had been said that on the High Plains a person could see for fifty miles in every direction, and if that person were to stand on a cotton row, then he could see for a hundred miles.

The two cars lined up with Lance standing between them. He had his shirt off and was holding it like a flag. The cars revved up their engines and held them at the sweet spot in a harmonious roar. When the flag came down the roar was drowned out by the wailing scream of the tires rasping against the asphalt in a desperate attempt to find some balance between hundreds of pent-up horses and the traction that was necessary to let them run free. A cloud of thick rubbery smoke formed so suddenly that it seemed to have burst from out of the earth. All that was visible from the starting line was the vanishing tail lights. The sound of the engines receded into the smoke and transformed into something lost and far away, like moans heard in dreams. The shouts nearby turned into coughs as the heavy smoke from the Bucron tires invaded the lungs of the spectators. There was an uneasy silence for a couple of minutes as everyone tried to see the finish line, but it was impossible to see through the rubber fog.

A dull pulsating haze of red seemed to have risen to the top of the smoke as the wind began to carry it away. Everyone looked around as if the sky were sending messages. The red cloud seemed to be circling them, and a tremor of danger quickly invaded the group.

Three cars emerged from the cloud. Sgt. Baylock was herding Mickey and Beetle back down the quarter-mile from the finish line with his patrol lights flashing and his spotlight eerily focused through the back windshield and on the back of Beetle's head.

> Baylock! Son-of-a-bitch! How in the hell— ?

Everyone scattered. They piled into their cars and made U-turns from shoulder to shoulder, using every inch of the two-lane width of 98th Street. The Noot-Noot Brothers were the first out of the shoot, fishtailing between bar ditches down a dirt side road that led to nowhere. Glen skidded a shade wide and wound up straddling a 3-pack of cotton rows, his rear wheels spinning desperately, digging himself his own grave as he pounded and cussed the steering wheel. John Silo backed into the door of Glen's car as he blindly scrambled for any way out. John did a half-doughnut into the dirt that turned into an out-of-control fishtail. Lance came running down the bar-ditch yelling for John to stop and then, realizing the futility of the situation, tried in vain to push Glen's car out of the cotton rows. By then Baylock had his spotlight trained on Glen's Dodge as Smallwood jumped out of the squad car with gun drawn to arrest the two. Dozens of tail lights zigzagged in the distance, scattered throughout the dusty cotton fields. The dust and the smoke, combined with the full moon and swarms of swerving lights, gave the scene the look of an epic in the making. It was hard to believe that it was only a broken-up drag race.

Lance and Glen joined the circle, heads down, expecting the inevitable. Baylock watched them with a smirk.

> They'll be opening up the Iron Hotel in y'all's honor tonight. I'll make sure all of y'all get a suite.
>
> We weren't bothering nobody.
>
> Contesting for speed, disturbing the peace, vagrancy—
>
> What peace? Nothin' out here but the moon and coyotes.
>
> Tell me where to find Gene and we might work something out.
>
> Only Gene knows where to find Gene.
>
> In the car, boys.

The last chord of the night rang across the KoKo dance floor as Vickie sang,

> *Together, at last, at Twilight Time.*

The audience—what was left of it—was far too drunk
to clap. They could only sway back and for, trying to keep their collective balance until some
outside force gave them a clue what to do next.
Tiny then went into a drum solo which led into
Wipeout and then more drum solos. Earle said
goodnight to the drunken audience, and the
band members all went to their table at the
side of the stage next to the dusty plastic coco-
nut tree that leaned helplessly against the faux
bamboo wall. Nicky was passed out, face down,
with drink umbrellas scattered about the table.
The owner, Mr. Jim, met the boys there, a look
of intent on his face.

Have a seat, boys. And young lady.

Wally pulled out a chair and sat beside Nicky, bumping
her just enough that she slid sideways off the table
and into his lap, bringing a mountain of half-full
drinks and umbrellas with her. Wally brushed
himself off with a 'damnit to hell' and propped
Nicky's limp shell roughly back on the table.

I hate to say this but I think y'all might
have outgrown this place. It just ain't
working any more. Our clientele is a
more sophisticated, older crowd looking for a quiet, romantic evening.

The band all looked at Nicky, drooling on the table.

You guys need to play the college
crowd where they don't mind yelling

over the music. Nobody in here can
hear each other talk. And the KoKo
is all about intimacy and elegance
and respect.

Bobby Lynne, the football star, walked up loudly and
announced to Big Jim that he was off to the
Eastside, to Neal's, for a night of cocktails and
gambling and would he like to join him?

Just a minute, Bobby.

Just a minute, hell, the night is leaving our asses behind! The whores'll
all be in church, singin' in the choir!
And by the way, boys, y'all play the
dogshit outta them git-tars.

He reached into his pocket and plucked a wadded up
hundred-dollar bill from the handful of cabbage.
He handed it to Earle singing, *Oh the night life...*

Jim rolled his eyes and shook his head—his original
intention had just been blown to shreds. Earle
spoke lightly.

Well, Jim, maybe we'll see you at Neal's.
We can probably make more in tips
than we can playing this drunk tank.

Earle gave Tiny the hundred-dollar bill to divvy up
later and he walked up the bamboo-studded
stairway into the stark and sterile fluorescent
lobby of the KoKo Palace. If there is a hell, this
must be it, thought Earle. When he reached the
dark parking lot, he let the summer wind blow

through his hair as he looked up into the cosmos. He felt strangely liberated as the sky ran freely in his eyes, with each new constellation suggesting possibilities of a new direction. The Milky Way spilled away from Lubbock from horizon to horizon like a farm road made of diamonds. The great Swan flew overhead unbound by the gravity of earth. Hercules played the Harp with a Dragon at his head and, just like Don Bagget had said, he simply played to his movements. The Scorpion crawled low over the KoKo Motel sign....

A pang of fear shot through Earle's spine when he thought about his rendezvous with Patricia. He had a feeling about her that he'd never had before, and felt he must go to her house to see if everything was all right. It was a little earlier than she had asked him to come but he was sure that her parents had long been in bed. He swung by the Hi-D-Ho on 50th on the way and saw the Legendary Stardust Cowboy on the trunk of his Biscayne, chaps and spurs clanking against the paint, screaming I Met My True Love Down At The Wrecking Yard at the top of his lungs. He smiled to himself and wanted to stop but it looked like the Ledge had an audience and he didn't want to disturb him at that moment. Besides, the blood was now racing in his veins in anticipation of seeing Patricia.

He parked around the corner from her house and walked the dark street in the shadow of the giant juniper trees that hung over the sidewalk at the two houses before hers. He could see that her light was on in the back of the house just over the fence. He knew just the place to scale the fence and went over it silently. As he approached her window he could hear her voice. Did her parents somehow anticipate his coming? He froze up flat against the cool brick by her window and listened. He could hear his heart, pounding against his back. He was afraid that she could hear it through the wall and he moved forward a few inches. Her tone of voice was not the same as she usually used when she spoke to her parents. In fact she sounded more like she usually did when she talked to him. He crept closer to the window.

> Yes, Dan... Of course, Dan. That's just the way I am. You know I do. I'm not seeing Earle anymore. Dan, believe me. I just thought he was funny. I love *you*. More now than ever. More than I ever have. I'll love you forever. I want to be with you. No, no, not tonight, it's too late. Tomorrow night.

Earle just stood in one place, stunned. Unable to move, breathe, or even think. Was this really happening? Maybe his ears were still ringing from the cymbals. But no, he knew that he had heard what he had heard, all right. But how could it be? It was beyond any and all of whatever could ever be imagined through logic or reason. He was numb. Where, just seconds before, there was a torrent of blood racing through his body, now there was nothing—no blood, not a drop, not even a puff of wind. Just a desert, no plants, just rocks. Dull gray rocks with no faces, no shape. His heart had quit beating and his lungs were not even in his body. Everything had rushed out of him at once. He could see shards of his feelings scattered high and low in the trees and bushes as if a bomb had gone off inside him. He felt as if he were suffocating, like he had been wrung out like a towel, twisted beyond recognition.

He staggered to the fence and threw himself over with one push. He was as light as a bag of sheets, and fell to the other side without a sound. He crawled to the juniper trees where he tried to throw up but only dry heaved, as there was nothing inside him, not even space. He thought he heard his name being called but couldn't figure how that could be possible. If he didn't know where he was and why, how could anyone else? The shadows on the street were pools of tar pulling him under and the tree limbs reached for him as he tramped near their grasp, delirious with emptiness. This is it, he thought, but it was not it...

CHAPTER 2

Earle could remember few details of the last hours and
had only brief recollections of walking all night.
Now he stood, facing east, tired and alone, holding a guitar in one hand and his echo chamber
in the other. As the first rays of the morning sun
revealed the Idalou Highway, the feeling began
to return to Earle's senses. He remembered the
grilled cheese sandwich that he had eaten a few
days ago at Gordon Moore's Drug Store. He remembered losing control of his motorbike at the
Athens Ranch and the pain that still followed
him when he walked. How long ago was that, a
few days, a few weeks?

The cool morning air felt good to his lungs. He was
not really sure if he had taken a breath all night.
With each ratchet of the sun, he could feel his
body return, although the back of his head and
his chest still felt empty and void. Like a snake
that had shed its old body, Earle felt that something similar had happened to him in the last
few hours and he remembered the signs he'd received last night from the heavens. God must
be watching after him.

A truck put on its brakes ahead and pulled over, lights
flashing. Earle had not gestured that he was
looking for a ride, but it seemed to fit into his
current plan of letting everything take its own
course. He ran to the cab, with his guitar slam-

ming his knees, and noticed the hand-painted sign on the door that read West Texas Demolition. How appropriate, he decided. He climbed up the ladder and on to the lathe platform over the chrome gas tank. When he opened the door, the first thing he noticed was that the driver's arm was in a sling.

You ain't the devil, 'r'ya?

Earle laughed and assured him that the devil would not be awake at this time of the morning. The man, who was missing most of his bottom teeth, just stared at him, full of suspicion, and did not acknowledge Earle's first attempt at humor since his past life had ended.

I can't handle no more devils. What's in them cases?

Just a guitar. And an echo chamber.

You better not open it or I'll echo your ass.

You couldn't hear it anyway.

Couldn't hear what?

The guitar.

How come?

It's electric.

What's electric?

The guitar. And the echo chamber.

What'cha carryin' it around for?

In hopes I'll find some place to plug it
in someday.

You runnin' from somethin'?

Runnin' to somethin', I suppose.

That *was* a good question, thought Earle. In all truthfulness, it was the first time he'd really thought about his destination. He didn't know what the word *destination* meant at this point in his life. He was caught up in the moment, looking up into the cab of a semi-truck, into another human being's strange made-up universe. A plastic Chihuahua danced on the dash, with a head that bobbed with each bump in the road. A strange picture of Jesus, who looked like he was about to sneeze, was stuck on the dash beside the Chihuahua. News of the war blared out of the radio speaker. Pieces of handwritten scripture, mostly from Revelations, and cutout headlines about recent tragedies were fastened all over the inside of the cab. Religious trinkets dangled from every knob and lever, which gave the impression that the trinkets were doing most of the driving. Everything in the cab was in motion, accelerating in symmetry with the rest of the truck. As they pulled onto the highway, Earle was in awe, watching this strange

man shift gears with the wrong arm while ma-
nipulating a steaming cup of coffee in the crook
of his broken arm.

What'cha haulin'?

The driver yelled over the thunder of the pipes and
the rattle of the trinkets.

Do what?

What are you carrying? What's your
load? Earle yelled.

Explosives, dynamite.

Did he say dynamite? A whole truck full of dynamite?
He looked in the rearview mirror. The trailer,
fishtailing down the dusty highway, might as
well have been a forty-five-foot-long bomb inches
behind them at sixty miles an hour. No, make
that seventy-five. Cold chills ran from his shoulder, down one arm then back up the other. Air
rushed into his empty chest and his heart raced
to keep up with the speedometer. Danger was
filling the empty spaces inside him with a fear
that was rising parallel to the increase in speed.

A thought came to him that perhaps all of the writings
that he had written to the sleepwalking masses
should have, in all reality, been addressed to
himself. Was it not true that the emptiness he
had been seeing in others, was in truth a part
of himself? Now here he was sitting behind a lit
fuse and feeling himself come alive. The truck

was flying past Silver Falls and everything inside and out was in motion. A tumbleweed blew
across the road and lodged in the clutches of a
barbed wire fence. A jackrabbit flattened his
ears as the truck roared past. Papers were blowing around the inside of the cab and the wind
roared in response. The dance of the trinkets
had become a raging frenzy of self-awareness.

The sleeping had arisen, the dead had awakened...

Maggie checked Earle's room on her way to the kitch-
en and was surprised to see Earle not there.
She looked in every room, then looked under
the blankets in front of the swamp cooler. She
looked out the front window and saw the car
parked in the middle of the front yard, on the
grass with both doors open. His band uniform
was wadded up on the dashboard. In the trunk
she found his Super Reverb amp and his work
apron from the Chicken Box. She went to the
phone and called Gary Bass. No, Earle seemed
fine last night, maybe a little distant, he said.
There were some people goin' to Neal's after the
show but Earle didn't seem to be the least bit
interested. Gary said he'd let her know when he
surfaced. Maggie put down the phone and felt a
sudden pain shoot through her insides like a ro-
man candle had just gone off inside her. Where
could Earle be? She went to the medicine cabinet to prescribe what might relieve her sudden
anxiety. *Where could he be?*

Lance woke up on straps of steel looking up at an
image of a nude woman that had been drawn
on the back of the bunk above with the smoke
from a Zippo lighter. He recognized that he was
in the drunk tank, the worst corner of the Lubbock County Jail and the place where Baylock
loved to accommodate his little buddies after
a night on the town. His hangover throbbed
against the steel walls and in between pulses
he asked himself why he was in this godforsak-
en situation one more time. He swore to some
far-away Heavenly Father that if he would get
him out of jail this time, he would give his life
to something good, like helping orphans and
lepers. There was something in his family history that caused him to make such outrageous
promises every time he was cornered or pinned
down. When released, he went back to taunt-
ing the very forces that determined his freedom, until some dark desire of his will would
lead him back into chains. He remembered that
Baylock had also arrested Mickey and Beetle
and Glen and he called out their names to see
if they were within earshot. There were a few
groans here and there but none that he recognized so he lay back down on his bunk and
tried to piece together a collage of the faces of
his mother and father.

Gene woke in a porch swing with the sun slicing
through the slats and into his squinting brain.
The smell of bacon and eggs stirred with the
smells of hay and horse shit. Buck Owens was
singing Tiger by the Tail which irritated Gene

enough to make him take a swipe at the radio. When his arm lurched forward the swing responded in reverse, throwing him face down onto a sleeping Dalmatian who answered with a sudden attack to Gene's groin area. Gene was trying to kick back the dog while screaming at the top of his hoarse throat for someone to come and pull this monster off of him.

Carol Ann and Biggars came running out to see what was going on and arrived just as Gene was about to pound the dog with an iron candle holder that he found beside the swing.

> Stop! Don't! Chuckie! Chuckie, you come over here right now! Oh! Are you all right baby dog? What are you trying to do to my Chuckie baby dog!

> He just tried to eat my crotch! You're takin' up for *him*? He oughta be chained to the clothesline!

> You just get your ass outta here. Where'd you come from anyway? Get outta here before I call the cops. Come here Chuckie baby baby.

Gene was still not sure if this was part of his dream or if he had dropped out of the sky into the middle of a dog fight. He tottered from the porch down the dirt drive to Strictland's Nomad. He opened the door and sat in the sunbaked front seat, looking down at the contorted reflection of himself in the sharp chrome center of the steering wheel. The horn ring floated above the grooved spokes almost like a halo and this gave Gene a temporary peaceful feeling. He sat like this for a long time for he knew there was nowhere to go, at least not any place that *he* knew of. The key chain dangled in the ignition switch and by the time he reached for it he was drenched in sweat.

After breakfast, Patricia called Earle's house, worried about why she had never heard from him last night. Surely he hadn't come by while she was on the phone to Dan. No, that would have been too early for him, she decided. Still, why does no one answer?

Outside of Dickens the driver of the truck started to confide in Earle. He told him of his recent divorce after his wife had driven off with his best friend on a coast-to-coast run leaving only a note saying she would not be back and would he take care of her goldfish? He told about when they met when she was a waitress in a truck stop in Clovis, New Mexico, and he was hauling peanuts from Portales to the ship channel in Houston. And about how he would bring her one bag of raw and one bag of roasted with a little note on it tied in pretty ribbon. And she liked the raw better and saved the roasted for him. As the details of the story unfolded the driver began to cry and the more he cried the faster he drove. He was taking the curves so wide that he was beginning to drift into the oncoming lanes. He was becoming delirious with the details of their broken relationship and forgetting the rather important fact that he was behind the wheel of a dynamite truck.

Earle glanced at the speedometer as they approached ninety miles an hour and began rapidly blinking his eyes, trying to conjure up an action to take. When the man came to the part about his ex leaving her Pekinese and the waterbed, Earle had had enough. He told the driver that he was also in the throes of a love gone bad and didn't want to be reminded of it right now and besides he had business to take care of in Guthrie, the next town. The driver blasted by the Four-Sixes stables with not even so much as an acknowledgment that he had heard a word he had said. Earle repeated himself but now realized that the driver was inside of a cocoon and was incoherent because his emotions had swallowed him alive. Something had to be done before their combined existence was nothing more than a crater in the Dickens-Guthrie highway.

Earle first turned the radio up as loud as it would go. He then took off his shirt, pushed open the door on his side of the truck with his feet and began reciting whatever came to his mind at the top of his lungs.

Sieze Cesar!
Sin Harder!

Silk Skinpaws!
Side Of Slaw!

Skin Scissors!
Silk Slammer!

Skertch Of Whrirr!
Slabber Dabber!

Sis Boom Batter!

The driver slammed on his brakes at the first curve
in Guthrie and stared at Earle in horror.

I knowed you was the devil, I knowed
it! Get thee out of mine house as
those who have trespassed against
me. Get out! Get out! Take thine soul
out of Babelousa and drink with the
slaves who lay with lions!

Earle smiled as he climbed down and couldn't resist
giving the driver a long, serious, squinty look.
He then rolled his eyes into the back of his head
and flicked his tongue spastically across his
front teeth.

The trucker gunned his engine, not even waiting for
the door to shut. Earle watched his smokestacks
snort as he made the curve by the pipe yard,
chuckling to himself and glad to be stranded in
a place so ancient and remote.

He walked to the 6666 supply store and bought a
Dr. Pepper and read the notices that the cowboys had thumb-tacked to the front of the store.
Some were in search of tack and saddle parts,
some were looking for tractor and truck parts,
and some were looking for anything to soften

the forlorn and lonely passage of time.

There was a wooden bench on the front porch and Earle sat for a long time observing the pace of the town. Nothing much was in motion besides what was being blown about by the wind. What movement there was, was slow and deliberate, disconnected from time. An old man sat in front of the store, seemingly made out of stone. A truck beside the flat-fixing area inched forward and stopped, then crept backward, then back and forth, inches at a time. A woman got out of the back seat, knelt down, reached under the car and walked over and threw something into a blue-and-red-painted oil barrel. The truck continued to inch back and forth until the driver appeared satisfied that the unknown conditions were met. The windmill by the feed store seemed to be spinning so fast that if it separated from its bearings it would buzz-saw the town in half. Sparrows darted from telephone line to Chinese elm. A dust devil blew in from the string of vacant lots and as it crossed the road an old rusted pickup truck emerged from its tail as if the swirling apparition were giving birth to antique farm implements.

The truck pulled up and skidded to a park in front of the Supply Store. A man got out, looked all around and crossed to the porch where Earle was sitting. He went inside and asked for something and Earle could hear the storekeeper say that they had not carried that product in seven or eight years.

The man came back out and looked at Earle, then down at his guitar case.

Play that thang?

Try to.

Hope you don't make a livin' at it. You could starve to death out here.

I bet you got that right. I'm just passin' through, though.

Where to?

Earle thought for a second.

Dallas.

Hop in. I could use a navigator.

Earle introduced himself.

Earle.

Dub responded.

Dub.

Nice to meet 'cha.

Earle put his guitar and echo chamber in the back and got in the truck. The dashboard was covered in dirt. In fact the whole inside of the cab looked like the truck had been sitting out in the weather for years. Earle tried the window. Sure enough it didn't work.

You cold?

The man was trying to make a joke but the way he
said it made it seem like he wanted Earle to
keep his hands to himself.

Just wonderin' how she got so dusty.

Good clean farm livin'.

The man put on a pair of sunglasses that did not
match his character in the least. He looked all
around the car and checked his mirrors several
times. Although he had only met him a couple of
minutes earlier, Earle felt there was something
about this person that was not exactly visible.
He was likable enough on the surface, but there
were ripples down inside him that criss-crossed
each other and seemed to cause him to be two
different people in the same body. Earle asked a
question just to see what he would say.

Where are you comin' from?

It doesn't really matter in the long run.

I guess not. We all come from the
same place if you go back far enough.

That's what I mean. It's all the same.

Before leaving the parking lot, Dub confided in a road
map. Earle watched as he bit his lip and looked
both ways yet again. And once again there
were no cars in either direction at least as far

as the horizon. He lighted out on the shoulder and gunned it down Highway 82 through Vera, then surprisingly took a right on a dirt farm-to-market road. Earle started to question this turn but decided to wait for an explanation from the driver.

The dirt became redder as they dropped from a slight ridge onto an open range of pigmy mesquites snarling for space. Myriad trails twisted relentlessly in an immense maze always turning in on itself. Small patches of buffalo grass tried in vain to hide between the cracks in the parched dirt, protected by rings of goat-head sticker plants and walls of cockleburs. Deadly nightshade was in bloom with its tainted purple flowers that would soon transform into bright yellow balls of belladonna, tempting the cattle with enlightenment. If its lure was successful, the drug reduced the poor fools to a subterranean state, chased through the prickly maze by ghostly bovine spooks until bludgeoning themselves to death by natural forces or until their veins exploded from fear and exhaustion.

Earle allowed himself to think for a few seconds about Patricia and wondered how he could have been so foolish to let himself fall so helplessly in love with someone who was so untrue. He felt the sky blowing out of his chest as the vast empty feeling began to return to his body. A sudden jerk of the steering wheel slammed him smack back into the present. A jackrabbit had crossed in front of them and Dub had turned and braked at the same time, sending them spinning sideways into the soft dirt of the bar ditch.

Son of a bitch.

Guess he showed us.

Fuckin' rabbits.

The inertia of the spin had sloshed the fuel out of the
carburetor and the engine had strangled itself.
Dub pumped the accelerator as the engine dry-
ly turned, sounding like a gaggle of park geese
barking for crumbs. Dub's face was contorted
in panic as he anticipated the engine to catch.
When it finally did he wasted no time slamming it down into first and popping the clutch.
The soft sand allowed no traction, however, and
the attempt at forward movement failed. Earle
jumped out and pushed on the tailgate. They
rocked the truck back and forth for several minutes until the traction wheel found a home and
the truck lurched forward. Earle ran back to
the cab, first stopping to get his instruments
out of the back and got in.

I thought that might 'a been it.

Wudn't as deep as it looked.

A rancher drove by slowly eyeing the truck at the edge
of the bar ditch. His brake light came on for a
second until their truck U-turned and pulled
back into the road.

Dub said that he didn't remember asking for any attention and watched the rancher's truck until it
disappeared around the curve in front of them.

A couple of miles down he turned left onto another dirt road heading east. Earle couldn't
hold it back any longer.

Shortcut to Dallas?

I don't recall you buyin' a ticket.

Just that I never been this way.

It's a way.

Every conversation with this mystery man seemed to
end the exact same way, in a circle, with nowhere else to go. Something was tracking him,
and Earle began to feel like he would have been
better off if he had stayed back in Guthrie. Dub
kept looking at his watch and then at the rear
view mirror. His speed increased as the pot-
holes got deeper, and the old pickup shook like
it was about to disintegrate. The water tower of
Seymour was a welcome sight.

You know, Dub, I got some people
here that I haven't seen in a while. If
you don't mind you can just drop me
off at some little burger joint in town.

He slammed on his brakes, and the dust passed them.

You know, you ain't done nothin' but
whine ever since I picked your ass up.
This here's the end of the line.

Wish I could say I enjoyed the ride.

Earle took his guitar and echo chamber and got out of the truck, relieved to be on solid ground again. He saw Dub's eyes flash in the rearview mirror and then down to his watch. He was grateful to be free from the confines of the strange webs that his last two rides had woven around him. The free hot wind felt good on his face and he said a silent thanks to be as lucky as he had been. He had no pressing engagements, neither now nor ever. The only thing pressing was his stomach against his back bone. The macaroni and cheese dinner from last night seemed like weeks ago.

He walked softly past the small houses on the outskirts of town. A lone dog began to bark which set off a chain reaction and within a few blocks he could hear dogs all over town warning each other of an incoming intruder. Eyes peeked out from behind Venetian blinds and curtains ruffled as Earle made his way to the stop sign several blocks up the street. Brenda's Dairy Dog was nestled between two closed filling stations and had a sign out front that called out HELP WANTED—NO NEED TO APPLY. He sat at a concrete table and was checking out his new environment when a voice yelled out.

Know what'cha wont yet?

Earle turned to the order window to see a perfectly framed woman's face so painted with makeup that he could not tell if she was real or not. In disbelief he studied the egg-white face painted with bright red, over-the-lines lipstick and fluorescent blue shades over her eyes. The upper lashes were as long as the legs of spiders, and the lower lashes curled like razor wire from the inside of her eyes to the tiny crow's feet at the corners. When he saw her rub her eye with her apron, he was able to let loose from his initial surprise and to respond to her question.

> Can I get a burger and fries and a Dr. Pepper for a dollar and a half?
>
> You can get more than that, she said mock-seductively.
>
> Well, that's what I want, then.
>
> Everything on it?
>
> Cut the pickles.
>
> Don't like pickles?
>
> Never have. Never will. I like 'em by themselves, though.

She said that more people cut the onions than cut the pickles but most people don't cut anything so that they feel like they're getting more for their money. Then they take 'em off themselves and throw 'em in the parking lot. And that was why the last car hop, Shachelle, was in the hospital at this very moment with a broken kneecap. From slipping on a pickle slice.

Earle replied.

I'll be.

She ducked inside her little cave and soon steam was
coming out of the grill vent on the sunny side
of the building and he could hear her singing
Gene Pitney's He's a Rebel.

Earle pulled the notebook from his back pocket and
fumbled some words around in his head. Since
leaving Lubbock this morning a melody had
been running around the inside of his head. He
usually wrote words by themselves and, come
to think of it, had never really thought of com-
bining them with music. The last twenty-four
hours were symbolic of both everything he had
lived for and everything he was trying to get
away from. He felt like it was his duty to capture it all, from now on, in story and song.

The girl from the window came walking out the front
door with his order on a tray. She had huge
breasts and a huge butt but had tiny feet and
tall heels. Earle could not believe that she, being built the way she was, could even walk at
all. She took tiny steps but walked quickly. She
reminded Earle of a miniature dog that had
been trimmed into ridiculous proportions. She
laid her breasts on his shoulder as she put the
tray on the table.

Anything else?

How do I get to 114?

Just up to the light. Wher'ya' goin'?

Dallas, I guess.

You guess?

I'm pretty much free to go anywhere,
I suppose.

Wish I was.

You are, but the right particulars
haven't showed you the way, yet.

I'm about sick of it, here.

You got a long way to go, yet.

Earle pulled out the dollar and a half that was left
over from getting his amp out of hock and laid
it on the table.

That your last money?

Lucky I got that.

Keep it, then. You're liable to need it.

Earle saw in her eyes that she meant it and realized
that he had judged her by her outlandish makeup rather than who she was, a small town girl
trying to be a grown woman.

Thanks, sweetheart, I might at that.

If you're ever 'round here again, stop
by. I'm open every day.

You never know.

The hamburger was delicious, a connoisseur combination of greasy ingredients. The buttered bun had been toasted on top of the grill just like the midget chef used to make at his neighborhood drugstore grill. The onions had been freshly chopped and were sweet and hot at the same time. The lettuce had been freshly shredded and the tomato was thinly sliced. Everything had then been assembled at exactly the right time and the outcome was nothing less than a masterpiece.

Earle walked to the highway and within minutes a brand new Oldsmobile stopped, rolled down the front power window and asked, first, what religion he was, and then, what his destination was.

First Baptist and Dallas, in that order.

Wrong answer.

No, it's true.

Wrong answer, get in.

Earle put his cases on the floor of the rear seat and carefully got in the car. Everything was spotless, not a speck of dust on any little thing. Earle wondered why this man had said what he had said.

Just curious, why did you say 'wrong answer'?

A Christian's destination should always be Heaven, not his earthly destination.

Well, Heaven then. I haven't been to church much since my daddy died.

And why not?

Mother started seein' spirits and such around the house and everyone thought she'd flipped out and had her committed to Big Spring. I always figured that it was only natural to become closer to the spirit world after someone they love has died because they have to learn a brand new way of communicating with them.

Angels are the messengers of God.

They drove my mother right on over the edge.

Her fears were reflected back to her as a result of her lack of faith.

She's been afraid of dying since I was born.

Where did you grow up?

Born in Amarillo, off Route 66. Came to Lubbock after that. Been there ever since.

I preached in Amarillo a long time
ago. We moved to Mesquite in '58.

Earle was barely listening. He tried to think of something to add but he was blank. The contrast between his three rides and the blur of the last
few days was stirring in his thoughts. His body
felt like rubber. The Oldsmobile rode like it was
hopping from cloud to cloud and soon the lack
of sleep caught up with him. His eyes closed silently on the heavenly highway....

Sgt. Baylock parked in front of Earle's house on 28th
Street. Maggie had been watching for him
through the front curtains for the last hour. She
had called Baylock after painstakingly calling
everyone in her address book. Virtually no one
had seen Earle since the parking lot at the KoKo
around midnight last night. She even talked to
several gamblers that had gone to Neal's after
hours. The car was still in the front yard with
the doors open, only now a small crowd had
stopped to rubberneck. Baylock examined the
outside of the car, looked in the trunk, then inspected under the seats, between the seats and
in the cracks of the seats. Earle's clip-on tie was
under the front seat but that was all.

Missus Maggie, I think Earle will
turn up. He don't usually go far.

I just have this feeling, with Gene
gone and all.

Maybe he's with him.

But you don't know where he is?

Now, now, the Lubbock Police Force
knows all. One of our birds has been
doin' a little singin'....

Baylock walked over to the onlookers and told them
to move on and then explained to them about
the superior vagrancy laws in the State of Texas. He turned and shouted to Maggie that if she
heard anything to let him know.

The news of Earle's disappearance had spread like
wildfire and several different accounts were
already going around. Lubbock loved a good
mystery and this weekend was brimming with
juicy gossip. Some were saying that after the
owner of the KoKo had fired the TwiLites there
had been a disagreement in the parking lot and
he had forced Earle into the trunk of his Cad-
dy and had him knocked off at Neal's. Others
were saying that Earle would be one of the only
people that Gene would talk to since they both
worked at the Chicken Box and that he had
gone to meet Gene somewhere. But most just
dismissed it with a shrug, knowing that musicians sometimes lose their way in the worlds of
sin in which they mingle.

Red and blue lights were flashing on the highway just
west of Jacksboro. The sun was almost down

and the landscape was immersed in a golden glow. The Highway Patrol cars looked almost like fancy candy bars wrapped in cellophane. At least that's what it looked like to Earle, who was just waking from an erotic dream that included Brenda, the Dairy Dog girl. The Reverend had slowed down in the expectation that his services might be needed. Four patrol cars had corralled an old pickup truck and another was flashing in from the direction of Jacksboro. As they closed in on the scene Earle recognized the truck as Dub's and seconds later saw Dub face down in the gravel, handcuffed, with two officers, guns drawn, keeping him covered. A knot formed in Earle's throat and beads of sweat erupted from his brow. Dub lifted his head and looked their way as the Oldsmobile passed. Earle thought he saw his lips move till the patrolman kicked him in the ribs, redirecting his attention, and they passed away from each other into the Texas sunset and on into the horizon, to their own destinations.

Looks as if that man's past is now his present, said the Reverend.

If not the other way around.

Did you get your nap out?

I'm sorry to be such rude company. My eyes just closed on me.

We must renourish our bodies in order to strengthen our souls.

The Reverend's words were soothing to Earle as they reminded him of the tone in which his grandfather used to describe different states of being. He felt protected against the elements both physically and spiritually and settled into the cushy leather seats of the big Oldsmobile. In the golden clouds up ahead he saw a winged horse raring against a dragon. An eagle swooped in with a baby on its back and in the distance thousands of soldiers waited to cross a furious river that led to a range of majestic mountains covered in palm trees. A mushroom cloud was in the far distance with the face of Jesus superimposed on it and rays of light coming out from behind. They traveled silently through Jacksboro and Springtown and as it was getting dark the rows of honky-tonks came alive with neon spilling into the slick streets like blood from a wound. It aroused a concealed place inside Earle's soul, a place dark with sexual mystery and alive with deathly intrigue much like the border towns that his friends had visited last year where pleasure turned to pain, and eventually, trouble. He added a verse to his new song.

They traveled through Fort Worth and across the nether lands of suburb after suburb that loosely tied Fort Worth with Dallas. The Oldsmobile seemed to know its destination without the Reverend so much as steering. Like being in a tunnel with the Golden Gates at the far end, the Reverend never swerved. Earle could feel a kind of menacing uncertainty as they approached the Dallas skyline. He hated to leave the womb of the Reverend but in the end his youthful exuberance was in need of worldly experience.

He had the address and number of his old girlfriend
Barbara who lived in Oak Cliff and he asked the
Reverend if he would drop him off there. The
Reverend smiled and said of course he would
and within a matter of minutes had found the
apartment building where she lived.

> You are embarking on a grand jour-
> ney, said the Reverend. Be sure and
> carry faith in the Lord with you
> wherever you go. Nothing will harm
> you if you have the light of God inside
> you to guide you through the darker
> moments. We meet as if by chance
> along life's weary highway, but it is
> no mere coincidence. We are here to
> share harmony with each other and
> with all our brothers and sisters and
> to help one another through the ob-
> stacles of life.

Earle felt as if his soul had been lightened and he
thanked the good Reverend for giving him more
than just a ride. He said he wished he could
give something in return but he had nothing
but the tools of his trade. The Reverend said
he would be needing them and to use them in
order to give his gifts to others, to lighten their
hearts, and to remind them that their life is a
blessing to share with all the world.

As he drove away the streetlight above him blinked off,
then on, then off. The parking lot was dark and
he could hear screams coming from one of the
apartments. The sound of sirens wailed in pain

across the bridge in the direction of downtown. The tall buildings tore at the bottoms of the low clouds. Earle was alone in a big city for the first time. But something inside him was protecting him and he had no fear. He closed his eyes and felt the cool night wind on his face and heard the cicadas chirping in the trees. After wandering through rows and rows of numbered doors he found the one that matched his piece of paper. He took a deep breath and knocked at the door....

Maggie and Mark sat in the front room lighting a candle with the Mormon minister. He was telling how Joseph Smith was an explorer who was guided by visions and that her son sounded like the same sort of person. He told them to pray for five minutes every hour until they heard from him.

The jailer opened the doors to Lance and Glen's cell. Lance said that it was about fuckin' time and Glen seconded it. Betty and Bill and John had gone their bail and were scowling at them, drunker than hell, when they came into the check-out room. The deputy at the desk gave them back their possessions at which time Betty began to go off on Lance.

We only got y'all out so's you can clean up our goddamned kitchen.
Bill, ever the diplomat, said in a slur,

Now Betty, there's another reashon why we got them out. I'd tell them now

but we might discriminate some one
who'sh already in trouble, beshides,
Lance hash every intenshun of—

Sorry, Deputy, said Lance, but this
is my drunk-ass aunt and she don't
know how to goddamn act in public.

You ain't never had to get *my* ass outta jail before! said Betty.

The Deputy had heard enough.

Ever *one* of you better get outta here
'fore I r'rest the whole lot of your sorry asses.

John Silo was out in the car, grinning from ear to
ear, his eyes bugging out and a smug look on
his face as if to rub it in that he was one of the
ones who got away. Lance and Glen lit into him
and blamed him for themselves getting caught.
John, who was a master at reversing the blame,
said that if Glen were not such a piss-poor driver to run him off the fuckin' road and to try
and drive in the cotton fields then they would
all have gotten away with no dents. John also
managed to change the subject by telling them
that Chicken Box Jimmy had heard from Gene
and that he was in Fort Worth. He went on to
complain that with both Gene and Earle gone
he was doing a triple shift at the Chicken Box.
He said that Jimmy himself was so exhausted
that he had dropped his own chef's hat into the
fryer at rush hour and could do nothing but

scoop it out with the onion rings and throw it in the burn bin.

Everybody laughed and John popped Miller High Lifes for everyone which, by the very sound of air rushing into the beer space vacuum, elevated the mood several notches inside the car. The stories started to flow with everyone chiming in at once. Betty started laughing about Bill sticking the kitchen knife into the phone jack and nearly electrocuting himself and Lance started laughing about Betty yelling to Gene on the floor with a dead telephone in her hand. Glen laughed at himself stuck in loose dirt between some cotton rows as Smallwood, with a bandage wrapped around his head, ordered him—with gun drain—to stay where he was. Everybody howled with laughter until their eyes watered, even as the radio played a sad Ray Price ballad. The ship of fools weaved around the deserted streets in downtown Lubbock until, once again like so many times before, they vanished into a sorry, dusty oblivion.

Barbara answered the door, ready for bed, in her nightgown. She was shocked to see Earle standing there looking like some specter from the past.

What in...? *This* is a surprise.
Good one I hope.

Where the... Well don't just stand there, come in.

Sorry to just drop in on you like this, but I left Lubbock sort of unexpectedly.

I wish you'd have at least called.

I been hitchhiking since sunrise this morning.

What have you been doing? How's the band?

The band's laid off. Everybody's glad, though. Lubbock's just the same. Baylock's after everybody's ass. Gene's on the run. Lance and KC are still fighting like crazy. Chicken Box Jimmy's still losin' his ass. Mom's gettin' stranger. Like I said, Lubbock's just the same.

Sounds like it. I had to get outta there. You need a place to stay?

Glad you asked. If I could stay on the couch for a couple of days....

Yeah, sure, but I go to work early in the morning and you'll be stranded here. Here's an extra key, don't let the cat get out. Anyway, you can't stay here long, my mother's paying for this place and she doesn't want me to have a roommate while I'm working at this job. I've got to go to bed.

I've got an early call in the morning.

I really appreciate this. I don't know what I'd've done if you hadn't've been here.

Earle dropped into oblivion the second he hit the couch and didn't wake until the afternoon of the next day. He stayed on the couch watching television with the sound off and the radio on. Barbara called and said that she was staying with her mother that night in Mesquite and to make himself at home. He went back to sleep and slept through the evening and night and didn't rise until the next morning. He walked across the bridge and spent the afternoon exploring downtown Dallas, getting lost, and then making a big circle back to Barbara's apartment.

On the six o'clock news were more stories of the draft forty thousand teenagers a month were now being called into service. As more families were being affected by the mass callings, America was starting to ask questions about the civil war in Viet Nam and the questions were becoming a public issue as well as a government problem. Racial unrest had spread from the South into virtually every city and had recently flared up in the Watts area of LA. Social insecurity was a hot news topic, being felt by everyone, everywhere.

He called his mother collect and told her where he was and how he got there and that he was all right. She broke down and cried out of relief

and asked him how he could do this to her and
that her blood pressure was up and that Baylock had come and that everybody had thought
that the KoKo guy had had him killed over on
the eastside and that Patricia was worried and
that Lance and Glen and Mickey and Beetle
had been thrown in jail and that Lance knew
where Gene was and that—

Wait, wait, what did you say? Lance
knows where Gene is?

He said he did.

I thought you said they were in jail.

John Silo got them out.

Where's Lance now?

I really don't care. All I care about is
that you're all right.

I'm fine. I'm gonna see if I can get
something going here—we got laid
off from the KoKo last night.

I know everything that all your
friends did last night. That place was
never any good, anyway.

I know. Anyway, I had to get out of
there, everything fell in on me at
once.

Just be careful, Earle, Dallas is a big
city. I love you.

I love you, too....

The next call Earle made was to Betty and Bill's
house to find out where Gene was. Lance got on
the phone and asked Earle what had happened
to him and told him about the drag race and
about Baylock busting them and about Gene
calling from Fort Worth. He gave Earle the
number where he was staying. Lance said that
he was going to have to get out of Lubbock soon
or he might lose his mind, what little there was
left of it. Earle asked Lance if he would explain
his situation to Chicken Box Jimmy and he said
he would. He also asked him that if he came
to Fort Worth would he please bring his Super
Reverb amp and he said he would.

Earle called the number for Gene and a pissed-off
woman answered the phone saying that she
didn't know where the son-of-a-bitch was but
she'd bet a hundred dollars that later that night
you could probably find him at the Cellar Club
downtown hangin' out with the derelicts.

Earle grabbed his guitar and left Barbara a note saying he had gone to Fort Worth to look for work
and asked if she would keep his echo chamber
till he returned. He walked down to the Bronco
Bowl, had a cup of coffee and, for an hour or two,
watched as customers vainly tried to entertain
themselves in an artificial environment, the
likes of which he had never seen before. When
the fascination wore off, he strolled outside and

stuck out his thumb and was in front of the Cellar Club within two hours.

The bouncer who watched the stairway could have just as easily been a granite boulder. There was a sign that said $2 cover and all Earle had was a dollar and a quarter. He somehow persuaded the bouncer that he was there at the invitation of the band and Gene Holiday.

Gene Holiday! What a crazy bastard!
He came in the last couple of nights.
You know Gene? Go on in. Said he'd
be back tonight.

Amazing, thought Earle. Gene's been here four days and they already know him at the Cellar. That was the way Gene was. He was spiritual in the way he attracted strangers. He saw the humor in most everything and took nothing whatsoever seriously. Nothing, that is, except policemen and poker hands.

Earle walked up the Cellar stairs into a fakely trashed out world obviously manufactured by someone cashing in on the recent popularity of bohemian culture. Out-of-context catch phrases plagiarized from the beat writers lined the walls, perfectly painted in a pseudo-poetical type-style. Clichéd pieces of beatnik paraphernalia, Mexican bongos, sombreros, and black-velvet-backed oil paintings of cartoon-like Dobie Gillis characters wearing Rayban sunglasses and trimmed little chingadero-style goatees were randomly hanging around the lightless room. The air was permeated with clouds of yellow nicotine, and chain-smoking was encouraged. Each table was filled with drinks that were not really drinks. The Cellar didn't have an alcoholic beverage license but sold drinks spiked with a kind of flavored artificial liquor imported from the Orient.

The waitresses who sold the imitation drinks wore nothing but panties and bras and walked around with a brash kind of daringly defiant pose. This attitude assured them of better than average tips from the more self-centered and free-flowing of the clientele. Signs were posted around the walls that warned not to touch the waitresses, or else.

The waitresses were protected by the bouncers. The Cellar bouncers were notorious for being the most barbarous, savage, bloodthirsty non-human beings in the tri-county area. It was said they were hired solely on the merits of their arrest records. The management surely searched the Tarrant County bail bond offices for newly freed convicts who were looking for a low-pay, high-contact position protecting scantily-clad biker chicks from liquored-up geeks. There was no shortage of bouncers at the Cellar Club.

Earle stood by the dirty curtains that hid the back door, watching the band from the side of the stage. They were playing a passable rendition of a Kinks song, Tired of Waiting. The singer obviously lived in a different world than the rest of the band, and when he went off into a soul-exposing tangent, wrenching his heart with his hands, the band looked down at their instruments.

A drunk customer who was sitting on the cushions on the floor in a rumpled, expensive suit reached up and grabbed at one of the waitresses as she walked by. She turned and threw a whole tray of drinks in his face and before the tray hit the floor the man was surrounded by the Cellar's licensed thugs. They scooped him up like a flapjack and carried him kicking and yelling through the dirty curtains. They then opened the back door and tossed him down a fire escape slide that emptied into a dumpster two floors down in the alley behind the club. The band played louder and within a couple of minutes the event had passed from the collective memory of the patrons.

Earle recognized Gene Holiday's laughing silhouette in the center of a commotion by the entrance. He made his way through the crowd and tapped Gene on the shoulder. Gene threw his arms around Earle and announced to his new friends that this was truly a night to celebrate. Gene got a glass from the counter and poured Earle a drink from the half-pint of vodka he carried in his boot. He already knew half of the waitresses' names and introduced Earle to them all. When the band quit Gene took Earle backstage and introduced him to the band. A couple of the guys were from West Texas and they exchanged names and places until they arrived at those they had in common.

The bass player invited everyone over to his place after the show. As they left the club, another band, the American Blues, was breaking into their last set of hard driving blues. Charlie's apartment was about the size of a cracker box with a broken couch covered in embroidered roses that had long since turned into weeds on a vacant lot. The refrigerator was well stocked with beer but not a bite of food. Earle and Gene talked long about Baylock's vendetta against him and laughed about the exploits of Betty and Bill. Gene was concerned that Lance knew his whereabouts, because that meant that soon Baylock's moles would get word.

The hosts of the house, Charlie Mitchell and his girlfriend Surrenda, invited Earle to sleep on the couch since everyone was leaving and the sun was coming up. Earle could hear them making love in the next room as the waking city rumbled the walls and vibrated the faded roses on the couch, lulling Earle into an uneasy, Fort Worth sleep.

KC honked at Betty and Bill's and was surprised when Lance came out of the house ready to go. It was eleven in the morning and it was strange to witness this enthusiasm coming from him at that time of the day. He bounced in the car, gave her a kiss, and even announced what a great day it was. He said if she wanted breakfast at the Toddle House that he would buy it with the money he had stolen from John Silo's wallet.

You stole money from your best friend who got you out of jail?

John wouldn't piss on a monk on fire.

Gene told him to get us out and that
he would pay him back.

Well, I guess that makes it all right,
then.

Look, bitch, you wanna stop at the
Toddle House or not? Or do you want
me to slap the shit out of you?

I ain't all that hungry, asshole moth-
erfucker.

A short silence followed which meant that both sides
didn't want to escalate the pointless feud.

We ain't even left the front yard and
the shit starts flyin'.

Let's have a picnic at Silver Falls.

O.K., sweetheart.

He French-kissed her ear and ran his hand up her
blouse and fondled her breasts for several minutes until she was breathing so heavily that
she thought she would faint. The radio station
had been tuned to a far away AM station and
the signal was beginning to fade to static. KC
felt like she was melting into the noise. Lance
sucked huge whelps on her neck and licked her
eyes like a wild animal. He put his other hand
up her dress and a wave of pleasure invaded
her body to the point that she began to pant
out loud and rub his hand harder and harder

against her boiling fountain. She loved it when his abuse turned suddenly from violence to sex. He imagined he was complementing her desires by sucking all the blood out of her body and then driving a stake through her heart. It took all her strength to barely whisper to him, asking, begging, pleading, if they could go into the back bedroom without waking anyone. He carried her across the front yard and around to the back door. They made vicious love for an hour and then helped each other like wounded animals back to the car and through the sad streets of Lubbock, past the Fair Park Coliseum, down the Caprock at Mackenzie Park, past Prairie Dog Town and the Purina Chow dog food factory and out the Idalou highway to the plain and uncomplicated horizon that seemed to drop off the edge of the known world.

At noon the rest of the band came over to meet with Charlie about the imminent departure of their front man. Gene had told them about Earle's ability to front a band and they asked him if he wanted to go down to the club and run through some songs. Within thirty minutes they asked Earle to join their band, the Neurotic Sheep. Earle was flattered, but had two questions.

> When can we rehearse and when would you like me to start?

> Today and tonight.

> You're out of your minds.

Mike gave notice a couple of weeks
ago so if you wanna jump in, now's
the time to jump.

Holy—

We know jillions of songs. At least
twenty or thirty.

They compared songs that they knew in common and
were surprised to find ten or so they both had
played before.

Combine those with a few instrumen-
tals and we got a set. Plus we can do
Jimmy Reed songs.

But don't you do more than one set?

We play every third hour between
seven and five. Tomorrow we play at
eight, eleven, and two.

Long hours.

Low pay.

Count me in boys, but wait, the second question ....

What's that?

About the name of the band, I mean
it's kind of an inside sheep joke.

Bad Bob sorta laid it on us.

Who's Bad Bob?

They looked at each other in disbelief that anyone that they knew could possibly not know who Bob Crump was.

You'll see soon enough.

Earle didn't like this nebulous kind of answer but there was little he could do about it.

They went over the songs they knew a couple of times each and had just enough time to grab a bite at the bus station before the show. Earle had a queasy feeling as he looked out of the dirty windows at the bloody sunset. An air of uncertainty dampened his excitement and the smell of diesel clouded what should have been an exciting event in his life. Something about it all....

Gene showed up right before the band went on and announced to Earle that Lance and KC were on their way. Earle didn't respond one way or the other since his total focus was on the fact that he was about to walk on stage in the Cellar Club with a band he'd never played with.

A waitress wearing white panties, a red bra, and a blue cowboy hat announced:

And now, cowboys and biker chicks, welcome back The Neurotic Sheep!

Earle felt queasy as he walked out into the black light to a smattering of applause. There were chairs

for the band to sit in, which also gave Earle a
strange feeling. He had never sat down to play.
It was as if he were in an environment invented
by someone else and he was merely dangling
there. The lights were controlled by automobile
dimmer switches in front of Charlie, and his
Beatle boots danced on the one and the three
which painted the stage red and green like a
Christmas tree with a short in the fuse. The
familiar riff of Walkin' the Dog roared out of
the dual Bassman speakers and soon the band
was pretty much in sync. They blasted through
their patchwork set and, surprisingly, got a rise
from the audience. In fact, at the end of the set
the whole place was stirring, not because of
what the band was playing but because of some
commotion toward the back of the room. He
saw a flash of Lance tearing his shirt off, fists
flying, and of Gene cold-cocking one of the giant bouncers. The red light in the middle of the
room started to flash, which was a Cellar code
that the Fort Worth Police Department would
soon make an appearance. People began to
scatter, and within a few minutes all that was
left were some bloody bouncers, the waitresses
and the manager, Pat, peering out of his office
with something silver in his hand. The band
coasted in for a landing like a toy whose spring
had unwound. Charlie put down his bass and
looked at Earle.

I won't tell 'em they're your friends.

You can't take them Lubbock boys
anywhere.

The set was just startin' to get in gear—

—till Gene tried to power shift without the clutch.

The band retired to the back room to smoke and talk while the next band, the American Blues, took to the stage. Earle stayed by the curtain to watch as these curious-looking cave dwellers walked on stage in bright blue hair and ripped into a Muddy Waters standard, I'm a Man. In a few minutes Charlie motioned for Earle to come in the dressing room, like something was up.

Pat, the manager of the Cellar, was sitting on the couch watching James clip his fingernails. Charlie shut the door when Earle was inside. Oh, shit, thought Earle, they must've figured out that Lance and Gene were his friends. Earle sat down and watched Randy's fingernails fly off the clipper like tiny boomerangs. Pat looked up and addressed the strange group. Earle braced for the worst.

Boys, guess what? It's your lucky day. There's a new Cellar opening up in downtown Houston and you and the Blues are gonna be the main attraction. Bigger club, bigger city—

Better pay?

Pay's the same. More skyscrapers. More girls. Bigger girls. More every-

thing. Some big tippers down in the
Bayou City.

When do we start?

Get packed. Tomorrow, a few days, max.

Pat left the room and everybody jumped up and down
on the broken cushions on the couch and pulled
the pint of gin from a hole in the plasterboard
and passed it around to celebrate. Everyone
toasted to each other with a kind of lost, far
away look in their eyes as if not quite sure what
to expect or from what range to gauge their expectations. In their insecurity they simply envi-
sioned a big, golden palace with a stage bathed
in a rainbow of light surrounded by luscious,
busomful girls with pure complexions holding
drinks in front of them on silver trays.

Earle called Barbara the next day to tell her the news
and to arrange to pick up his echo chamber.
She told him that somebody had broken into
her apartment and taken her TV, radio alarm
clock and his echo chamber and that she was
very sorry but that Oak Cliff was getting a reputation for break-ins. Earle was silent for a long
time and she asked if he was still on the phone.
He said that he was but that he had worked at
the Chicken Box for a year and a half paying for
that echo chamber and that he was beginning
to lose faith in his fellow man. He told her he
was sorry that she had lost her TV but that the
preacher who had given him a ride to her house
had told him not to value worldly possessions

because they were unnecessary in the world beyond. She thanked him for his words and they said good-bye.

Earle had, in truth, loved that echo chamber because it reminded him that the moment can be repeated forever unless you move forward. Or at least an illusion of the moment. Shit. One third of his worldly possessions had just vanished in the Dallas suburbs and he thought he better call Lance before another third did the same.

KC and Lance and Gene met him at Charlie's and brought him his Super Reverb amp that they had hauled from Lubbock. He told them about losing the echo chamber and about his offer to open the Houston Cellar, and Gene said that he had worked out a deal with the girl where he was staying and it looked like he would be there awhile and to call him collect whenever he felt like it.

There was a sadness in the air as they drove away. The leisure days of their youth were slipping away without so much as a warning, and it appeared as if they would be a long, long time returning.

CHAPTER 3

Opening night at the Houston Cellar brought out the best and worst of Houston nightlife. The Banditos, a notoriously badass version of the Hell's Angels whose headquarters were in hideouts around the ship channel, came out in force. Harleys circled Market Square as the bikers paraded with their mamasitas straddling the rear wheel, looking like goddesses of some long lost underworld surfacing on some strange new planet for the first time. As they rolled together in a rumbling pack, they personified the very image of rebellion and defiance, yet Earle saw in their eyes the glint of desperateness that an outsider always wears, and felt a strange, although distant, kinship with these roaming refugees.

Cool Daddy Winter, his snow-white pompadour frozen hard in an invisible shell of spray net, arrived in a white limousine with a gaggle of slinky blondes at his side. His pink albino eyes squinted when the press fired their flashbulbs at him as he entered the doors of the new dungeon, and he ducked behind the curtain that concealed the band from the world.

The Neurotic Sheep parked diagonally across the street from the front of the Cellar in a fire zone. The old Chevy they arrived in was covered in so much rust that it looked like parts from an old railroad bridge drug up from some gulf salvage yard. No one had told them about any press party. The band looked so beat up that the press thought they were the clean-up crew and stepped aside to let them inside, all the while scanning Market Square for the possibility of another VIP or band member who may be late and newsworthy.

The inside of the club was just the same as the Fort Worth club with double the size and half the imagination. In fact the same clichés adorned the walls, the same flat black paint job with the same black burlap covering on parts of the walls and ceiling. Even the stage was made the same, down to the automobile dimmer switches used for the lighting system. Maybe it was designed so that neither light nor the blues could ever escape. There was a group of musicians going down to see the hotel and Earle jumped at the chance to break from this brand spanking new dungeon.

As they were about to leave, a vague and dangerous-looking man walked out of the front office and gave them a discriminatory looking-over as if he were some military officer inspecting the new recruits.

You the Fort Worth boys?

Yep, that's where we come from today.

Bad Bob. Welcome to your own private hell, where you'll be livin' and tryin' to breathe seven nights a week.

I guess we should say thanks.

You better wait on that. You might change your mind. You know the rules—nobody can be late, ever; no dating the waitresses, 'specially Candy; no alcohol inside the club; and a one-month notice if you decide to escape.

Sounds like the Army, said Earle.

You might be wishin' for the *Marines* after a few weeks here, fuckface. I used to break in little shits like you in Fort Bliss. Don't ever fuck with me.

He turned back into the office and slammed the door.

They didn't spare no expense on the welcomin' committee.

You said he was no picnic, but I didn't expect him to be a fuckin' bucket 'a scorpions.

Best to take the long way around him.

The Milby Hotel had seen better days. It was obvious that the mural of the fabulous locomotive on the wall in the lobby had not always faded into a water stain, and that the painted plywood around the lobby windows used to be windows. But it was convenient, being only three blocks from the club. There was a cheap little diner next door.

Each musician made ten dollars a night and since the hotel charged forty dollars a week for rooms, it was instantly decided that the band would only rent two rooms and share them accordingly. Since Earle's entire wardrobe was on his back, he needed very little in the way of accommodations. He only had to jump in the shower and splash some water in his face from time to time and he was ready for the night.

The Cellar was packed. The Banditos took up the entire floor section sitting on cushions and having their ladies sprawl across their laps. The bohemians gathered at the tables on the side of the stage and smoked roll-your-owns and stared expressionless. The college kids sat on the other side of the room and talked to each other, laughing carelessly between themselves as if no one else existed.

A local band, the Treeks, opened the night and then the Neurotic Sheep went on and stumbled through most of their early set. The American Blues made a grand entrance, bursting through the front door, spilling drinks and crawling over the audience to get to the stage. They had only played two songs when a particularly surly biker grabbed a waitress and began popping the elastic on her panties while grunting through his beard at his compadres. Rocky had been watching from the bandstand and suddenly threw down his instrument and leaped onto the unsuspecting customer. The bouncers were close behind. A chain reaction began, with skirmishes popping up around the floor. The band went into a drum solo that built in intensity like a runaway freight train that was a perfect soundtrack for the mayhem. Rocky returned to the stage, slightly bloody, to a rousing encore. By the end of their set, the Cellar had been christened in the style that it would repeat over and over and over again.

Earle and the band had just enough time to eat their first meal of the day before going back to the Cellar. Their next set started at eleven and the American Blues went on at midnight. The crowd was starting to come in from other clubs all tanked up and ready for trouble. Earle and the Sheep played their best set ever (in less than a week) closing with Midnight Hour, and looked at each other in surprise at the ovation they received. The Blues were feeling their oats on the back side of the clock as Cool Daddy Winter joined them for two songs.

By the third set the crowd had evolved into a drunker, sleazier bunch and the real underground of Houston was beginning to appear. The Banditos, who had left after the fight early in the night, were back—double in size and triple in defiance. The waitresses were visibly afraid to walk between them and the bouncers were beginning to wonder if they were current on their insurance policies. The musicians dug in as if to find the source of their inspiration and to use it as a shield against any outside force that might cause them harm or humiliation.

As the band began to play, the music seemed to come, not from the surface, but from a deeper realm where the players felt a bond between all those who have come before. Now here they sat in the present moment, circled around a stage in a dive in downtown Houston. The more tribal the music became, the more unified the crowd became, until at 3 a.m. there were no differences between the most sophisticated and the most heathen in the audience. Everyone was connected to everyone and by the time the American Blues hit the stage the bikers on the cushions and the beatniks at the tables were making out with their women, squirming here and there, flowing with the passion. Everyone stirred as if on cue at about 4 a.m., when the bedroom called and the mass exodus began. When the Sheep went on for the 5 a.m. set, the Cellar had become a graveyard and the band felt like they were playing to zombies as one by one the audience nodded and were escorted to the front door by the bouncers. The main exception was the rather large gathering of the meth-headed Banditos who were just staring to kick into gear. When closing time came at 6 a.m. they raced for their scooters and zipped away into the dawn, to the warehouses in the ship channel where the week-long day was just beginning.

So much had happened in Earle's life in the last twenty-four hours that it was hard to remember what *had* happened. When he landed on the couch at the Milby he was out cold, dreaming of a place far away, of a green slope that rolled down to the sea, where the clouds floated by and all the world was as simple as that....

The next afternoon Earle woke up at two and went out to explore his new neighborhood. Every bar

around Market Square had their jukeboxes
blasting away, churning up the brutal heat. In
fact it felt as if the music itself was creating the
100-plus degrees that was turning the sidewalks
into griddles. George Jones sang his blues out of
a hillbilly bar while next door Lightnin' Hopkins'
voice wailed his own tales of woe from a jukebox
speaker aimed at the street. From the shoeshine
parlor came Sam and Dave and from a pawnshop
came the Rolling Stones singing Time Is On My
Side. Earle wondered how it had all evolved to
become such a diverse center of sadness. No answer came to mind so he stopped in for coffee at
a burger joint on the south side of the square.

The sign said St. Paul's Cafe but there was nothing to
suggest that any church or charity was involved
in the management of the rundown cafe. Earle
sat on the ripped Naugahyde stool at the counter and found a piece of yesterday's paper at the
booth behind him. He noticed that the ashtray
was so packed with cigarette butts that it had
become a pyramid. Earle lit a smoke and slid a
Carling Black Label ashtray from down the bar.

Earle heard the waitress come up to the counter but
he kept reading the paper as he ordered coffee
and toast.

Anything else?

Who's Saint Paul?

Was my old man till he bled to death
in my arms.

Earle looked up from the paper and was stunned at
the face of the old waitress. Her skin was the
texture of sunbaked leather and the creases and
folds seemed as if it had taken nature thousands
of years to create such a masterpiece. There was
a strange beauty to the old woman, yet there
was a sadness as deep as the cracks around her
eyes. There was a kind of symmetry to each line
that curled and twisted like eddies in the Rio
Grande. Each ravine had its mirrored equiva-
lent but not always in the same part of her face.

Oh, my God. I'm sorry.

He saved me from a mad robber.
Would'a killed us both if Paul hadn't
'a wrestled him down. Bullet went
clean thorough the son-of-a-bitch,
bounced off'a the hard top, went back
through him and into Paul's heart.

They ought'a make a saint out of him.

We already have.

She pointed to the sign above the ordering window
that said 'Saint Paul's Kitchen'. It had been
stitched by hand, embroidered with crude roses
and placed in a substitute frame that had previously bordered a beer sign.

And your name is?

Paulina, Santa Paulina. That's what
everybody's called me since Paul's gone.

Earle, here. I just moved into your town. Playin' over at the Cellar every night.

People ain't too pleased about the Cellar movin' in.

How come?

That gangster who runs it has warned everybody in ten square blocks about what a bad ass he is. He don't scare me none. Them kind'a fellers usually get what they deserve.

I just met him, and I don't care if I ever see him again. 'Cept at paycheck time. I'm just a musician, and I don't get involved in the business end of things much.

You ever hear of Lightnin' Hopkins?

He's the King, far as I'm concerned.

He plays sometimes over at the liquor store and sometimes at the bar next door.

I can't even believe that.

He's got family down here.

Maybe I'll catch him one of these days. Damn, Lightnin' Hopkins!

Never really knew if he was real or not just because he's too real. You know what I'm sayin'? Well, guess I better run. Nice meetin' you, Pauline.

I make the best French toast in Houston.

I bet you do. I'll see you mañana.

Sayonara, cowboy.

Earle walked back to the hotel expecting to take a shower, but when he walked into the room every square inch was occupied by the musicians and the waitresses and other employees from the club. The smoke was so thick you could hardly see the dreadful pictures on the wall. In only twenty-four hours their room had established itself as the official hangout spot of the Cellar. He walked down to the lobby and found a gigantic couch covered in ragged gold chenille and he sat at one end, imagining all the millionaires that had sat there in the Milby's heyday. He found a piece of paper by the house phone and wrote:

The Comfortable Dead, The Happy Dead
Those who deny in public,
Deny that they are dead
Let the Dead Wake Up!

Let the Dead Watch Out!
Drowsy memory perforated!
Soon the dead will rise!

Let the Dead Wake Up!

Down the tracks of insomnia
Let the Dead Wake Up!

He heard the elevator door open and a wall of conversation spilled out, mixed with smoke, perfume and guitars. It took him a second to realize that these were the same thirty people
who had just come from his room. He glanced
at the clock and saw it was close to seven,
time to go to the Cellar.

He walked with everyone, straggling behind, and was
greeted by two women who had dropped to the
back of the pack and introduced themselves.

Hi, I'm Pam and ...

I'm Loretta and we ...

Like the way you sing and ...

We dance around the corner from ...

The Cellar and we live ...

On the same floor as you guys and ...

Sometime, if you want ...

Come by and visit Prince Albert ...

They turned at the corner, giggling, and waved good-
bye, bumping into each other and dropping this

and that like a slapstick team improvising try-ing to walk in a rolling funhouse.

Randy dropped back and made a commentary.

It's a wonder they can make it through a day.

What's with them?

Stoned titty dancers from the Stag.

They could still see them two blocks away, weaving and laughing.

Good thing they don't drive airplanes, Randy said.

Or run the government.

After a couple of seconds Earle recanted his last statement and they both decided that the gov-ernment would, in fact, be better if these goofy girls were running the planet. They would most certainly not be involved in an obscure civil war in Southeast Asia.

They walked through the Cellar door and felt all patches of time peel away and remain outside as the blackness inside forbade any forward ad-vancement. In fact, the evening progressed very much the same as the night before and Earle was amazed to see a pattern emerge in such a short time. It seemed there was nothing any more fulfilling about this night than the night before, much to his dismay. He had hoped that it was only himself that was disturbed by this impression, but everyone he talked to seem to have some feeling that there was something not right about this place. Of course they would then dismiss their testimony with a shrug and a nervous laugh and change the subject to something a little lighter.

Earle began to cherish the time between sets, walking the streets, getting to know the characters around Market Square. He listened to countless stories about how each person happened to land in this stewpot of a city.

He walked to the liquor store that Paulina had mentioned and went in and engaged the man behind the counter.

Y'all carry Southern Comfort?

Half-pint, pint, or fifth? You of age?

Just seeing if y'all carried it or not. I'm new in town. Heard Lightnin' Hopkins shows up now and then.

You never know what Lightnin's gonna do. He's like Texas weather, only more so. It might be rainin', might be cloudy. Might be blowin' like all get out. Free as the four winds but less predictable.

Maybe I'll get lucky.

Mondays, 'round dark. He sometime git thirsty on Mondays.

Name's Earle.

Yeah, Little Bell, here.

Pleased to meet ya.

Likewise.

He walked back to the Cellar and slipped into the darkness. Nothing had changed. He played the next set noticing that the band stumbled at the same places each time. Each set was like a live rehearsal only they could not go back and fix what needed fixing. The magic from the night before was missing. It seemed that they were just going through the motions. He missed his Lubbock band.

When the set was over he strolled around the square and walked over to Main where he watched the buses load and unload. The city wound down as the oil company skyscrapers flicked whole floors of lights on and off. As the last of the workers trudged out, the night crawlers arrived, one by one, to see what they could scavenge from the scene. They had an air about them that was cautious like mice, yet sinister like scorpions. Con men, dealers and pimps snaked around the dark streets, sitting low in their cars waiting to make a play.

Earle realized that since he had ventured away from West Texas and out into the world, everything around him seemed to happen in a speeded up time frame, and as a result he had ignored his daily habit of recording his thoughts. He sat on a concrete windowsill that was lit by several pulsing advertising lights. He read backwards through the pages of his journal and it felt like he was reading someone else's life, not his own. He did not feel even remotely the same person as the one from a week ago. It made his heart hurt to read his references to Patricia, as he allowed himself to reminisce about her for a beat or two from his empty chest. God, how he had loved her.

He saw himself as a fly in a huge, maniacal cowtown. He thought about his home far away and the events that led him to this unreal city and he decided he needed to jot down a couple of lines that had been rolling around in his head before going back to the Flat Black Inferno.

> The Cyclone
> The Hurricane
> The Tornado berserk!
> The Living, The Dying
> Trudging on to Work...
>
> O Volcano, Frost and Freeze
> Wild fire of mad disease
> Tidal Wave of the weary
> Let the Dead Wake Up!
> And the Dying!
> And the Dying!
> And the Dying!

During the next five hours the Sheep played twice
more and Earle escaped to the streets after
each round. By the end of the night he had met
most of the Market Square regulars. They were
all curious about the Cellar management and
they all wanted to know if it was really as bad
as its reputation. Earle said that he didn't know
much about it but that he figured it was worse
than they had heard.

The Cellar emptied out after the four o'clock set and
everyone filed out joking about going home to
the 'Chateau Debris'. Charlie invited everyone
over to the band's room for a party. As they entered the lobby Earle saw Pam and Loretta, the
two strippers from the beginning of the night,
still giggling and bouncing into each other.
They saw Earle and asked if he wanted to come
up to their room. It seemed like a sensible alternative to his only other option.

They had obviously been living in the hotel for some
time. Their room, although huge, was jam-
packed with stage clothes, hangers, props, trinkets and other things that had no name. Pam,
the redheaded one, told Earle to make himself
comfortable on the couch while they changed.

When they returned arm in arm they were dressed
in East Indian outfits and giggling hysterically.
Loretta, the larger of the two, asked the room
to be quiet as she had an important announcement to make. Earle, since he was the only other person in the room, did not say a word.

Loretta proceeded.

Please rise.

Earle stood up.

The Prince has arrived.

She pulled a tin from her feather boa purse, and both
girls mock-ceremoniously walked the can over
to the coffee table. It looked to Earle like the
thin kind of Prince Albert tobacco can that had
a hinged top and would fit in your hind pocket.
The two girls took a pipe out of an elaborate
wooden box and asked Earle if he would like
to do the honors. Since he did not know what
they were talking about, he shook his head and
mumbled that he was the guest and he reckoned that the hostesses were supposed to initi-
ate all honors. Pam suddenly blurted.

Your accent is so cute.

It's luscious and delicious.

After slurring her similar words, Loretta laughed
herself into a ball on the floor.

Is that word inside a word?

It's a wordy, wordy, wordy world.

The two girls howled with laughter and several minutes went by before they were able to contain
themselves. Earle had never seen any two creatures quite so absurd in all his life.

When Pam was able to crawl to the coffee table, she pulled some green crushed leaves from the can and put them into the pipe and handed it to Earle. Earle smoked it just like his uncle Willis used to smoke his pipe.

No, don't let it escape. It has to bloom in your body.

Pam took a long draw from the pipe and held the smoke inside her lungs for a long time until a thought flew by and caused her to laugh. Earle followed her directions but found that, except for being a little dizzy from holding his breath, he felt nothing unusual. He even told the girls that very few things had ever had an effect on him.

They passed the pipe around again and he noticed that the room had become so quiet that his thoughts were beginning to turn inward, away from the circumstances of the situation. He closed his eyes, partly out of exhaustion and partly to concentrate on what was inside his head. He heard a rustling in the room and opened his eyes to a nude Loretta who looked like she was ten feet tall bending to soft music that seemed to be spraying out of the walls. Pam then stood and dropped the sari from around her shoulders which twirled her glitter-covered pasties as it fell in a heap around the sparkles on her chrome high heels. She began to caress Loretta in a slow swish of her hand that left trails of light behind each movement, embedded into Loretta's skin.

When he turned his head, he noticed that the candles left streams of light that stayed in his
vision where he stopped his eyes. The shapes
would turn into smoky spirits that seemed to
dance in midair against the rolling blue and
purple shadows that made up the dark space
of the room. As their colors turned to blue and
green, their shapes elongated and divided, giving themselves legs and arms that bent and
twisted like some kind of taffy that became
infinitely thinner as it stretched into the dark
corners. He could hear the dancers' skin as they
rubbed against each other across the room, but
the streams that were in his vision had com-
manded his attention. A groan faded into a
train whistle which faded into the rattling of
the fan which gave the impression that each
sound was being played, on cue, in time to the
dancing spirits that were now passing through
the wall. The glass doorknob on the closet door
seemed to beckon him and he was unable to do
anything except to obey.

When he looked closely inside the glass he could see
what looked like a contorted Shakespeare play.
Ladies in tall pointy lace hats were watching television on a balcony above a huge ball-
room filled with dancing shapes. Rubber Great
Danes sat stretching their necks at the moon in
huge spirals as if they were singing it a silent
song. The ladies were fanning themselves with
fans that spewed off dozens of the ghostly spirit phantoms that Earle had just seen dancing
around the room. They dove in and around the
waves of whirling blue velvet that had, only sec-

onds before, been a hall full of dancing people. Golden falcons flew out of the windows of the palace and into the driveway where bishops sat on white Harley Davidsons in white robes and tall hats, revving their engines in time and in tune with the unseen orchestra that seemed to be playing just behind a wall of juniper trees at the end of the driveway. In the distance, large bonfires were burning on the tops of each of the many hills that surrounded the palace. At least it used to be a palace. Now it looked more like a huge gazebo surrounded by flagpoles hundreds of feet tall with ridiculously tiny flags attached to the top of each.

Earle watched this amazing event for what seemed like hours, only to be distracted by the smell of candle smoke from a candle by the couch that the girls had blown out before going to bed. Earle crawled over on the couch and closed his eyes to watch green and blue fluorescent road graders pave a road that seemed to be a perfect mirrored surface across the flatlands and into a crimson sunset next to a gazebo surrounded by flagpoles....

Sgt. Baylock woke at his usual time of 11 a.m. and drove downtown to Chandler's Cafe for breakfast. Hernando was just getting up to leave when Baylock walked in.

Mornin', Mr. Baylock.

Hernando scuttled towards the cash register, looking down, hoping that Baylock wouldn't grill him on anything current.

> Mornin', Hernando, can I buy you a cup of coffee?

> Drank my coffee, all the drops. Must meet the boss to take delivery of this month.

Baylock stopped and gave Hernando a persuasive glare. Hernando surrendered.

> Maybe just one more cup.

> I thought you might join me. Heard from Gene?

> Still in Fort Worth. Working at a club. I no know the name. Living in a house with Lance. KC sometimes. Earle play the guitarra in the bar that is under the ground. That is all I know. Es todo.

> Piense, cuál es el nombre del night-club?

> No sé. Si supiera, le diría.

> OK then, who would know? How about Chicken Box?

> Si fuera usted, hablaría con Jimmy.

Baylock got up and tossed a quarter on the table and told Hernando to keep his nose clean and reminded him that his probation was coming up in a couple of months. Hernando told him that when he was free again, he would not be subject to Baylock ever again.

I'll make sure your probation officer knows your plans.

He knows I am a man, not a rodent.

But you still bend over and take the cheese.

Hernando looked down at the table ashamed and humiliated. He heard Baylock shuffle away. He quickly reconstructed the plan in his head that had been brewing for years. Someday he was going to get even.

Chicken Box Jimmy rolled his eyes in futility as he stood by the flour sifter watching his new employee create havoc out of a task that Jimmy figured a dead man could do. Since Gene and Earle were gone he had to resort to hiring their worthless friends to train them in the art of cooking chicken.

Glen, you're trying to separate the powdered flour from the damned little dingleberry balls that the egg batter makes. That's all you're trying to do, not form a fuckin' one man dust storm.

I'm sorry Mr. White, I was thinkin'
about somethin' else.

I'm sorry. I don't mean to pick on you.
But we got a lunch rush about to
descend on our asses and they ain't
nothin' to do but face it. When I find
Gene, I'm gonna kill him. You wanna
go to Fort Worth with me, Thursday?

I can't. I gotta work.

I'm the boss, you dumbass. If I ask
you to go you're supposed to say yes.

OK. I guess I can go then.

Maggie walked over to the drug store to have a cup
    of coffee with PD and Jose. Just as she reached
    the door she saw Baylock who saw her and
    pulled into the parking lot and cocked his head
    partially out the window.

Mornin', Mrs. Maggie.

Good Morning, Mr. Baylock, I do believe we could use some rain.

It's gonna be a hot one. Heard from
Earle?

Oh, yes, didn't you hear? He's playing in the fanciest nightclub in down-

town Houston. Seven nights a week.
He says they can't get enough of his
band.

So he's not in Fort Worth? That's
strange. My little bird said he was in
Fort Worth.

Nope, he's livin' in a hotel with digni-
taries from all over the world.

Well, I've been thinkin' about takin' a
trip up there to visit all the Lubbock
refugees. Things are so quiet around
here that I'm startin' to miss 'em.

Well you just do that. And tell Gene
that I've still got his mother's hair
dryer whenever he wants to pick it
back up.

I don't thank he's gonna need that
dryer where he ends up. He's gonna
wish everything was a little wetter.

Earle woke up with the afternoon sun slicing
straight through the middle of his head. He
was not sure if this was still his dream or if
it was something left over from last night. He
raised up and looked around the room. The
glass doorknob caught his attention and he
fell back into the scene he had witnessed inside its shell. He laid back down and closed
his eyes, slipping back into recent events that

now seemed mellow and unthreatening. In fact he slept for another three hours, waking when the giggling girls came out of their bedroom and asked if he'd ever been to Sugarland. When he asked where Sugarland was, they, of course, died laughing for at least another fifteen minutes.

Earle groaned at the thought that it was almost time for the first set at the Cellar. He decided to go to Saint Paul's and see if they were still making breakfast at 5 p.m. He tiptoed out the front door, hoping the girls wouldn't hear him leave.

There was an old black Cadillac in front of the cafe when Earle arrived. It had a mysterious, handmade air about it and, when he saw Paulina, he asked her about the car.

It's a friend of Lightnin's. They were here a couple of hours ago. Saw 'em gettin' Lightnin's guitar out of the trunk. Might be over at Little Bell's. You want a menu?

How could I eat knowin' Lightnin' might be wailin' around the corner? Why don't you shut this joint down and come over?

Cain't. Paul would be reproaching me all the way there and back. Ain't nobody else to run the place 'cept Willow. And she cain't run a toaster, much less a register.

Earle skipped down to Little Bell's and, sure enough, he could hear the refrains of Lightnin's guitar from a block away. A few people were milling around out front; some listening, some smoking, and some tapping their feet and singing along. Earle was surprised there weren't more people around and most of the ones that were there were from the neighborhood. He made his way into the bar next to the liquor store and there was Lightnin', his gold tooth shining in the beer-sign light, sittin' on an old cane chair wailing away with a half-pint of gin on the floor by his chair. He was in the middle of a revved-up rendition of Mojo Hand, grinning from ear to ear like he had finally made it home after a long hard journey. There was something familiar, almost grandfather-like about Lightnin', as if his soul had merged with his music and been passed on through a tweed amplifier for the world to share. He played song after song and in-between talked and laughed with his friends in the bar. Little Bell came in the side door with a chocolate birthday cake with a sparkler implanted in the top. It appeared that Lightnin' had ordered the cake for his friend, Napoleon, the bartender. After they mumbled assorted versions of Happy Birthday, Lightnin' dedicated a song to Napoleon and as he played the floor began to shake. Earle could have spent the rest of his life in this spot had he not glanced at the clock to see that he was to be on stage in ten minutes.

He ran two blocks to the Cellar and saw Bad Bob eyeing him as he panted in the door.

Cuttin' it purty thin, ain't ya?

Always have.

Just don't fuck up. The Cellar ain't forgivin'.

That seems to be the consensus.

The Sheep played an all right set that ended a few minutes early when Charlie busted a bass string. Earle hit the door and made tracks for Little Bell's. The bar had returned to its pre-Lightnin',' sleepy self. The light was still on the amplifier that Lightnin' had played through and an empty half-pint bottle stood at the side of the chair. Napoleon was wiping the bar in a slow circular motion as Earle asked when Lightnin' might return.

If I knew that, I might be one rich fool. He pop in like the Jack 'n a Box and he pop out the same way. He done gone 'bout 'da time the woid get aroun'.

Name's Earle. I caught a little of Lightnin' earlier before I had to run and play my set over at the Cellar.

Nice to make your acquaintance but I wouldn't brag about my place of employment if I were you.

Somethin' strange all right. I can feel it here, blocks away.

Bob ain't got much of a name 'roun' here.

We crossed swords the day we met. He don't seem to care much for the very ones that pay his bills. It sure as hell ain't *his* playin' that brings in the door. Funny guy. Well, Napoleon, guess I better grab a little breakfast 'fore my nex' set.

Breakfast at eight in the night? You keepin' *my* hours now....

Earle sat in a booth by the window at Saint Paul's drinking coffee and watching black clouds bury the sun. Within minutes the rain came, turning to steam as it hit the broiling Houston asphalt. The windows fogged up and puddles of rain formed under the holes in the roof. Paulina was doing double duty, cooking *and* serving; Willow had to leave early to pick up her husband at the refinery. The radio was blaring that a half-million soldiers were now fighting in Southeast Asia and the war was escalating. President Johnson was saying that if America doesn't stop the Communist aggressors in North Viet Nam they will be soon be trying to take over our neighborhoods. The station played Eve of Destruction and the chorus played differently to Earle now; everything that he had taken for granted, freedom, liberty and the pursuit of happiness, was now being challenged by a war 10,000 miles away.

You look like you're lost 'cross the ocean.

You ain't far off. I'm gettin' more and more worried that I might get called for the draft

You shouldn't fret, you should pray. Pray you get called up. It'd be an honor to serve your country.

That's just it. I'm in a dilemma 'bout this whole deal. I've tried praying and the answer I get is the one that everybody says is the wrong one.

We had to stop the Germans from taking over the world.

I don't see that this is anything the same.

Well, you just follow your heart and everything else will follow along.

My heart tells me to run.

That's just what you're doing. And it's what I better do 'fore I git swamped in the kitchen. If that Willow does this to me one more time....

California Dreaming came on the radio and set a series of wheels off inside Earle's head that spun like the pointer on a compass. He remembered the times he traveled on the Santa Fe Chief with his parents, across the desert, to the palms of sunny Southern California. He remembered seeing the barracks in San Diego where his daddy had been stationed in World War II, and he remembered the ride up the coast on the Sunset Limited past great cliffs that dropped off into a wild, frothing sea. He remembered the lady who sat behind him and told his fortune by reading the bumps on his head. He remembered the fog that slithered around Alcatraz as he wondered what imprisoned killers ate for breakfast.

The other night in Fort Worth, Gene had mentioned something about knowing some people on the beach in L.A. and that he might go out there soon to see if he could find them. Earle thought that maybe it was in his fortune to see the beautiful West Coast again. On the other hand, maybe it was time for his next set in the pitch-black hellhole down the road....

The days and nights crawled by and very little changed. The routine that had been established upon arriving at the Cellar soon became a deep rut. The insanity of having to be around that place for eleven hours a night was starting to take its toll on everybody. Not to mention the tension that was building at the hotel. The management had reprimanded Rocky and Dusty and Frank for turning their towels blue when they dyed their hair. In return the musicians were beginning to take out their own frustrations on the hotel's outer appearance. Several of the landscape paintings in the halls had been manipulated to include such things as flying saucers landing in the distant hills while long-tongued dogs fornicated in the foreground.

If it weren't for his friends around the square, Earle might have lost all hope. He began inviting them to drop by the club for the honor of having them as his guest. During the course of one evening he invited Bo Peep and Too Slim from the shoeshine parlor and Julio and Hector from the pawn shop. He stopped by Little Bell's the next evening on his way to the Cellar and saw Napoleon polishing the bar.

> You're liable to rub a hole in it and then what would you do?

> Have to shut this joint down and go fishin' I suppose.

> Might be too hot, the locks might melt.

> Or the fish be hangin' on to a root down on the cool bottom.

Earle looked through the glass to the liquor store.

> I don't see Little Bell.

> His gal friend swooped him up and they done flew to Red Bird City.

> I gotta go there someday. Hey, listen,

I'd like to invite you guys over some night as my guests.

That's mighty kind of you, but the word on the street ain't too favorable towards that place.

I'm out to make it better. The place is a little too wrapped up in itself, that's all.

Thursday's our only night loose.

Good, that's the new moon. Tell Little Bell or I will if I see him first.

Why, thank you Mr. Earle, I'll let him know. I'd like to see the inside of somewhere other than this bar.

Bad Bob's girlfriend, Candy, showed up that evening from Fort Worth and there was a general red alert around the club that night. No musician was to even glance at Candy, or Bob would have them vaporized by his pack of hoodlums. There was only one problem. Candy was nuts about musicians and ran around the club in a red miniskirt begging for their attention. Earle crossed from one side to the other several times to avoid this new threat to his well being and slipped in the far backstage dressing room while she was on the other side of the club. He was sitting on the couch, looking down, tuning his guitar when he heard the volume level rise in the room. When he looked up, his heart skipped a beat when he saw Candy slither into the room like a coral snake. There was no way out of the room so he stood up and faced the corner and started humming Saint James Infirmary. He could hear her slide across the room toward him. He stopped playing and began making his plea as if he were on trial.

I really really think you better leave
this room.

She came back in a low seductive voice that struck fear in Earle's heart.

What if I don't want to. Are you going to make me do something I don't
want to do?

I'm just asking—no, begging.

A nice boy like you shouldn't have to
beg.

Look, Candy....

I didn't know you knew my name.
Say it again.

Earle turned around to find a creature more drenched in sex than any girl he'd ever seen before. Her pale flesh was bursting out of her clothes and she writhed before she spoke.

Say my name again.

Earle tried to say her name but the sound choked in his throat. The volume level rose suddenly in the room again, and Earle thought it was a reaction inside his own body until he saw the silhouette at the doorway. Bad Bob glared into the room.

Candy, I need to see you out here.

He stared a hole into Earle as Candy swiveled to leave the room.

And you....

He slammed the door so hard that the sound in the room imploded and collapsed into a vacuum between Earle's ears. He fell in a heap on the couch and wondered how he was going to finish out the night. Larry came in and told him it was time to go on. Earle asked for a slug of the half-pint that he had stashed in the wall. He took two giant swigs and then tottered, rubber-legged, to the stage.

He felt dizzy and disconnected as he walked to his amp. The weight of his guitar had doubled since the last set. The red and green lights burned his eyes, and when the band hit the first note he could feel the kick drum slugging him in the back of his neck. He opened his mouth to sing and the sound that came out was nothing like his normal voice; it was guttural like the sounds animals make when they are cornered and about to die. As he was singing he was also making a huge conscious effort to not look at Candy. But in every direction he turned she was there. It was as if she had premonitions of which way Earle's head would be facing on each particular verse. She moved around the room and stood in whatever light happened to be there.

Bob was at the office door watching Candy priss around the room while watching Earle's every move. The two bouncers at his side were following the direction of their boss's head. They even shuffled their feet and moved their toothpicks at the same time.

From Earle's viewpoint they resembled a three-headed viper trailing a grasshopper around a dry creek bed. He needed to escape this grave situation but had no idea how to get around the hazards at the front door. After the set, Earle told the band what he was up against and how he was truly at odds over what to do about it. Larry ran out and came back in with the news that Rocky and Dusty had offered their dressing room as a refuge. It was the room with the safe in it and it had both a deadbolt and a padlock on the inside of the room. Earle thanked them for their kindness and locked the door behind them as they went out for their set. For the rest of the night he jumped back and forth from stage to backstage and by the end of the night he was a wreck. He asked Rocky if he would bring his amp and guitar back to him so to avoid Candy and Bad Bob. Rocky not only brought his gear but offered him a ride back to the hotel with him and his girlfriend, Misty. They left out the service entrance around back and attracted no attention.

At the Milby, it took all of Earle's strength to wrestle his amp upstairs. Rocky's girlfriend said she would lock his guitar up in her car and he could get it in the morning. He had a key to Pam and Loretta's room and fell out on the couch without even removing his boots.

In the morning he went down to the lobby for a cup of coffee and noticed some commotion outside on the street. He saw through the window a couple of Houston police cars with their lights blinking. Misty, who had given him a ride last night, was crying on the curb and a policeman was trying to comfort her. Rocky was pacing up and down the sidewalk ranting and raving. Earle walked out to investigate and immediately noticed the pile of broken glass by the side of the car.

He told himself that this could not be happening. Someone could not have taken his guitar. It was impossible. Not his guitar. Not his staff, the main tool of his holy trinity of tools. No, he decided, the police were there for some other reason; there was a shooting and the perpetrator, perhaps, missed. Maybe a gargoyle fell off the hotel roof. Each made-up explanation fell short upon his logic, although Earle refused to accept that which was obvious.

Rocky turned to find Earle staring at the scene in shock. He ran over to tell Earle what was going on.

> Some son-of-a-bitchin' junkie-assed
> bastard broke in Misty's car and got

> your guitar, Misty's suitcase, and my
> fuckin' pistol. What in the hell is this
> fuckin' world comin' to?

Earle felt sick at his stomach and thought about the good Reverend who had given him a ride to Dallas and who had told him to use his tools to make the world a better place. That was less than a month ago and he had now lost two-thirds of his tools and, in his eyes anyway, the world seemed to be a considerably worse place. Anyway, he told Rocky not to worry, but after he said it he wondered why he had said something so mundane at a time like this.

> Worry, hell, I just hope the asshole
> shoots off his own little pecker with
> my .38.

After the cops had gotten a description of the guitar from Earle, he walked down to the square stunned and bewildered. Every building looked hollow with rows of dead, sunken eyes. The storekeepers seemed to physically avoid him as he walked by. This was it. It was time to move on. He walked, slightly relieved at his decision, down to Saint Paul's for coffee.

Paulina was reading the Bible when he sat down at the counter. She got up and brought him a cup of coffee before he had a chance to say anything.

> Somebody shoot your horse? You
> want to tell me about it?

Thieves stole my guitar last night. I've pretty much had it. That was the instrument I used to speak through. I washed dishes for two years to pay for that guitar. I feel like my soul's been stolen.

No one can steal your soul but the devil. You lost something dear, but it can be replaced.

There's something about that place that's rubbin' off on me. I gotta do something before it gets too late.

That's your best call yet. You know Little Bell and Napoleon went by there last night to see you and that thug at the door pointed to a tiny sign way up by the roof that said: Cover Charge $99.

Earle jumped up in a near panic.

That son-of-a-bitch. That *son*-of-a-bitch! That lowdown .... I've got to tell them—

I think they knew all along.

Earle thanked Paulina and ran out onto the square. He felt like he might never see her again and a wave of sadness ran over him. He walked with his head down, watching the sidewalk cracks, wondering what to say to his friends that he had invited the night before.

When he walked into the liquor store Little Bell glanced up and quickly glanced away. Earle went to the counter.

> Paulina told me y'all came by last night. I had no idea that those guys were *that* low down. I've had it with them. I quit today. Right now. Right this minute.

> You mean to say you didn't know about that place before now? You ain't got ears?

> I had a bad feelin' when I first walked in the door. I thought it was just me, though. Most of the musicians are happy just to have work and a roof over their heads.

> Us black folks been havin' situations like this for a long time. Maybe you seeing something for the first time.

> Maybe so.

There was a long silence between them as a police siren wailed thru the city streets.

> Is Napoleon around?

> After we got turned away, he started drinkin' heavy. Reminded him

too much of his upbringin'. He ain't showed up to open the bar yet, neither. He don't handle hangovers too well at his age.

Tell him I'm sorry about what happened last night and that I'll come by when I figure out what I'm gonna do. Thieves stole my guitar last night. Broke out a car window in front of the hotel. Reckon I'll have to start all over. Well, guess I better run.

Earle turned to leave.

Earle?

Yeah?

Me and Napoleon ain't blamin' you.

Earle looked straight into Little Bell's sincere eyes.

I know you ain't.

It was painful to walk away but Earle was glad that he had heard compassion in Little Bell's voice. Not that it made anything on the outside any better but it did make the understanding better.

Earle went by to see Bo Peep and Too Slim but there was a sign on the door that said 'Gone off—Be back'. He walked on down to the pawn shop and saw Hector by the back curtain but when he asked the cashier inside, he told Earle that

neither Hector nor Julio was there and that
he was not expecting them today and probably
not tomorrow either. Earle could see the rage
in the young cashier's eyes and could see that
a considerable amount of damage had been
done. He asked him to relay the message to
Hector and Julio that he was sorry for not realizing any sooner that the people he worked
for were bigots and racists but that he did now
and that he had quit the Cellar and was leaving the city soon.

He walked back to the Milby to try and catch the
band but there was not a soul in either of their
rooms, though smoke still hung thick in the air.
He went over to the window and opened it as far
as it would open and sat on the ledge and looked
out over the cruel city. An approaching storm
blocked the sunset and the neon signs came on
as the rain lashed out and splashed into the
glazed streets like molten lava. The whole city
steamed and hissed like a wildcat defending
something sick and unborn. The city's incessant bass pulse came from somewhere deep and
secret and the two sounds were pulling at one
another as if some gargantuan force was being
twisted inside. It sounded as if the city itself
was seeking a breaking point in order to rid
each part from itself. He scribbled in his book.

> Flood Light Blind Eye
> The Power Within!
> Mad dogs follow
> Where Fools rush in
> Let the Dead Wake Up!

Oh Plastic Clock
The Timex cries
Alarm the World
Warn the Dead to rise!

Dead in Spirit, Dead in Nerve
Dead in Mind, no King to serve
Dead in Spark, Dead in Gut
Dead in part, Dead clear-cut
Lift your eyes, O Shaft of Light
Abandon Ye O Guillotine
Let the Dead Wake Up!
And the Dying!
And the Dying!
And the Dying!

Some insane impulse made Earle decide to walk to
the Cellar and confront Bob Crump. He had to
tell him what was on his mind and ask for the
money that was owed him. When he walked in
the door he was whisked into the office by the
bouncers at the front door. Bob sat in a well-
worn office chair and raised his brow and froze
his eyes on Earle when he came in the room.
Earle could hear the Sheep playing on-stage
and he waited for Bob to blink. Finally Bob
shifted back in his chair and crossed his arms.

Maybe you don't recall our lateness
policy. You've damned near missed
the first set.

I ain't late. I'm quittin' this hole. Ain't
my idea of a good time. That ninety-

nine dollar cover charge bullshit
didn't set well with my amigos.

We don't like niggers and meskins
in here and don't care whose friends
they are. And maybe you don't recall our quitting policy. Nobody
quits the Cellar.

Bob reached into the top desk drawer and pulled out
a .45 automatic and aimed it at Earle. He then
grinned the evil grin he always used when he
intimidated someone. Earle felt his ribcage suddenly rise through his throat and lodge in the
roof of his mouth. The bass notes hammered
through the wall and matched the pounding of
his heart, beat for beat. The door opened suddenly on his left and when Bob's eyes darted
toward it, Earle dove for the bottom of the opening. The bouncers were in the process of throwing someone out as Earle flew past them and
sailed out the front door and across the inter-
section with cars' brakes screeching all around
him. His vision blurred at the edges of his eyes
and his head felt like a spark-gun blowing fueled sparks from every cavity into the thick humid air. He could feel his lungs beating him in
the back as the liquid light rippled beneath him
on the wet, glassy sidewalks. As he rounded
the corner his shirt caught on a piece of torn
chain-link fence, causing him to fall and to skid
across the asphalt. He stayed there, not moving,
feeling that the pain of the fall was like a res-
urrection. He no longer heard footsteps behind
him. He could feel a new dawn on the other

side of the pain. He closed his eyes for a second and thought about the sweet girls back in Lubbock asleep in cotton quilts in rooms with little paintings hung on the walls of furry kittens hopelessly tangled in balls of twine.

He could hear Lightnin snappin' his strings way back in the back of his head. He kissed the smooth sidewalk and when he lifted his head he could smell the bus to Fort Worth idling nearby.

CHAPTER 4

Earle sat at the back of the bus numb and motionless.
He had somehow retrieved his amplifier from
the hotel and put it on the seat next to him. He
felt a pang of emptiness run through him realizing that he was leaving his guitar forever
behind with some faceless chickenshit thief in
Houston, Texas. He might have broken down
then and there if it were not for the pain that
surrounded his body. His elbows and knees were
throbbing and his chest and ribs hurt when he
breathed. His chin and bottom teeth had taken
part of the fall. The hot rain smeared down the
bus windows as Earle watched the distorted
skyline fade into a humid blur of wasted light.
He wished he could have explained to the band
what all had happened to him but there was
no way to get through to them without going
through Bad Bob.

He remembered talking to Gene from the hotel and
hearing Gene slur something about going to
California. When he had asked him how he
was going to get there, Gene had told him not
to worry, that he was rich. Earle himself had
maybe five dollars left after buying the bus
ticket. He thought about the seventy dollars
the Cellar owed him that he would never see.
He was just glad he got out of there with most
of his body intact.

As the bus rolled north through Spring and Conroe
it rocked back and forth, wrapping Earle in an
uneasy sleep. He dreamed about the ladies in
the pointy hats that he'd seen in the glass doorknob—only now their hats were bent and the
Great Danes with the rubber necks had melted into a pool of brown glue. The golden doves,
once symbols of freedom, had turned into scrag-
gly black crows raiding a drought-blasted South
Texas cornfield....

Sgt. Baylock pulled into a motel on the Jacksboro
highway where a partially burned-out *Vac
ncy* sign flashed red to black erratically on
the hood of his pickup truck. He was to meet
the Fort Worth authorities to discuss the details of the planned raid to bring Gene back
to Lubbock. He stood outside stretching his
legs and taking in his new environment. The
cicadas were screaming in the trees and he
could see lightning in the far southern sky,
past the Fort Worth skyline. A few prostitutes walked between motels and he followed
them with his eyes until they disappeared. A
trucker honked and blinked his lights and
downshifted around a turn and out of sight.
Baylock wondered if he should think about
moving to Fort Worth to help them clean up
the vice he was now witness to, but discarded
the idea as impractical. He had been under
the wing of the Lubbock Force for so long that
he couldn't even imagine leaving now. Besides, if it weren't for him, the whole damn
copshop might just go haywire.

The desk clerk gave him the key to his room and a handwritten message that said the Fort Worth team was looking forward to working with the Lubbock team as the two cities were sister cities in heart and spirit. Bullshit, thought Baylock, that's a crock of bullshit...

It was barely early morning when KC slammed her car door, locked it, and fumbled to get the key in the ignition before Lance came out of the house. In her panic, she couldn't find the hole for the key and when she looked up to take a reading, a body slammed on her hood. Lance's face slid past the windshield wipers as he attacked the windshield with an animal-like viciousness. KC screamed and her heart wrapped into a knot. She fumbled the key before it slid into the ignition switch. The car would not start the first few tries and KC watched in terror as Lance tried to beat out the windshield with his fists and then with his bare feet. The fact that Lance was nude lent a surreal slant to his irrational fury. When the car leaped to life it was his same nude body that spun from the hood to the asphalt as KC floored the accelerator with the wheels locked hard left In the split second after Lance slid off of the hood, KC wondered if maybe she had run over him. When she felt the swelling in her eye and the blood run down her face where he had slugged her moments before, she actually entertained the idea, did a U-turn and drove through the yard leveling everything in sight before spinning back into the street, out to the highway, and back into the landscape where she stopped and prayed that she would be rid of that sorry son-of-a-bitch from now on.

Maggie sat on a stool in the kitchen and stared at the sea of prescription bottles that she had arranged on the kitchen table. It was as though her life stretched out before her like a horizon of disconnected highways. Even the pieces that were meaningful were beginning to crumble. The thought of her precious Earle being exploited by thugs in a far away Gulf Coast city only fueled her hysteria. Each part of her life was packed with elements that she had no control over. She could temporarily gain some control by changing her personality in order to deal with the problem at hand. She tried to connect her present situation with her carefree childhood years but stumbled at every event where a death occurred. The loss of her baby sister still filled her with guilt although there was nothing that anyone could have done to stop it. Losing her brother in a submarine in World War II and her mother soon after were two events that twisted her life into a descending spiral that later became uncontrollable when her husband died. The doctors had prescribed acres of drugs to divert her attention, but they only made the situation worse. She used combinations of pills to balance each circumstance but it had created the opposite effect and had turned her into a human roller coaster. At one point her father had even gone to visit the doctors to try and dissuade them from issuing any more prescriptions, but discovered that she had a half dozen doctors whom she played one against the other until she got what she wanted.

Gene had pulled himself up from the couch when he heard Lance and KC fighting in the other room. He made coffee while looking out the kitchen window and laughed when he saw Lance's naked body being thrown off KC's hood. Lance had limped in the door and was pouring hydrogen peroxide on his scrapes when KC came roaring back through the yard turning Gene's favorite lawn chair into splinters. The phone rang before Gene had a chance to show his anger.

It's me, Earle.

Where are you?

Fort Worth bus station. Just got in.

You bring your surf board?

Ain't got nothin' left 'cept my old Super Reverb.

I got just enough for a couple of tickets to LA. Lance is comin' out when his scabs heal up.

Lance gave him the snake-eye.

He get hammered on?

KC liked to have run him over.

They're like gunpowder and matches,
them two.

I'll swing by in about an hour.

I ain't goin' nowhere.

Everything that Gene owned fit in a paper grocery
sack. He called a taxicab and told Lance to meet
him in Venice after he had time to get his con-
tacts in order. Lance paid no attention to Gene;
he was looking backwards into the mirror trying to pull bits of gravel out of his hind quarters. When the taxi honked, Gene said good-bye
and ran to the car as if he were running on air.
He had been thinking about California for his
whole life, and today was his day to change the
future of his history....

It was less than ten minutes after Gene left when
a swarm of police cars surrounded his house.
One group of officers ran to the front door and
one group ran to the back. When the ones at the
front knocked, the ones at the back door yelled
for them to come on in. Although this procedure
was considered unlawful, the 'Texas Search
Warrant' was seldom contested in court simply
because it was next to impossible to prove who
it was that said to come in.

Baylock was in the front of the pack as they broke
in the door and was as surprised as the rest
of the officers to find a naked man pouring hydrogen peroxide on his bloody, naked
butt. It took Baylock a couple of beats to
recognize Lance.

> Why, Billy Lance Copeless, fancy
> meetin' you here.

> What the hell are you doin', bustin' in
> while a man is mindin' his own busi-
> ness? Damn, Baylock, you're kind of
> far from home, ain'tcha?

> Cut the chit-chat, fuckhead, where's
> Gene?

> Am I losin' it or did you ask me the
> very same question in a Lubbock pool
> hall a few weeks ago?

Baylock fumbled for an answer, but his better judgment told him to avoid the question.

The officers searched the house in a matter of seconds
and came up empty-handed. When Baylock saw
the look of disappointment in the officer's eyes,
he grew furious and pulled Lance up from the
couch by the hair.

> I'll give you five seconds to tell me
> everything you know, you little shit,
> and then I'm gonna drop the hammer.

Lance didn't say a word. He just stared a hole through
Baylock as if to dare him to lay a hand on him
in front of so many witnesses. Lance knew he
had Baylock over a barrel and played it like a
fine poker hand.

Baylock dropped his grip on Lance's hair and walked
out of the house. He couldn't figure out what had

gone wrong. The car that Gene had been seen driving was still in the driveway and the informant had seen the two of them the previous night, driving home from a bar. This was a devastating blow to his credibility, especially in Fort Worth. He hoped it wouldn't hurt his chances of running for office back up in Lubbock.

Earle saw Gene's smiling face pop out of the rear window of a taxicab. He threw his heavy amp in the trunk and hopped in the back.

You're a damned welcome sight.

You're one, too. Funny how we just sorta veered in different directions.

Let's veer outta here, driver.

They had to wait several hours at the airport before there was a flight available to Los Angeles. The sun was sinking low in the west when they finally got on the plane. The stewardesses were uncertain as to what to do with Earle's amplifier, but since it had no case it could not ride underneath the plane. They asked Earle to strap it in the seat next to him as if it were another passenger.

Before they took off, Earle was apprehensive about the possibility of such a huge airplane being able to rise above the earth. He had only flown once before, and that was with his uncle J.B. in a four-seater Cessna, years ago. He remembered he and his parents had driven from Amarillo to Petersburg to see J.B. and Lola B. There was something intriguing about this side of his family that was vastly different from any of his other relatives. They were, in fact, the only ones who were rich. J.B. had just bought a new plane and offered to take Earle's family for a spin around the huge expanse of land that he called his 'little farm.' Earle sat in the front and his parents sat in the back. When they became airborne, J.B. asked for orders and opened up the bar between the seats and poured himself a shot of whiskey in a new glass. He flew around the farm, bragging about his crops and telling stories about his fellow farmers. No matter where he was, even in the middle of a story, when his drink was empty he would open the window of his Cessna and throw out his empty glass. The roar of the 180 m.p.h. wind would be deafening and the force would whip the inside of the cabin into an insane frenzy. Earle remembered that moment as one of his life's greatest thrills but also remembered seeing his parents in the back seat frozen in fear, their knuckles white from clutching each other's hands. They looked as if it were their last moment on earth. When J.B. closed the window, he would pour himself another whiskey and continue with his story as if nothing had happened. At the end of the ride J.B. flew his plane thirty feet over downtown Petersburg and encored his performance by flying sideways between his very own grain elevators at the end of town.

The stewardesses served Gene and Earle a delicious meal of game hen and green beans which was better than anything either of them had ever eaten and by the time they stopped in El Paso both of them were sound asleep. The plane stopped again in Phoenix and Gene woke for a minute to see a jackrabbit run along the back of the landing lights and then disappear into the darkness. The next time he woke up they were descending over Los Angeles into a flat field of lights that seemed to go on forever. A tinge of fear sparked through both of them when he saw that they were about to land in a sea of humanity, not knowing but one person between them and having nothing but a few bucks and a Super Reverb amplifier to get them by.

When the plane touched down, Earle—so to protect his Super Reverb from harm—held his right hand straight across the seat, instinctively, the same way his mother did when she put on the brakes in her Mercury Comet. He wondered how she and Mark were getting along and became afraid in his wonder.

As they walked from the plane to the street there was a silence between Earle and Gene. It was the kind of silence that was born of uncertainty and as they came to the realization of where they were, the silence grew louder. Taxicabs prowled in front of the airport like June bugs around a porch light and when they inquired about the fare to Venice, they were shocked that it was three times what they counted between them. Earle joked to Gene.

I thought you said you were rich.

I was, but it didn't last for shit.

How far is it to Venice?

Flash said it was just a beach or two
down.

Who's Flash?

The guy who might put us to work.

Beach or two, my ass.

You feeling tough?

Guess we gotta git that way. Ain't got
much choice.

They asked the taxi driver for instructions and he di-
rected them to follow Lincoln Boulevard north
until they dropped from exhaustion and then
he laughed sarcastically at his own joke. Gene
kicked his door and told him to beat it before he
whipped his ass. As they began their journey out
of the airport they talked excitedly about being
in California. The palm trees overhead swayed
in the nighttime ocean breeze and everything
looked more intense than it actually was. Every car was overly clean and shiny and all the
lights and signs were much brighter than they
were back in Texas. The city buzzed with a kind
of false energy like adrenaline or Benzedrine
and the billboards begged to distract their vic-
tims from the steady open spigot of traffic. As
they walked and the hours ticked by, their ex-

citement steadily waned as they passed Earle's sixty-pound Super Reverb amp back and forth. At one point they agreed that he should have left it in Huber's Pawn Shop. The excitement returned briefly when a jacked-up hippie gave them a ride in a beat up truck, but he only took them a few blocks and told them Venice was still a 'couple of miles' up the coast.

At 3 a.m. they turned west on Washington Boulevard and trudged toward the beach, their mouths parched and their hands and shoulders burning with pulled muscles and newly-formed blisters. At the pier they were stopped in their tracks by the sliver of a moon that glistened above the silver Pacific. They looked across the sand while the clouds floated in front of the moon like lost ships in search of a familiar beacon to steer them on their way. Earle and Gene felt as if they were dreaming, so unreal this sight was, until their aching bodies slapped them back in the present and begged them to find a spot to rest for the short remainder of the night.

They walked the boardwalk toward Venice and noticed shapes sprawled on park benches and randomly dropped in doorways. There was occasional music coming from windows and voices talking from behind hidden places and, though it did not seem to be threatening them at the moment, it awoke the question of whether they were intruding or not. When they reached the Sea View Cafe, Gene said he was going to look for Flash and Earle said he might lie down for a minute till he got back. Gene headed down the alley and Earle limped out on the sand to

the breakers by the shore and watched a million shreds of light shimmer on the surface of
the ocean. He put his Super Reverb backside
down on the sand and laid his head on the amp
so, in case he fell asleep for a few minutes, he
could feel it move if someone were crazy enough
to try and remove it. The roar of the surf took
him under within minutes and he dreamed of
that same green slope that rolled down to the
sea, as the clouds floated by until ripped in half
by a monster jet plane in route to an advertised
paradise some place—somewhere not nearly as
blissful as the idea of it all....

Earle woke to the sound of flutes and conga drums.
He was stiff with pain and shivering from the
moist morning chill. There was sand in every
crevice of his body. When he opened his eyes,
a crab scurried by inches away and he popped
straight up, having never seen such a creature.
His bruised body froze as his cold stiff muscles
contracted into the recent damage. When his
eyes landed on the morning ocean, his discom-
fort withdrew into the view of something so immense and endless that it caused him to gasp
in awe. Golden clouds floated far away on a
shiny silver vision of something immeasurable.
Seagulls suspended themselves in midflight.
The beach curved away in both directions and
was broken by a pier at each end, but survived
until it faded into the pale lavender mountains.
Around him, on the sand, small groups of hippies formed around rhythms that sounded like
they had come up from the sea during the night.
He listened as the groups intertwined with each

other and with the sea as it pounded the shore low and merciless and then retreated with the roll of a thousand cymbals.

As he lugged his amplifier across the sand toward the boardwalk he felt the same kind of excitement he had felt as a child, as if each moment was unfolding and each step was a new adventure. He bought coffee at the deli and sat on a bench taking in the myriad life forms that made up Southern California. Venice was nothing like he had imagined; it was poorer and more bohemian than he had expected, with music being played on every corner. Hair had become a kind of status: the longer the more. People dressed the way they felt, with no regard for convention. And, since Venice was a bohemian beach town, people often didn't dress at all. When Earle saw a beautiful, unadorned, angelic looking girl in a see-through white gown he dropped his amplifier on his foot and gaped in disbelief.

He wanted to explore the area (and maybe meet the girl in white) but he was hobbled by his amp. He could not walk around gracefully with a sixty-pound weight tied to his body all day. He wondered if Gene had found his friends and where he might be. He walked a block down to find the Sea View Cafe still closed and parked himself on an empty bench across the boardwalk. He again positioned his amplifier as his pillow and lay on his back and watched the tops of the palm trees sway until he dozed off to the lazy whispers of the wind...

The dust was blowing through the locust-ravaged elm trees as the rusty swamp cooler beat a low rhythm against the back of the windowsill. Maggie opened the Government letter thinking that it might be pension checks from the Navy. She had not noticed the words 'Selective Service Department' at the top of the letterhead. She was first surprised in that it was addressing her son, Earle Jr., and later was horrified that it was a request for him to appear for a physical examination for induction into the United States Armed Forces. She fell back in her chair and cried, asking God how could He do this to her. She called the Mormon preacher and told him he better come over immediately. She called Bob the Turk and told him about the letter. She then called her father in Houston and told him that there was an emergency and asked if he could drive to Lubbock. Last of all she called her doctor and told him she needed something for her nerves and asked if he could call it in to the pharmacy for her.

Bob the Turk was the first to come over. He first tried to cheer her by cussing the government and doing his cartoon impersonation of LBJ. Bob knew that Maggie enjoyed his company because he knew how to make her laugh, and laughter was the thing she needed most. He had helped her through her husband's death and had tried to help her keep the store open. That is, until the bills stacked up higher than the bales of used clothes. He could see the difficulty ahead because her sons were the only ones she had left and now the Army was threatening to take one of them away. He did a take on politics, religion and the high cost of living, and watched as Maggie laughed hysterically one minute and cried the next. When she asked him to tell the story of how he came to Texas he first balked but then relented if she really wanted to hear it again.

Though he had ranted and raved about everything political, Bob actually felt lucky to be a legal immigrant in America. He had come with his parents at the end of World War II after suffering the loss of his house and land as a result of the consequences of that war. He remembered entering the city of New York and being with his parents at a busy market in Brooklyn. He became distracted for just a second and when he turned around they were gone. He waited for the longest time and when they didn't return, he walked the streets looking for them the rest of the day and into the night. He looked for days, weeks, then months. He spoke no English and there were few in America who spoke Turkish. He made his way the best that he could by sleeping in abandoned buildings and eating what had been thrown away. All the while, he spent every waking minute learning English by mimicking sounds and studying signs and devouring the contents of periodicals, matching the pictures with the words. It was in a National Geographic that Bob saw a feature on Texas and decided, after months of searching in vain for his parents, to head to the Southwest and become a cowboy. It took weeks to work his way to Texas but when he arrived he was hired on the spot as a roughneck in the fields around

Floydada. With the money he made he bought a horse and became as good a cowboy as any of the locals had ever seen. His reputation brought him to the attention of the XIT ranch in the Panhandle where he worked keeping calves away from the Canadian River's quicksand. After a spat with the foreman he moved south to Lubbock where he met Maggie and Earle when they hired him to drive their delivery truck for the D.A.V. Thrift Store.

The door knocked and it was the Mormon preacher. Maggie introduced him to Bob and Bob swiftly offered a measly excuse for not being able to stay and enjoy the sermon—that is, conversation—that they were sure to share.

The mama cat appeared that Earle had not seen since he was a child. Her tongue was out and she was panting as if she were having problems breathing. He went over to see if he could assist her and was surprised to see that she was giving birth. He watched in disbelief as she gave birth to twelve little pink erasers....

Gene's cheeks and nose were bright red when Earle opened his eyes and tried to figure out what was happening. Gene was singing *Come on baby light my fire*, bobbing his head back and forth and grinning from ear to ear. A flute player nearby was playing the melody from In the Hall of the Mountain King and a radio blasted Coltrane from an apartment window on the boardwalk. Gene shouted as he danced in a circle.

We're free! We're free! Free from Lubbock and Fort Worth! Free from re-
pression! Free to fly across the sky....

Earle was suspicious.

Are you stoned?

I'm free!

Earle followed Gene as he danced down the boardwalk singing and spinning, oblivious to everyone he passed. He turned up Westminster and
then down Speedway for a couple of blocks. He
turned east across Pacific for a block. Earle had
to carry the amp with his fingertips to keep
from opening the blisters from last night. When
Gene danced up a sidewalk and into the front
door of a small bungalow, Earle sighed a sigh
of relief.

The air inside of the house was thick with incense
and Indian tapestries and a hookah sat on the
table amid bowls of dried herbs. At a table in
the corner of the front room, a young girl wearing a tiny bikini and a paper crown sat playing
chess with a bearded old man in a military outfit wearing a torn green beret. People came and
went of their own free will, but no one who entered the house acknowledged anyone else, as if
they were traveling through a different galaxy
in a different time. Gene showed Earle a basement where he could store his amp. When Earle
asked if it was safe, Gene replied that this was
Venice and it was different than most places.

There was a code of honor among the hippies, and everyone here respected each other's space.

Earle went for a walk around the neighborhood happy to be free from having a weight tied to his body. As he walked in the sun in the cool ocean breeze a sense of freedom rolled in waves over his body. He was filled with a feeling of ecstasy as if he had somehow entered a new body that perceived its surroundings with greatly enhanced senses. Each puff of wind on his cheek, each faint scent he passed through, and all the sights and sounds were magnified in the more subtle openness that surrounded him. As he walked up Pacific Avenue he realized that everything he experienced was opposite the place he had come from. Every tree, plant and weed seemed to radiate a carefree attitude that was mirrored by the people that he passed on the street.

At a bus stop bench on the corner of Venice and Pacific he noticed a wild-haired hippie sitting and playing an old Gibson guitar covered in seashells. He crossed the street to hear what he was playing. As he approached the bench the man stopped playing and looked up at Earle with reckless, beady eyes.

You need something?

Earle was embarrassed that he had interrupted the man's concentration and apologized.

Sorry to have broken your train of thought.
Just thought I could hear you play.

Well, I don't play for anybody. They can read your mind. That's how they get'cha.

Earle was surprised at this reply. He had never been around any musician quite so paranoid.

Why would anybody want to cause you harm for playing music?

They send signals through your body and the government can intercept them and then destroy you.

It was time to change the subject.

What year is that old Gibson?

It has no time. Time can be traced.

Did you put them seashells on it or did someone else?

I camouflaged it to attract less attention. Why? Are you one of them? Why are you asking me these questions?

I've never seen a guitar covered in seashells.

Everyone has been forced underground. Some still ask questions. That's how they get'cha.

Even though the conversation was fascinating, he felt

it was time to split. He couldn't help but leave
the poor fellow a few tidbits to think about.

> Sorry I opened the door. I've been
> living on a mirrored roof exposed to
> radio signals and satellites. You have
> no idea where I come from. You think
> you're the only one that's vulner-
> able. The whole universe is vulner-
> able. But who gives a shit? I'm on the
> verge of turning myself in. But first
> I have a secret meeting to attend. If
> you'll excuse me....

As Earle started to walk away, the guitar holder
turned to him and replied in a meek voice.

> It's for sale ... ten bucks ... cash. I
> need the money. I think you're the
> one... You understand.

Earle told him that he only had some change and
asked where he could find him tomorrow.

> I'm always here. If I went anywhere
> else, they'd find me.

> See you mañana.

Within a block, Earle had decided that he needed
this guitar to fill the hole in his life that had
been created in Houston. As he walked toward
the boardwalk, he wondered how he could ever
come up with such a massive amount of money
by tomorrow. He counted his change. Thirty-

seven cents. He walked out to the edge of the beach and looked across the water to the edge of the horizon. It could be done, he thought. Anything can be done.

The next twenty-four hours found him in an all-out collection mode. Gene could spare a dollar. He told Earle that he had a job at the Sea View washing dishes but that it wouldn't start for a couple of days. The consensus on the street was that the people in Santa Monica were more prosperous than the Venice bohemians. He walked the shore past Pacific Ocean Pier to the Santa Monica Pier. Sure enough he found lots of coke bottles that had been left on benches where the lines ended for the rides. He took them to the grocery store and cashed them in for another seventy-five cents. Throughout the day and into the night he followed every hint that might lead him to his goal of ten dollars. He collected seashells under the pier and traded them for a kite, which he traded for a barbell, which he sold for a dollar at Muscle Beach. He sang on the boardwalk briefly, but without a guitar no one stopped except for an attractive older woman who offered him twenty dollars to go home with her. Earle drew the line right there but asked if she would contribute a dollar to his cause. She took him to an open- air restaurant and bought him dinner and wine and talked about writers and painters who lived tragic lives. He walked her home by the dark canals and when she opened the door he saw that her front room was full of colored lights and tropical birds. She offered to lie naked on the couch and cover herself in mynah birds but the whole idea was just too weird for Earle's West Texas mentality and he declined. She contributed two dollars to his cause for walking her home and told him that her offer would haunt him in his sleep and that, someday, he would be back.

He walked down the Carroll Canal by the bungalow where he was earlier. He peeked in the door and didn't see Gene so he walked on down to the boardwalk past a group of winos circled around a blind accordion player howling garbled country and western songs while stumbling around in the sand. Earle walked down the dark coast to the Venice Pier where he found a dry spot and dropped from his feet to sound asleep in a matter of seconds.

He knew it was Jimmy Durante's house but he was shocked that Mr. Durante himself was selling marijuana in the bedroom at the back of the house. He wanted to ask him a question about Hollywood, but a splashing sound at the window was distracting him. He went to the window and looked out. The house was surrounded by the ocean in every direction.

Earle was shaken from his dream by the sound of a thunderous wave followed by the splash of cold salt water that lifted him up and pushed him higher up the shore. He cussed to himself as the water shoved him rudely from his subconscious state, but had no choice but to laugh when he was dropped, unceremoniously, face down in a pile of seaweed. The ocean simply retreated with a hiss to begin its ancient ebb and swell all over again.

Soaking wet, he looked up and down the shore to see who had witnessed his miscalculation of the tides. There were only a couple of beachcombers and their dogs walking in the first crack of morning light. He quickly shook off his embarrassment when he remembered his mission and counted the booty from the day before. He had a little over five dollars, mostly in change. He walked up on the pier by the Cheetah and found a few stray bottles and went down to the market to sell them. The cashier was from Oklahoma and gave Earle a donut and coffee when he heard his familiar accent.

He sat on a bench and watched the boardwalk come alive with people from the city who invaded the coast on the weekends. Successful-looking men draped with gold chains strolled arm in arm with girls half their age. They wore the latest tropical swimsuits and had perfect tanned skin and their faces were masked with glued-on eyelashes and thick makeup. He had seen many different Californias in such a short while and each one seemed to have multiple personalities. The serene paradise that made up his first impression was beginning to become a facade disguising a mental hospital surrounded by palm trees.

He walked to Pacific Avenue to see if the guitar guy was there. Sure enough, he sat at the same bus bench grinding his teeth and scratching out

crude sounds hacked out from the old Gibson.
He approached the man cautiously.

See you're still here.

You know me?

I'm the Texas rooftop refugee from
yesterday. I've been collecting bottles
that they left behind so I might be
able to buy your guitar.

Did they follow you?

No, there's a tunnel under the sand
that they don't know about.

I've heard about it.

Earle reached in his pocket and pulled out a pile of
change and two crumpled dollars.

That don't look like ten dollars.

It ain't. It was all I could come up
with.

Damnit, I need ten dollars. I'm out. I
need the whole ten.

You could think of it as being over half
way there. It's more than nothing.

The hippie's speedhardened eyes locked on Earle and
held his gaze like a statue. Earle held his stare

and did not blink even though he could see the pain that had burned deeply into the man's shattered pupils. When the wild man spoke, it was in a yell.

Son-of-a-bitch! Damnit to hell. This
is the way they get'cha. All right.
O.K.! But I keep my seashells!

He scooped up the money and stuffed it in his shirt pocket. He then laid the guitar in his lap and began to rip the seashells off one at a time. There were five on the front and four on the back that had been held on with airplane glue. The glue had been sprinkled with glitter before it had hardened which gave it a sort of cheap circus look. Earle cringed with each shell that came off and thought he was going to pull the top wood off of the body. The old Gibson creaked and moaned but held firm. Finally he pulled coat hanger wires out of the drilled holes in the neck that had been twisted into a makeshift harmonica holder. He threw the guitar at Earle.

Here! Take it! Now get the hell out of
here before they find us. Go on, get!

Thank you, sir! I will deliver messages to those who control you and
ask them to leave you alone with
each note of music that I make on
this guitar.

Damn you!

Earle backed away as the speed freak stood up and
walked in circles stamping his feet and cussing
himself. He suddenly stopped cold and within
a second had changed his expression to a kind
of sly grin. He reached in his pocket and pulled
out the money and ran off down the street,
turning up the alley at Speedway.

Gene was putting on his apron when Earle walked
in the Sea View Cafe with the old guitar at his
side. He cheered as Earle walked in the room.

    You got it! Hot diggety!

    Was not easy. I walked off half my
    shoe leather.

    You needed it more'n Mr. Spaceman.
    Guess what? Lance oughta make it
    in by tonight. He's comin' from Dal-
    las with his new girlfriend. And her
    mother.

    Southern California, watch out. Did
    you say somebody's mother?

    They got an apartment on Brooks.
    Guess the mother's footin' the bill.
    Speakin' of mothers, yours wants
    you to call home. Something about a
    letter from the government.

    What d'ya mean the *government*?

    Chicken Box Jimmy said your moth-

er come in to eat last Sunday. Was
all upset about somethin'. Didn't
know how to find you. You hungry?
I'm cookin'. Doors open in thirty minutes. If you wanna work, you're on.
Flash was supposed to have been
here an hour ago. Sit back while the
chef prepares!

Yeah, I'll work. This guitar flat broke
me. I'm gonna walk to the market and
call home. Be back in a few minutes.

There was a pay phone on the boardwalk next to the
market where the Okie worked. Earle dialed the
operator and asked to make a collect call. Maggie accepted the charges and started crying.

Oh sweetheart where are you? We
have been so afraid. You got a letter.
I opened it, I opened it by mistake.
The Army wants you to report for a
physical. I don't want you to go. Remember, you had a borderline case
of rheumatic fever, rheumatic fever
when you were a child. You had to
take penicillin for seven years. You're
not well. In the letter they say that if
you pass, if you pass you will report
for military service, soon. They can't
do this! Our family has given too
much. And do they give a damn, do
they give a damn if I die from lack of
care? They told my doctor that they
would not pay for any more medicine!

I told them that one brother died in one of their damned submarines and then they had the nerve to send an idiot to Amarillo to bring the word to my mother who didn't believe him, she didn't believe him because he stuttered so the idiot told my mother, stuttering even more, four or five times that Frank had sunk, Frank had sunk to the bottom of the ocean in a submarine. She ran screaming into the street in nothing but her slip, nothing but her slip and they put her in the hospital later that very day and—

Mother, I've heard all of this.

And then I told the sorry son-of-a-bitches that my brother Carthel was a colonel who led the last raid on Berlin that ended World War II and that their sorry asses would be speaking German and eating turnips for breakfast if it wasn't for Carthel and was this any way to show their appreciation after all that?

Mother, I ain't likin' this any more than you are. Did it say when I had to appear? And where?

In three weeks and that was almost a week ago. To Amarillo. That's where they destroyed our family! Of course

they'd say Amarillo. That's where all
this started. They can't do this to
us....

Do you know where I am?

Mr. Jimmy at the Chicken Box
thought you were in California.

Yep. Venice. Now how am I gonna get
to Amarillo?

Your grandfather will just have to
wire you some money, that's all. I
mean, he'll have to. We miss you so
much. You've been gone and little
Mark misses you and all your friends
miss you. I'll call Dr. Benjamin and
Dr. Weir. And what about the chiro-
practor that you went to for all those
years. And what about Dr. Milner,
your friend's psychiatrist, what about
him?

Mother, I'm not sick. I just don't believe that we should be killin' people
for something we don't even know
about. It's a moral thing for me. I
can't go fight somebody else's war.
That's insane. I better go now, this
is gonna cost a small fortune. I'll call
y'all in a day or two.

You have to call, or I'll lose my mind.
And there ain't that much left to lose.

I will. Good-bye.

He listened but there was no reply. She was crying
the second he said 'good-bye.' He should have
said 'farewell' or 'take care' or something like
that. She spent half her waking hours crying
over one thing or the other. He didn't want to
go back to sad ol' Lubbock but he had no choice.
When he hung up the pay phone he stared at it
for the longest time as he surmised his uncertain future and wondered what could be done to
change the course that was being mapped out
for him by outside forces.

Back at the Sea View a few stragglers were coming
in for lunch. Earle put on an apron and walked
toward the kitchen when he was stopped by the
images on television. There were two groups
picketing the White House. One was led by a
Reverend Newhouse who was head of the oppo-
sition group. Earle cupped his ear to hear.

> Clergy and laymen concerned about
> Viet Nam are here today holding a
> silent vigil, we'd like to think, rath-
> er than a picket, in order simply to
> express a cry of anguish about what
> we believe to be an immoral and self-
> defeating course, which our country
> finds itself increasingly bogged down
> in in Viet Nam.

A reporter asked the preacher across the street about
the differences between the two Christian
groups. Reverend Reynolds took the mic.

They believe the war in Viet Nam is immoral and inhuman, and we believe it's essential to defend our freedom and to keep our word and our commitments made to the South Vietnamese. It's immoral to keep our boys over there in a battle where they're suffering and dying if we're not going to win!

The next clip was of dozens of coffins draped with American flags coming out of the back of a military transport plane. The newsman was live at the Los Angeles airport and, although the blender made it too loud to hear the sound, the staid images told the story too well. Earle felt a large bar of steel form in his throat and he felt the blood crystallize inside his veins. He stumbled to a chair and collapsed in a heap, trying to breathe in enough air to melt the ice. He could hear the French fries sizzling in the hot grease and Gene laughing with a customer. He thought he heard rifle shots but it was only someone swatting flies against the glass window by the front door. When he was able to stand again, he tottered to the bathroom and splashed water in his face but almost didn't recognize the pale reflection in the mirror.

How did he get in this situation? Where was Viet Nam anyway? No one even knew it existed until it started chewing into the news a couple of years ago. Everyone assumed it would fade out of memory just like any other bad dream, but instead it had swollen to the top of the page.

Every teenager's life in America was suddenly threatened with a situation that neither the President nor the Pentagon really understood and the stark images of death and destruction on the television were demanding answers from an entire generation. The generation of soldiers who had fought World War II were now in power and their children, who had been force-fed images of a planet-erasing nuclear holocaust, were now in line to fight a war that didn't belong to them.

When Earle came out of the washroom he felt as if he were a changed person. Everything looked different, more impermanent, more superficial. The restaurant was getting busy and Gene handed Earle the order tickets while he went back to cook. Earle tried to keep up but he was unfamiliar with the layout of the Sea View and he slipped further and further behind. Flash finally showed up, glassy-eyed, in a swim suit and cowboy boots, wearing a huge Mexican sombrero and an Army dress shirt with Hawaiian flowers around his neck. About all he could manage to do was bring water to the customers and sprinkle flower petals on the tops of their tables. When the smell of marijuana began wafting from the kitchen area, the food that arrived on the counter began changing in appearance. A grilled chicken breast arrived with about a hundred toothpicks stuck in it with an English green pea carefully impaled on each. A salad arrived for a sweet old Jewish lady on a plate of shredded lettuce with two whole tomatoes and a whole, very long, cucumber arranged in such a suggestive manner that the woman gasped and nearly fell out of her chair. She stood in the middle of the restaurant and loudly demanded her money back and it was up to Earle to convince her that she had not yet paid, so it would be impossible to refund her money. He did offer her a take-out bag at which she cried out that she was going to see her rabbi first, her lawyer second, and the sheriff of Santa Monica third, in that order, and that she doubted that the Sea View would be in business by this time the following day.

The three employees retreated to the kitchen and laughed until their sides hurt and then laughed some more. They might have laughed for hours had it not been for Lance walking in the front door looking dusty and windblown. Behind him was his new entourage, a tall pretty girl named Vickie and her mother Pearl. Gene was the first to speak.

> Well kiss my ass. Look what just blew in from the desert. Y'all musta made good time.

> The girls wanted to sleep in Gila Bend but I was too jacked up to even think about it. Oh, this is Vickie and her mother, Pearl. I been shackin' up with both of them.

They blushed and mock-slapped at Lance. He danced away with his tongue flicking like a snake.

> Well, Gene, what kind of recreational
> activities have you arranged for us?

Gene rolled his eyes and arched his eyebrows like Clark
Gable and smiled mischievously. He wiggled as he spoke.

> Only the best for my friends. Flash
> will take care of us tonight, right,
> Flash?

Flash was drawing designs on a linoleum table using
his finger and a glass of water oblivious to the
rest of the world.

> Like I said, only the best. We'll meet
> by the ocean at sundown. At the
> rocks.

> How 'bout you, Earle?

> I'll bring my new, old guitar.

Lance led his party out the door and down the boardwalk, his long black hair looking dangerous in
the afternoon sun. He walked like a dare, almost on his tiptoes, head high, unafraid, cock-
sure and dead certain that no one would challenge his authority while he inhabited this
stretch of coastline.

The sun was going behind a bank of purple clouds
and the ocean was more calm than it had been
this morning when it had roused Earle with a
rude dousing. Gene arrived, skipping through

the sand with Flash and a few of the people that he recognized from the crash house. Lance and Vickie meandered up with the girl he had seen on the boardwalk dressed in white and introduced her as their new friend, Snowflake. Flash passed out tiny folded packets of tinfoil and everyone unwrapped them and swallowed the minuscule contents. Gene bragged that it was pure LSD, Owsley 25, just in from Berkeley, the best in all the world. They sat in the sand facing the water as the last light of the sun faded and the sky turned the color of fresh peaches and the clouds radiated sharp slices of golden light. There was a slight sense of apprehension among the group as many did not know what to expect from the tiny dose. But no one asked any questions.

After a few minutes as Earle was watching the light shimmer on top of the ocean he noticed that a wave was starting to form in slow motion from the far left of his vision. It was as if he had never seen the birth of a wave before, and he was amazed that his vision was seeing every detail take form as if he were watching it on film. Then suddenly, as the wave reached its crest, a bolt of electricity seemed to traverse the length of the wave and glow an eerie blue-green from inside the wave below the surface of the water. Earle watched the line shoot all the way down the beach, even past the pier into the Santa Monica mist. This astounding sight was followed by a roar of sound like an orchestra of timpani drums doing a roll followed by the crash of cymbals and the fizzing sound of carbonated water fading into total silence. Everyone in the group let loose a collective *'wow,'* putting Earle's mind at ease, that perhaps he was not the only one that had experienced this amazing event. When he turned to look at the group of people they were all a different color than they had been only minutes earlier. Even the subtle features of their faces had changed such that Earle was not sure if he had ever really looked at any of these people before. Lance's face was contorted like he had just eaten a lemon and was not very happy about it. His girlfriend, Vickie, looked as if she had been stretched to an uncomfortable shape, not unlike Silly Putty. These contortions were beginning to irritate Earle slightly because his senses were playing tricks on his natural knowledge. Not only was everything different but it was actually changing as he watched. The sand was shimmering from gold to blue and the houses by the boardwalk were now dripping in rich dark colors. A large Golden Retriever ran by, splashing water in a slow spray followed by a woman who appeared to be tethered to the dog by an invisible line, running together in a strange harmony that Earle would not have deemed possible before this evening.

Someone asked if Earle would play his guitar and he began by playing slowly, one note at a time in rhythm to the swelling of the sea and the crashing of the waves and he realized that he had never really heard the sound of this guitar. The notes stung his fingers as he played and seemed to come from out of his chest instead of from out of the guitar. When the waves crashed on the shore, the body of the guitar magnified the force and throbbed against his rib cage. He could feel his heart moving in a circle as if it were suspended like a pendulum, pounding on the opposite ends of the orbit. He began to use this rhythm as a counterpart to the drone of the ocean. The elements and the cycle of it all began to take on a life of its own. The sandpipers and the seagulls added their parts to the symphony and for a long time the gathering hovered in sync with everything else. It was not until a pair of throbbing helicopters flew overhead that the serenity was rattled into a shambles. As the harsh sound retreated into the distance, everyone stood at once, turned away from the ocean, and slowly ambled in the direction of the boardwalk. While walking in the sand, Earle had the strange sensation that it was not a solid substance and that it might not be able to support the weight of all the people that were walking on it. Gene had the same feeling at the same moment and blurted out,

Hey everybody, I'm sinking.

The surfer guy assured him that it was just sand.

No, really, I'm sinking. I can feel it.

One of the beach bums made light of Gene's remark and began to sing.

We're sinking! We're sinking! We're sinking in the sand!

> In the sand! In the sand! We're sink-
> ing in the sand!

The song was contagious and soon everyone including Gene was dancing in a circle, singing with
total abandon at the top of their lungs. Some
twirled off like planets while others joined
hands and skipped wildly in a circle across the
beach. After what seemed like hours of romp-
ing in the sand, everyone slowly gravitated
back to the spot where the street lamp was
now radiating arcs and arrows of rainbows
against the purple sky. There was a feeling
among the group that they were all traveling
on the same ship and a kinship had formed
to help each other through the intense experience they were sharing. Gene seemed to be the
only one preoccupied with other thoughts. He
was looking out toward the dark waters when
he asked the group if anybody had seen Flash.

The old chess player replied that the last time he
saw Flash was when everyone was walking
back from the water, before the dance, which
by now seemed like centuries before. An instant worry descended over everyone's previous enchantment as they turned to walk back
to the dark ocean. The sand felt completely different now; it was a burden that slowed everyone down as if they were traveling through an
endless bog. The line of phosphorescence still
flared down the waves but now it appeared to
be menacing, like a power line that had fallen,
twitching and spitting sparks down a dark
neighborhood street.

About halfway to the water, a dark shape appeared
that was dragging something behind it wrapped
in a sheet. This person was struggling with
something very heavy, leaving a furrow in the
sand that caught light from down the shore. A
deep fear scattered among the party and a few
of them were frozen in their tracks and refused
to go forward. When the shape got closer it was
Gene's voice that recognized the bowed shape.

> Flash! Where in the hell have you
> been? What are you dragging?
>
> A shark.
>
> A what?
>
> A shark. This fisherman gave me his
> shark.

Everyone stepped back.

> You mean it's a real shark?
>
> Of course it's a real shark.
>
> What are you going to do with it?
>
> I'm going to keep it.

The sheet shook back and forth.

> Where? Where are you going to keep
> a shark?

At my house. In my bathtub.

He was obviously out of his mind, but so was everyone else.

You're going to keep a shark in your
bathtub.

That's right, in my bathtub.

He lugged the weight the rest of the way across the
sand and right into the front door of his apartment.

Why are you going to keep it? Why
not just let it go?

It was a gift. Nobody's ever given me
a gift like this before.

But sharks need seawater.

There's a whole ocean full of it right
behind us.

Flash must have made a convincing argument because most of the group of people committed
themselves right then and there to making
the shark as comfortable as possible in Flash's
house. Several people got pots and pans and
ran down to the ocean to collect seawater. Another committee decided which way to position
the shark in the bathtub. It was decided to put
it toward the faucets so that his tail could swish
on the slope at the back of the tub. When the

first brigade returned with the water it just barely covered the bottom of the tub.

What's he gonna eat?

Flash said there were some hot dogs in the refrigerator. The surfer guy threw two weenies into the bath tub and they twirled foolishly in the shallow water.

More water. We need more water.

A little tap water couldn't hurt. Somebody bring me some salt.

As another group headed for the dark ocean, others scoured the pantry for salt. Flash mixed the solution by tasting the seawater and then trying to approximate it with bowls of tap water and a saltshaker. Gene held the sheet out as far from his body as possible and screamed whenever it wiggled. There was blood at the front of the sheet where the shark's mouth would be. Flash decided it was time to go ahead and put the shark in the tub.

As Gene lifted the front of the sheet, Flash lifted the back and Earle tried to find a spot in the middle to help move the heavy bundle. Just as they maneuvered the shark over the tub the bottom tore out of the sheet and the shark fell into the tub like a bag of concrete, hitting the side of the tub and landing upside down, thrashing violently with his tail and rocking the tub as if it were a toy. Water was slung everywhere and everyone in the room was screaming at the top of their lungs.

We've got to flip him over!

How do you flip a shark ?

We got to!

More water! We need more water!

Snowflake, the Chess Player and Lance and Vickie collected jars and cups from the pantry and headed for the ocean. The returning brigade passed them at the door, sloshing pots full of seawater as they ran to the tub. They suddenly screeched to a halt when they saw the size of the shark. Flash ordered them to pour the water in the tub and when they did the shark wrenched his spine sideways with such force that it moved the tub several inches away from the wall, severing the plumbing connections. Scalding water shot up in a jet to the ceiling and within seconds the room was filled with steam. The shark was upright now and was able to spring himself off of the bottom and everyone could see that he might clear the sides of the tub at any time.

Meanwhile, the commotion had attracted the attention of the neighborhood. Some peeked in the front screen while several dozen stood out front discussing how a live shark could have crossed the sand and made it into someone's bathtub. Flash's landlord arrived in a dirty terrycloth housecoat and looked stunned as he cussed to himself while watching the steam drift out the front door. Damned idiot, he thought to himself, damned goofy bastard! He turned around and kicked at the flowerbed, knocking the bloom off of a chrysanthemum and into the fountain. This only fed his anger. He then ripped the concrete fountain out of the ground and smashed it to pieces while swearing wildly about the mentality of his tenants.

When the fire department arrived, the scene took on a more serious dimension. The original group backed away from the apartment and side-stepped toward the boardwalk. Gene had to physically pull Flash away from his house as Flash was crying and saying it was against his morals to abandon his shark like that. Gene reminded him that not only did his landlord want to kill him, but soon the place would be crawling with authorities trying to figure out how to get a pissed off shark out of an apartment.

When they passed the Okie Market, Gene took up a collection for a bottle of Red Mountain Vin Rose, saying that they all deserved a drink after a night like tonight. They sat by the park bench at the edge of the sand and passed the bottle around. Most of the group was still visibly shaken and it took several rounds of the Red Mountain to break the grip of the acid. Soon they walked in the cool air down Speedway to the crash house off Pacific and passed a police car and an animal shelter truck that looked like they might be headed to Flash's place.

At the bungalow, Earle played his guitar as people took turns telling others of their strange ordeal. Soon everyone was laughing, except Flash, as the story of the shark grew more ridiculous with each telling. It was only when someone fired up the hookah that the room became quiet again and, one by one, the newly bonded group drifted backwards onto the huge Indian pillows to finally let loose of the long, long night...

For the next few days Earle and Gene spent long hours at the Sea View serving food and fixing the place up. Remy, the Frenchman who owned both the bungalow and the restaurant, would come in occasionally, make a few suggestions and leave. Earle spent much of the time wondering what to do about his impending situation. Several people that he asked suggested he could take refuge in Canada, but, Earle thought, then he would be in *Canada*. What in hell's name would he do there? No, he would go back to Texas, take the damn physical, and figure it out from there. He wanted to stretch his time in California for as long as he could but he knew his days were numbered.

The Okie at the Market told him he should hop freight trains back to Texas. He said that one went straight from San Bernardino to Amarillo and that he had jumped it several times going back and forth to Tulsa. The idea ran rampant around Earle's mind but he knew that he couldn't drag his Super Reverb amplifier on such a journey. Back at the Sea View, Gene assured him that he would take care of it until Earle returned.

You *are* coming back, aren't you?

Of course I am. You think I'm going to spend the summer in Lubbock? After Venice? I just gotta figure out this draft thing.

They're probably gonna knock on my door any day now.

Ain't it the shits?

If it was like World War II we'd be the first in line.

It ain't.

I know it ain't.

When he got back to the Sea View, Gene told him that his grandfather had called and was wiring him fifty dollars for a cab and a Greyhound ticket back to Lubbock. Earle told him about the Okie's transportation tip and how it sounded like a pretty good deal. If it was good enough for Woody....

Ray Charles was singing Crying Time as Bill sat at the kitchen table staring at his beer can. Betty was crying in the living room when she heard Bill yell out.

You damn near run everyone away.
They ain't hardly anyone come over
no more.

You're full'a shit, Bill. Everyone left
cause they cain't stand you a' pissin'
and a' moanin'. You're a fuckin' ghost.
Everybody got sick of your dead ass.
Don't blame me for your fuck stick
bullshit.

John and Glen sat on the couch in the living room obviously enjoying every second of this everyday
soap opera. As long as Betty and Bill could cuss
each other out and the refrigerator had cold
beer, the world was a pretty good place after all.

Sgt. Baylock sat in his squad car at the Hi-D-Ho
parking lot reminiscing the past. Since Gene
had left, the nightly scene was more quiet and
he found himself missing the action of earlier
days. Deep inside he actually liked most of the
kids that he constantly harassed. When he was
young, he was just as much a hell-raiser as
these kids were. Now that he was in the position of authority, he thought of himself as their
savior, the one who would guide them by force
to the straight and narrow path to redemption.
He thought of old Sgt. Dupree and how Dupree
had thrown him in jail for stealing watermel-
ons. This thought led him to Dupree's wife the
night before the big graduation party, and he
pictured her slowly crossing her tan legs and
how she had him walk her to her car while

laughing and confessing that she had had a little too much to drink and how she had asked him to help her start her car and how—

The rude crackle of the police radio interrupted his guilty memory with a call about a domestic disturbance on 37th Street. Before the dispatcher could finish the sentence, Baylock had started his car and peeled off to Betty and Bill's.

Earle's new beach friends heard about his plan to travel to Texas and threw him a little party at the crash house. Everyone brought gifts for his upcoming journey. Flash, now homeless, brought him his old Army canteen and told him he might need it when crossing the desert. Snowflake brought him some incense and a bouquet of wildflowers. A small stack of gifts on the kitchen table included magic rocks, a ginger root, an antique knight from a chess set and some brownies wrapped in tinfoil. Gene and Lance had gone in together and had the sandal maker sew a bag for Earle's guitar made with material from Pakistan that was covered in tiny mirrors. Harlon, the Okie from the market, brought him a half-pint of Night Train Express and told him that the desert gets cold at night and he might need something to warm him up. Earle thanked everyone for their kindness and told them he would be back to Venice soon. He took his guitar and his worldly belongings, said his good-byes and graciously made his exit.

He walked along the dark canals listening to the patchwork sounds of other peoples' lives. When he got to the house where the bird lady lived, he hesitated. He walked to the porch where he could see colored lights radiating from every room. The doorbell played an abbreviated version of Für Elise and he could hear the birds inside reacting to the bells. Amethyst came to the door totally nude and when Earle saw her he apologized for coming by so late and that he was sure she was already in bed and that he should let her sleep. She simply opened the screen and told him she knew he would be back...

A cacophony of shrill sounds woke him in the morning and it took him a few seconds to make out where he was. There were birds everywhere, in cages, out of cages, woven into tapestries and embroidered onto pillow cases. In a few minutes Amethyst came in, nude, with a tray of tea, fruit and scones. She asked how he slept and if he enjoyed the night before. He told her he thought he might have dreamt it all because he had never experienced an evening so strange and full of pleasure. She said that he had been guided by winged creatures all his life and if he kept his faith and followed his dreams they would lead him away from trouble and into bliss where, in the end, he would become one of them.

She then laid her perfect body beside him and they made love again surrounded by the sounds of birds and the feeling of each other's warm flesh melting into one. When the doorbell rang, he looked to Amethyst to see her reaction. She simply called out for whoever it was to come on in and that she was in the bedroom. Earle's reaction was to panic and pull the covers over his naked body, especially when the person turned out to be an equally beautiful woman. Amethyst spoke gently.

This is my sister, Emerald. Would you like to join us, love?

Emerald smiled and took off her dress and got into bed and began tenderly kissing Earle's surprised body. He tried to be modest and resist this heavenly new creature but found that his will had become the consistency of warm butter. As the ripples of pleasure trickled over his body, he became utterly powerless. He thought about asking for forgiveness but figured it would be better to wait awhile until he really needed it. Though he was equidistant between bewilderment and nirvana, he remembered what Amethyst had said about being guided by winged creatures and so he decided to just float with the current to see what kind of bliss waited for him. He went back and forth between them before collapsing in a pyramid of translucent flesh.

As he slowly came back to earth he remembered what he had set out to do today. To cross the Mojave, Arizona and New Mexico deserts by freight train. He had surely lost his mind. When they all walked to the kitchen for water he told them about his mission. As they had never been out of California, they were surprised that anyone would leave of their own free will. Earle described Lubbock to them and said that it was not, by any means, a beautiful place but that he had many friends there. He decided not to tell them about being called for the draft so as not to spoil an otherwise perfect morning. Emerald had her Volkswagen out front and offered to take him to San Bernardino. He told Amethyst that he would see her when he returned and then kissed her mouth and both breasts. She gave a sign with her hand like the wing of a bird flying away, which he interpreted as a good-bye gesture.

It took them a while to find the San Bernardino train yards, but when they did they were amazed at its size. Hundreds of pieces of trains lined up on dozens of tracks going off to God knows where. He kissed Emerald goodbye and told her that he would never forget this morning for as long as he lived. She said that some people can handle pleasure better than others. She then asked if he was sure about what he was about to do and he said that some people can handle misery better than others. They laughed together, uneasily. As she drove off, he looked out where the tracks met a thousand miles of desert and breathed a deep breath. He took one of the magic rocks from his bag and balanced it on a fence post. He took one step forward, then another, and when he saw the red-tailed hawk flying toward a section of stacked up boxcars he headed in that direction.

A switchman with a ponytail and a huge handlebar mustache stopped him short of his aim.

It's against the law to be walking the rail yards.

I was just wondering where they all go.

That a guitar in your bag there?

Yep, bought it down in Venice from a wild man. It's a Gibson J-45 that'll be all right when I get a bridge and a fret job done on it.

Where you goin'?

Gotta get back to Texas to appear for my Army physical.

Sorry about that. Guess I'm a little too old. They're calling the young ones first. Don't tell anyone I told you, but see that third set of cars over there with the stack of gondolas on it?

I see it.

That's the eastbound 4:42. The cars closest to the front should go through Belen Junction and on to Clovis. Watch out at Valley Junction by Barstow and at West Williams Junction by Flagstaff. Those are the places where they change. The back cars might get dropped along the way and more might get added at the junctions.

Thanks for the tip.

I play a little myself. Know any Woody?

Just learnin' Tom Joad.

Woody rode right through these very yards. The depression days were tough. Freights were the main ride for a lot of those guys.

Main one for me. Today.

Here's a few tips—don't catch 'em on the run. One slip and you lost a foot. And don't cross under while they're building a train. Go through an open door if you have to.

'Preciate it.

Be careful.

Earle walked to the line of gondolas where the box-cars began and found an open one about twen-ty cars back from the engine. The second he climbed through the door he heard a far away boom, and then a distant clatter grow closer and closer in a matter of seconds, like a wave, until it reached his car and jolted it a few feet forward and then passed on through before waning away. For the next couple of hours the locomotive went forward and back, switch-ing track, playing tag with the switch engine, building itself into a mile long, diesel-drinking, desert- crossing machine.

As the train eased off, his heart raced with excitement, but as they picked up speed he had the dreadful feeling that he might have bitten off more than he could chew. Since the boxcar was empty the suspension was worthless, and any unevenness on the tracks was transferred into bone- jarring, unsprung energy. There was no place to sit and no place to stand. After a few miles into the desert, the train was screaming down the track, thrashing violently in a deafening roar with an oven-like wind blowing through the open doors. He could not put down his guitar for fear that it would be in splinters after a few rough spots in the track. He found that near the middle of the car the rumbling was a little less brutal and he put down his Levi jacket and sat with his legs straight out to absorb some of the impact.

The train slowed through the edges of the mountains and blew its whistle at Hesperia. Earle made a point to read the town signs and watch for anything familiar. Oro Grande passed in a blur, as did Hodge, but at Valley Junction just west of Barstow the train finally came to a stop. The desert sky was turning pink in the west and a small dust devil skirted the fenceline out toward the mountains. Earle took a long drink of water from his new canteen and chuckled at the memory of Flash and his shark. He lit a cigarette and a stick of Snowflake's incense. He wanted to jump off to find a cardboard box or anything soft to rest his poor

ass, but was afraid that the train might take
off without him.

The train screeched away after a short stop and
crawled east through the sad burg of Barstow.
As the train picked up speed the full moon rose
over the hills out the open door. It seemed as if
the moon were hitched to a temperature gauge
that reacted contrary to its own inclination.
As they picked up speed on the long straight-
away, the temperature fluctuated ten degrees
in a matter of seconds. Earle could tell the train
was going faster than it had been before, as he
was bouncing several inches off of the floor on
the rough parts of the track. He had to keep
kicking backwards with his legs to stay in the
middle of the car. The open door loomed like a
hungry mouth to oblivion. The light was gone
now and the only thing visible was the moonlit sand, blurred fence posts and pale rocks. He
braced for a long, long night and pulled the tinfoil package out of his guitar bag to stave off his
hunger with one of the brownies.

Within twenty minutes the wind had become visible
shades of blue and purple and the roar of the
steel wheels had taken on a new intensity. He
couldn't believe that someone had spiked the
brownies! This was not a good time, he thought.
A panic descended over him as he inched himself backwards, away from the open doors and
into the recesses of the boxcar. He pushed himself into the corner where gales of wind, straw,
and cinder dust sandblasted him from every direction. He managed to put on his Levi jacket,

put his face down the front and hold his guitar over his head, allowing the corner walls to keep him in place by jabbing him in the side. He felt as if he were falling down an endless well, skidding helplessly off the sides as he fell.

The train slowed to climb the jagged foothills outside of Needles and stopped in the town long enough for Earle to pick a trio of splinters out of his ass. For the rest of the night the train alternated between straight track and winding climbs and by the wee hours of the morning the temperature had fallen drastically, cutting through Earle's thin jacket with ease. He pulled the bottle of Night Train Express from his bag and, just like Harlon had said, it took some of the chill out of the night and wove it through his ribcage.

By the light of the morning he knew he had left California when he saw signs for Kingman and Walapai. A couple of hours later the train stopped at a sidetrack in Seligman and waited two hours until a westbound freight passed. As they climbed up the mountains an exhilaration came over him, and the next few hours were the most pleasurable of the trip. Dazzling vistas opened up as the desert came alive. As they rose in elevation the vegetation bloomed with color and the pines began to appear again.

Earle remembered the switchman talking of the Williams Junction and when the train stopped there, it only took a second to decide to leave the battered mother ship and to find coffee and something to eat. He hobbled around the yards, barely able to walk, and found a tiny cafe down the road. He sat in a beat-up over-stuffed booth to which he compared his bruised body. His lungs felt like battered punching bags and the lack of sleep made him feel scratchy, like his insides were filled with brambles. He was covered head to toe in soot and dust. There was no way he was going to climb back on that train. Not today, anyway.

After he ate, he asked the waitress how to get to Flagstaff. She said the Greyhound bus sometimes stopped at the gas station and pointed down the road. She then said that her brother worked at the Sinclair at the other end of town and that he went to Flagstaff every night to get drunk and fight and that he might give him ride after work. Earle left her a quarter on the table and said he thought he might just take the bus.

Earle used the garden hose at the back of the station to give himself an in-clothes shower and laundry. He wrung himself out and sat facing the sun to dry. By the time the bus arrived, it was late in the day. After a thirty-minute stop in Flagstaff the sun was setting over the Frisco mountains just as the Greyhound slowly turned onto Route 66 and rolled—suspended between the East and the West—like a hammock on wheels. Earle sank into a cushioned seat and was asleep and dreaming even before...

Maggie and Mark and Bob the Turk were in the front room with the television blaring the theme music to Bonanza. Each of them had a TV tray in front of them with a plate of fish sticks and a huge clump of Kraft Macaroni and Cheese. A bowl of red jello with fruit and marshmallows sat nearby. Maggie was telling Mark and Bob the Turk about how Hoss was from Tahoka and they both nodded in agreement. When the phone rang, Maggie jumped up and ran into the kitchen to answer it. She thought it might be Earle but it was Patricia Loney asking when Earle might be coming back to town. She sounded a shade distraught but said that she was fine when Maggie asked if anything was wrong. Maggie told her that Earle would call her when he came in. When she went back to the TV room Bob quizzed her.

Who was that, Marco Polo?

No, it was Earle's nice girlfriend.

The one with the new car?

That one.

He oughta marry her. That car probably ain't got more than a thousand miles on it.

She gave him a look.

Bob.

He smiled slyly.

She in trouble?

She just wonders when he's comin'
home.

Must be in trouble.

Some gunfire came from the direction of the TV and
pulled everyone's attention with it. When Hoss
reappeared, Maggie wondered out loud if the
town of Tahoka would ever erect a monument
to their native son. Then came a commercial ex-
plaining the benefits of new, improved Tide and
Maggie asked Mark to remind her to buy a box
at the store tomorrow. He said that he would
just as the theme music resurfaced.

*The camping gear department was on the mezzanine
floor of the department store, up one flight on
the escalator. The sleeping bags were all laid
out in a row on the floor. The salesman came up
to Earle and offered his help if he had any questions. Earle asked his opinion as to what was
his best bag. The salesman walked him to the
end of the line and pointed down to a large silver tube with black rubber boots protruding out
of the end of it. Earle commented that it looked
heavy. The salesman said that it was made of
asbestos and weighed over a hundred pounds.
When he asked why it was made of asbestos the
salesman replied that if there was a forest fire,
you would be protected in this sleeping bag. The
explanation sounded logical to Earle and he
went on to question why the rubber boots were
sticking out of the end of the tube. The salesman
said that when the firefighters came to douse the*

forest fire, the boots would keep your feet from getting wet. This made perfect sense to Earle and he said that he would take it. When he gave the man the money, the salesman clapped his hands together and two boys came out of the back, each with a hand dolly. They loaded up the sleeping bag and rolled it to the stairway leading down to the first floor. They kicked the sleeping bag off of their dollies and let it tumble down the wide stairway. Earle watched in horror as the heavy tube tumbled and turned and flipped end over end violently down the stairs, causing shoppers to toss their belongings and run for cover. When it reached the bottom of the stairs it rolled helplessly to the revolving door at the front entrance of the store. Earle ran down the stairs and studied the unwieldy tube, staring at the revolving door, perplexed that it was too large to fit through the door, much less into a car and out to the forest—

The driver was shaking him, trying to wake him, telling him he was in Albuquerque and would have to change busses or else end up in Bangor, Maine. Earle could not quite shake off his dream and nothing the driver said could be connected with the department store scene where he had just come from. Only when he looked out the window and saw the mountains and the morning sky over the bus station did he cross over into consciousness. He walked like a zombie into the station and sat on a wooden bench with his eyes closed trying to get back into his strange dream but he kept ending up in different settings with different people. He finally gave up and wrote down as much as he could remember in his notebook.

The coffee shop was an interesting assortment of vagabonds and locals. He could not be sure whether the characters that came in and out were waiting for a bus or if they simply had nowhere else to be. Perhaps they arrived from somewhere else and this stop was as far as their ticket took them. Or maybe they just came to the station as a reminder that someday their journey might continue. The more he wrote, the more he tried to untangle mysteries that maybe weren't mysteries at all. In frustration he turned the page and began sketching a picture of Amethyst and Emerald holding beach balls and floating on inflatable rafts covered in mynah birds.

When the bus arrived Earle's first inclination was to not get on board. All the places where he had traveled had filled him with intrigue and adventure and now felt he was going back to gloom and dread. He watched as the driver clicked people's tickets at the door of the bus and wondered why no one turned away at the last moment while proclaiming to the driver that they had suddenly changed their minds. He remembered one autumn at the South Plains Fair where he had waited in a long line to ride the Death Wheel and had jumped through the chains after seeing a tattoo of a hideous Cyclops on the arm of the ticket taker. The combination of images had been enough to trigger a premonition that something was wrong. The next day in the paper there was a picture of a fire engine ladder truck backed up to the ride which had suffered a mechanical breakdown and the firemen were guiding people one by one down the ladder.

The bus driver gave the 'all aboard' call and Earle climbed on knowing his life was headed for a crossroads and he, like his ancestors before him, was diving straight into the uncertain middle of it all. As the mountains and curves turned into prairies and straightaways he prepared himself with a deep breath for what was to come. All through the day and into the night the Gray Dog galloped through Vaughn, Fort Sumner, Clovis, Muleshoe and Littlefield, and arrived in downtown Lubbock within minutes of midnight.

Not wanting to wake anyone, he walked the cool, dark streets toward his house. Millions of cicadas were singing under millions of stars and the longer he walked the more elated he became, flooded with childhood memories triggered by smells and sounds that he passed. The smell of fresh- cut grass mixed with the early morning smell from the bread factory. The combination was so intense that Earle likened it to a religious experience. Each tree had its own smell: the Chinese elm, the sycamore, the blooming mimosa and the juniper. Even the smell of Looter's stockyards triggered a certain comical nostalgia.

After a couple of hours, his house came into view. His mother's turquoise Mercury Comet slept under the trees on the driveway and he walked the familiar steps, skipping the missing step even in the dark, around to the back of the house. The key was, of course, still up on the ledge and he opened the door to the musty, humid kitchen and went in. The pile of blankets was exactly where it had been when he left and he made himself a pallet in front of the swamp cooler and slid into a windy sleep, safe in a maternal womb kind of way, but distraught in an uncertain gypsy kind of way.

In the morning Earle walked around his neighborhood feeling a tinge of nostalgia even though he had only been away for a couple of months. He gazed with fond memories at Phil Nick's old house, his good friend, where he had learned to play electric guitar. He walked down to the park and around his old grade school and then went into the drug store and ordered a Coke at the soda fountain. PD Sykes and Josi were still there, looking like the most mismatched workmates in all of history. PD was a midget who looked like Edward G. Robinson and smoked an oversized cigar. He cussed constantly and was a bookie on the side. Josi was skinny and shy and talked in a whisper. All the neighborhood kids gave PD hell, and he returned the favor by setting up numbers games to sucker them out of their lunch money. He would advertise a special on 25¢ banana splits by making a sign that said 'Take A Chance—From 3¢ To 33¢.' Of course nearly everyone would draw numbers near the 33¢ maximum. Only when the place was packed at lunch hour would PD slyly exchange folded numbers with an unsuspecting shill. He would ask for everyone's attention and announce the 3¢ winner, like someone at the racetrack might announce the winner of a horse race. Josi would give PD the evil eye, but PD never looked her way until after he raked in the money.

PD asked Earle if his barber had died and gave him the location of one just around the corner. Earle had not had a hair cut in almost a year, but he had not been really aware of its length while he was in Houston and California. Josi didn't acknowledge him at all and Shelly, the cashier who had always been friendly to him, didn't even look up from her movie magazine.

When he got back to his house, Maggie and Mark were ready to celebrate his return by going to the Dixie Dog on Avenue Q and having lunch at a picnic table under the dinky awning on the side of the building. Earle told them about his adventures on the road, his band in Houston, his good luck and his bad luck and about his long journey home. They all wailed with laughter at his extended story of Flash's shark although he left out many of the details.

He asked to see the letter from the government and Maggie dragged it slowly from her purse. A knot formed in his throat as he read the stark wording and he looked down at the ant bed in the sidewalk crack for a long time. The PA system snapped him back in the present to announce that their order was ready. An uncomfortable silence hovered over the table while they ate their corn dogs and onion rings in the bright sun as the cicadas in the trees screamed at a steady, maddening pitch.

For the next few days Earle made the rounds to see
his old friends and visit the spots where they
hung out. He went by Alice's Restaurant to say
hello to Charlie Ray and ended up playing a
short set in the upstairs room the next night.
It was after the show that he met an intriguing
woman who was the first girl since Patricia to
command his total attention. She seemed as if
she were from another galaxy even though she
spoke like a Lubbock girl. She lived so much
in the moment that Earle felt like his conversation was perpetually in the past. They talked
and laughed for hours about things that were
seldom discussed by any other people, and they
would have laughed all night had Earle not been
so bushed from his journey. As they parted in
the alley she told him she was sure they would
meet again. Then she told him that someday
she would have his children. Earle looked at
her to see if there was any facetiousness in her
face and was shocked to see that she was completely sincere.

As he walked away in the dusty night, he realized
that he, in his fascination, had not gotten her
name. It seemed as if he had known her all her
life and did not need to ask. He did not feel in
a panic to go back and find her. She had said
they would meet again, and he had no reason
to doubt.

He noticed at once how the length of his hair changed
the way some friends reacted to him. Some
shunned him altogether. Even Pete at the pool

hall and the crosseyed waitress at the Hi-D-Ho did not greet him as before but instead seemed to go out of their way to make him feel unwelcome. In a mere two months a demarcation had taken place among his friends that was symbolic of what was happening in the rest of the country.

Most had broken into two groups, the hawks and the doves: those for the war and those against it. And the hawks in Lubbock outnumbered the doves a hundred to one. No one dared to dispute the government's stance on the war and those who questioned it were considered traitors, plain and simple. By now, the media, who had originally painted the image of hippies as being anti-American outcasts, were starting to show the other side. They were covering events that the status quo thought should not be seen on television.

That evening, Dan Rather's news crew showed protests from all across the nation and presented the disturbing statistic that over half of the population now considered the war a mistake. The newscast then showed a Viet Nam war hero with no legs leaving his Purple Heart on the steps of the capitol building and denouncing the war as impossible to win. A half-million kids were now fighting in foreign jungles and the feeling of desperation was spreading among both civilians and the military. Earle thought about the fact that there was no 'bad guy' like there had been with Hitler—there was only the fear of an abstract concept and that concept was Communism. Instead of the military dealing with a handful of chickenshit dictators with Napoleon complexes, they were fighting an invisible enemy, camouflaged in their own environment. In trying to flush out enemy soldiers they were killing innocent villagers who were running scared, trying to survive inside a corrupt government. Meanwhile, most of America remained unconvinced that the president and the military were capable of making a poor judgment call on a scale as massive as the Southeast Asia situation. Why did America feed so much money and attention to an uncivil war in this previously unfamiliar part of the world? Did they not know it was public knowledge that most of the South Vietnamese supported the other side, the Vietcong, and not their own corrupt government?

The images of the news report troubled Earle to such an extent that he filled his bathtub with scalding hot water, encircled it with dozens of glowing candles and, for some unknown reason, poured a half-gallon of milk into the water before sliding in through the steam and chanting Buddhist chants that he made up on the spot. When his mother and Mark came home from the store they were alarmed at what they heard and beat on the bathroom door to see if everything was okay.

CHAPTER 5

He had been raised on the Amarillo Highway. He could name every small town, in succession, beginning at either end. Earle's life had originated from that desolate piece of road and he knew every bump and fence post along its length. It was a road straight and flat, maybe a swell here and a little curve there. It only gained a few feet in altitude in the one hundred and twenty miles between Lubbock and Amarillo.

When he reached the Army Induction Center there was a waiting line around the corner. He drove around the block several times out of sheer anxiety, weighing his total lack of options. He parked on the east side of the building closest to the end of the waiting line so as to attract the least attention. The first thing he noticed upon joining the line was the amazing cross-section of West Texas civilization that was represented. There were red-necked, freckled-faced farm boys, haughty and arrogant, next to shy and terrified black kids who had never stood so close to a white person. There were sons of junkyard scavengers and store clerks next to sons of preachers and police. The make-up of the line reminded Earle of the time he had applied for his driver's license, except for the uneasy silence that accompanied this group. A bulldog- faced Sergeant patrolled the file, staring knives through anyone who made light of the situation at hand. As Earle got closer to the head of the line, his appearance began to attract attention. Apparently no one in modern times had ever witnessed anyone with long hair before. The murmur began with a small group and then spread like a grass fire. Even the bulldog Sergeant was amused and asked Earle if he was aware that he was in the line for men and that the women's line was around the block. Earle looked the Sergeant straight in the eye for a few seconds and found nothing there— no compassion, nothing inside of him that resembled a human being. He therefore did not want to challenge such a creature and so looked down at his feet. He could only counter his repeated goading with silence. He knew that he was preparing himself for a long, hard road and his spirit had to remain strong or else be broken like a matchstick. He had never been prone to fight his way out of uncomfortable situations, and, unlike most of his friends, he kept most of his thoughts to himself.

Earle's situation didn't improve when he reached the head of the line. The officers at the desk felt compelled to crack jokes about his appearance and all the office workers came from their cubicles to take a look at him. To keep his humiliation from turning to anger, Earle kept playing the news clip over and over about the dozens of caskets arriving draped in flags mixed with images of Lyndon Johnson defending the war.

Even the military doctor who examined him had a slew of wise cracks to make about his hair. He said he was supposed to ask everyone to remove their clothes but in this case he wasn't sure. He said that transvestites usually didn't show up at the induction center because they usually traveled in the circus. Earle asked the doctor if that meant he was free to go and the doctor told him to shut the fuck up and take off his clothes. As he was removing his shoes he asked the doctor what he knew about Southeast Asia. The doctor said that he reckoned that it was full of little slant-eyed gooks that needed killing. Earle closed his eyes and breathed in, shocked that these words were coming from someone in the medical profession. Could it have been, because of fear, the military had been pumped up with misinformation and that the ignorance of actuality was not only expected but rewarded during war time?

The doctor listened to his chest, took his blood pressure, counted his pulse, looked down his throat and up his ass and told him that he might as well pack his clothes and cut his hair because he was fit as a fiddle and the Army would be calling him back soon to make a man out of him. He wrote a few things down on a sheet of paper and told him to get the hell out of his office.

When he signed out of the building, Earle had to swallow his anger in practice for what he imagined was to come. He said a prayer and drove away from downtown as fast as he could. He figured that the war had given license to those in power to create a hierarchy of zombies so as to convince inductees to participate in such an unpopular cause. He began to look at this episode in his life as if he had been sucked up into a drama that was being played out by the authoritarian maniacs of the world. If he gave in to his own anger, he would be on the same level as the warmongers.

He spent some time driving around old Amarillo, by the old house where he used to live, out to the graveyard to the plot where his family was buried and then across town to the house where he moved when he was nine years old. He went by his old school and to the vacant lot where he whiled away the afternoons in childhood bliss with his neighborhood friends. He remembered playing war using rolled up newspapers as ammunition, never expecting his daydreams to turn into nightmares. Usually he enjoyed conjuring up the nostalgia of those days when his family was truly happy, but today it weighed heavy on him, to the point of making him feel that his whole life had been wasted and that his current situation was caused by his own apathy.

The experience at the Army Center had made him ill and he soon found himself driving down the steep entrance to Palo Duro Canyon Park. He stopped at one of the low-water crossings and walked 50 yards down the creek and laid himself down, clothes and all, in the warm pungent water, letting the creek carry the sum and substance of today's unpleasant ordeal downstream. A pair of cardinals landed in the cottonwood tree and he watched them for a long spell, wondering why only humans create wars with each other and why each adversary aligns their position with their ruler or their deity. The birds flew into a patch of salt cedar at the creek bank and as he watched for them to emerge, a long water moccasin slithered into the water just a few yards from where he was lying. He popped out of the creek and walked briskly to his car, startling the nearby picnickers who had not been aware of his presence.

When he started the engine he realized that for the last few weeks he had felt as if he were being chased by some invisible force and now he was seeing the parallels of this pursuit in nature. Was God responsible for setting loose a wrath upon the world, or had it been brought on by mankind's stupidity? He thought back through thousands of years of wars perpetuated by the translation and interpretation of ancient texts. As he stared into the center of his steering wheel, he saw death and destruction being played out around the world even though the reasons for continuing this insanity had long been forgotten. He saw priests, politicians and those who made a living studying war kneeling over holy manuals that described the archaic differences of the sects and clans that now roamed the earth looking for old enemies. He saw, inside himself, the horrors of war he had inherited from ancestral memory and he heard the cries of the innocent who had always, since the beginning of time, been the ones who paid the price of war through their pain and suffering. He wondered if, someday, his species might annihilate their future simply because they were not able to let go of their past.

The threat of global war had cast a foreboding veil around everyone's life since the time he was born. Fresh out of a world war, the world went straight into a cold war. He thought about the nuclear bomb drills that had taken place each year since he had been in school. At three rings of the bell, he and his classmates would rush into the school hallway and put their heads between their knees. Although they had seen the pictures of the skeletal aftermath of Hiroshima and Nagasaki, everyone went through these drills as if they would actually, miraculously, save those who performed this ritual in the event of a nuclear war. Now, years later, this fear had manifested itself into taking sides against an unknown enemy. Communism, like a shadow figure on a giant movie set, loomed large on the world stage and the western world had resorted to napalming native jungle villages in Asia in a futile attempt to eradicate it.

Earle returned to Highway 87 absorbed in trying to define what it was that he actually believed. He knew exactly what he didn't believe. Snippets of the day played back in his head and he tried to bat them away like mad red hornets. He was losing strength with each town that passed by his window and by the time he reached his Mother's house he was empty and exhausted. After briefly telling his mother about his fiasco, he burrowed into a stack of blankets in front of the rackety old swamp cooler and imagined he was flying away, across the sad border of these flatlands, to some Shangri-La full of shy maidens, motorbikes, milk and fortune cookies.

When he awoke, the house was quiet except for the
rattling of the cooler and the morning TV quiz
shows. Earle took a walk down 26th Street and
saw his friend Kyle washing his '57 Chevy station wagon on the lawn in front of his house. In
the conversation that followed, Kyle wanted to
know everything about what was happening in
California. He was approaching draft age and
was curious about the political events on the
West Coast. His mother was the head of the music department at Texas Tech and he knew that
Earle had played some of the anti-war events
on campus. He wanted to know what was happening at Berkeley and if the news stories he
had heard were accurate. He said you can't ever
believe what you see on TV.

When they entered the house, Earle was overwhelmed
by the decor of the interior. He had passed by
many times and had always noticed the wiste-
ria growing on a trellis in the front yard. He
had been curious about the occupant even as
he attended the grade school across the street
many years earlier.

Inside the house everything was connected to music
and everything seemed to be alive as if there
were something invisible animating each object.
A huge piano took up the front room and books
and pictures were placed, not for decoration,
but within reach, as if they competed for your
attention. There were pictures of old composers
and violin players and stacks of sheet music everywhere. As they walked into the den, Kyle's
mother, Lortha, was walking in the back door
with a huge basket of flowers in her arms. She

was singing an aria while culling the wilted petals from her freshly picked bouquet. When Kyle stopped her to introduce her to Earle, she seemed surprised to have company and then tried to comb her hair with her fingers and apologized profusely for being such a mess.

> I ... I've been in the sun picking flowers and Kyle—Kyle never tells me when company is coming over and I ... I do want to apologize for my... my dirty hands and I ... I am very pleased to meet you.

> I was only passin' by and saw Kyle washin' the car in the front yard and didn't really plan to come in....

Kyle opened two Cokes and told his mother that Earle was a musician as well.

> Oh, you are! In Lubbock that's almost like saying you want to start a revolution.

> I think one's already begun, it just ain't made it here yet.

> What instrument do you play?

> Electric guitar till it got lifted in Houston. I picked up an old Gibson acoustic in Venice a couple of weeks back, so that's what I'm playin'. Played violin when I was eight till I

moved to Lubbock. They didn't have orchestra in the grade schools here.

There's a lot they don't have here. Well my, my, how fascinating. You mean you just travel around and play wherever you go?

Last few months, anyway. Hit some bad luck and had to go out and see the world.

I must put these flowers in some water. Please come and see us again. Bring your guitar and we'll play together.

I'm not great at reading the notes, but I can jam pretty good.

Do come again.

I will.

Kyle led Earle out the side door and the two of them jumped in Kyle's station wagon and went for a drive around the town. They talked about the war and Earle's Amarillo ordeal and about the California coast and The Doors. They talked about Stanley Owsley and about the LSD that he had manufactured and about his relationship to Ken Kesey and the Grateful Dead. He told Kyle the shark story and they laughed all the way down Quaker to the Brownfield Highway. They stopped at the Char-King and ordered onion rings and cherry-limes. They laughed again when they heard the drive-up speaker repeat their order. Earle could see that Kyle wanted nothing more in his life than to go to Venice but it was Kyle that popped the question.

> I think this old pile of bolts can make it across the desert. If you're game.

> I need to get out of the Hub and do some serious escaping from myself.

> Got any dough? I know where I can get twenty bucks or so. Maybe Chapman wants to go, too.

> I got some left over from my last trip.

> Well?

> How 'bout Monday. I need a couple of days with my family.

Kyle sang.

> *Monday Monday....*

Early Monday morning Sgt. Baylock watched a tan '57 Chevy station wagon with three people inside turn right onto Flint from 26th Street. At first he thought he saw Earle riding shotgun but remembered that his sources had informed him that most of the troublemakers who usually gave him grief were still either in Fort Worth or California. Even so, Baylock had a strange premonition about the old tan Chevy and he followed it all the way out the Clovis Highway to the city limits sign. He decided not to pull the car over only because, as he was turning on his flashing lights, his radio lit up with a burglary report that needed attention.

The boys in the car sighed relief when Baylock's squad car did a U-turn and raced back toward Lubbock. The huge hookah that Kyle had brought for the trip took up half the back seat and would have been a difficult item to explain to Baylock.

To celebrate their reprieve they pulled the hookah into the front seat and fired up a bowl. By the time they reached Muleshoe, they realized that they had been going under thirty miles an hour for the last 45 miles. They stopped at a roadside park and looked at a road map. They laughed hysterically at the minuscule amount that they had traveled and decided that at the rate they were going it would take three weeks to get to California. Marginally concerned, they pulled the guitar from the back and strummed a few songs.

When Maggie saw the empty covers in front of the air conditioner, she sensed something wrong. Her fears were confirmed when she picked up the note from the old leather trunk.

DEAR MOTHER,
I'M SORRY BUT I HAD TO
LEAVE AGAIN. THERE IS

KNOWLEDGE
OUT IN THE WORLD
THAT NEEDS
TO BE KNOWN.

WHEN I FIND IT, I WILL
RETURN.

I LOVE YOU AND MARK
VERY MUCH

EARLE

P.S. DON'T CRY

Maggie broke down into a deep crying spell that lasted until Mark woke up and asked what the matter was. Bob the Turk came to the door, rang the bell and, as usual, walked in before the door was answered. When he saw Maggie crying he started to scold her in his mock, whimsical way. He made himself a cup of coffee and told them that he had just become a rich man by selling his old couch and that he was going to celebrate by taking them out to lunch at the Lubbock Country Club. He hit his forehead with his open palm and cussed, saying how he had forgotten that the Country Club's kitchen was closed on Mondays so he would take them to Chandler's cafe instead.

Maggie's tears turned to laughter at the absurdity of Bob's announcement and soon the three of them were bouncing down the old brick streets of sad Broadway in lower downtown Lubbock. They

pulled up and parked in front of Huber's pawnshop. Bob bounced out of the truck, opened the
pawnshop door, and called into the long, skinny
building.

> If anyone's still alive in there you
> better come out with your hands up!

Maggie and Mark came up behind Bob as he continued.

> On second thought, don't come out.
> I'm hungry and I'm only buyin' lunch
> for the civilized!

Old man Huber and Hernando came to the front and
told Bob to hold it down, that the cats in the
attic were trying to sleep. They greeted each
other and remarked about how long it had been
since they had seen each other and that they
should come by more often. Bob cut into the po-
lite conversation.

> Y'all can small talk some other time.
> Chow's cookin' and my stomach is
> ringing a bell.

Next door at Chandler's Cafe, Bob made his tradi-
tional entrance.

> Every rat in the neighborhood is in
> hiding. Is this a concentration camp
> or just a plain ol' cafe?

Mrs. Chandler greeted the trio.

What a surprise! I haven't seen y'all
in so long.

Bob rolled his eyes in disgust.

Can we get some service here? This
dump'll never change. Hell, I can do
it myself. Here, y'all sit right here.
I'll get the menus and the water....

Gene Holiday's eyes were the size of quarters. His
cheeks were sunken and his skin had taken
on a pasty hue. He'd been up for three days
straight on a strange combination of bennies,
alcohol and amyl nitrate. He was talking with
three drug runners about muling some Oaxa-
can across the border at Nogales. Their conversation led off into spidery tangents that never
echoed back to the ears of the speaker and,
since no one was listening to each other, were
never fulfilled upon other ears. There were
guns scattered about the room and the sunlight
was blocked by tattered blankets nailed to the
window jamb. A police band radio was squawk-
ing away, sitting next to the half-empty gallon
of Old Granddad on the slatted crate that sub-
stituted for a coffee table. One of the runners
suddenly turned his attention to the radio and
put his finger to his lips to motion the others to
keep quiet. He whispered his interpretation of
the code coming from the radio.

They're coming down Pacific. One's already on the roof. Nobody make a sound.

All their faces became frozen in fear as they looked up to the ceiling, imagining the whole LA police department combing the roof directly overhead.

There's three more cars coming down Speedway....

The sun was low in the sky as the Chevy station wagon crept through the Billy the Kid town of Fort Sumner, New Mexico. The clouds were flaming red when they pulled into the truck stop where Route 66 met Santa Rosa. The waitress, who was from Lubbock, brought them huge bowls of freshly made green chili stew and an unopened package of saltine crackers. The New Mexico water she brought had a fresh, sweet taste to it, unlike the hard water they had grown up with on the High Plains. Chapman ran to the car and brought in three canteens for the waitress to fill. She was highly amused by this, and asked them if they were miners or something. They said that they were of the 'or something' kind.

She came back and filled their water glasses three times and replied that she'd never seen any three men drink so much water. Kyle told her that he had heard that there was a desert up the road a piece and that they were imitating the ways of the camel. They said they were headed for California and asked if she would like to go. She said that she would love to, but her life had changed since her baby had been born four months ago. Earle drew a picture of a station wagon driving down the road. He put a baby's face inside the face of the moon held lovingly in the arms of the waitress. He left it as a tip when they said good-bye.

They took turns driving all night across New Mexico and into Arizona, occasionally stopping for naps on the side of the road. Earle was at the wheel when the red sun popped over the purple mountains in the rear view mirror. A few miles east of Flagstaff he pulled into an Indian curio shop to see if they had coffee. The store had not yet opened but there was a coke machine outside that coughed up half- frozen cokes. Kyle woke up in the back and asked where they were and why they were stopping. Earle told him with gusto.

> We're in Winona. Winona, Arizona. We're in a damned Chuck Berry song! And a Wynonie Harris song. And a Nelson Riddle soundtrack. I've sung this word a hundred times thinking that somebody had just made it up! And here we fuckin' are! Winona, Arizona.

Earle repeated the town's name again just to savor the feel of the words on his tongue. Kyle gave him the snake-eye and rolled over and pulled his Levi jacket over his head.

Chapman took over at Flagstaff, slowly descending into the Mojave Basin as the old Chevy sputtered and swayed in the brutal desert wind. By the time they reached the Colorado River, the three of them were starting to evaporate from the combination of heat and lack of sleep. They drove to a spot by the water and Earle and Chapman jumped in, clothes and all. Kyle finally woke up all puffy and red and hopscotched down to the water, barefooted, dancing in pain on the burning rocks and pavement. The blue water was too much temptation and he, too, jumped in. When Earle pointed out that California was just across the water, they all shouted and splashed and twirled in circles. They shook off the water like wet dogs and within minutes were baked dry by the solar oven that surrounded them.

They drove into the lonesome town of Needles hoping to find something to eat. The town looked like it had been abandoned for years but they did find a cafe/gas station that looked to be open. Its only desirable trait was that it was the only spot to eat in a hundred miles.

The station attendant was so skinny he could hardly stand in the wind and had to hold on to the Chevy tail fin while pumping the gas. His wife, on the other hand, was so huge she could barely make it from table to table in the tiny restaurant. There was something about the couple so tragic and comical that the boys sat in wonderment at the myriad possibilities of the universe. She brought out two of the greasiest hamburgers they had ever seen but, in their semi-starvation mode, tasted as good as anything they had ever eaten. Nonetheless, Earle swore after the meal that he would become a vegetarian.

They filled the radiator with water, paid for the gas
and food, and Kyle jumped behind the wheel
for the last vacant stretch across the blistering
nether lands of Southern California. Chapman
rode shotgun, making his hand into a wing and
riding the hot currents of wind. Earle climbed
into the back, took a drink from his canteen of
the hot, sweet New Mexico water and passed
out in a soup of sweat and burning air. He soon
began dreaming about a wet green hillside that
sloped down to the sea....

What do I do now?

Huh?

I'm in quicksand. Where to, now?

Earle woke from his dream confused to find himself
in a sea of automobiles. Only when he saw his
sparkled guitar bag did he see that he was in
the back of Kyle's Chevy stuck in a suburban
traffic jam. He could see, in the far distance,
the San Bernardino freight yards were he had
caught a train only weeks ago. Had it been only
weeks? It seemed like months. His world had
flipped on its side and was wobbling trying to
right itself. Back then he was running toward
something and now he was running away from
it. Earle asked Kyle if there were any markers
posted to tell him were to go.

Did you see any signs?

Couple a' thousand.

Just keep followin' the sun. The
ocean'll stop ya.

The sun was setting behind the skyline of downtown
L.A., making it look as if it had been attacked
by hostile invaders and leaving behind diffused
red clouds and thick brown smoke. As they
neared the coast the sky became clearer and the
colors more saturated. When they reached Venice, the sky was purple and orange with pink
on the bottoms of clouds that seemed to scrape
the silhouettes of palm trees gently swaying in
the ocean breeze. They walked out to the beach
and scooped up a cup of ocean in their palms
and splashed the salty brine in their faces and
washed away a thousand miles of desert. When
the colors faded they walked across the sand to
the Sea View Cafe see if Gene or Lance was
around. Even before they opened the door, they
could feel a strange vibe around the place. Inside, Remy, the owner, was bouncing around
doing this and that and told them they could
sit anywhere. They ordered coffee and crackers,
and, in the same breath, asked Remy where
they could find Gene.

He gave them a double take and paused to see if they
were serious about asking this question. Had
they been living under a rock? He raised his
voice several notches as he went off on Gene.

Where is Gene? Do you make a joke?
He may be crawl through the drains
of Paris with the salamander, or,
more likely, cold-mooning in the Ba-

bushka morgue. Three days in the
past he look like blood letter zombie
with no word from him since that
time. I'm in the chilly here, damnit,
no chef, no adieu, no even a tip of the
hat. He hangs with the dope dealer
even after I pull him from the street
and devote him my home!

The boys looked down at the table and fumbled with
their silverware.

Sorry, didn't mean to bring up a bad
subject. We just drove in from Texas
a few minutes ago.

What is it flying with these Texas
men? One day they do anything for
you, the next day they are wild. They
are not civilized, they are unridden
horses.

Kyle snickered.

That's probably about right.

Remy's anger suddenly changed to fear. He pulled up
a chair and scooted up close to the table and
engaged the trio with his eyes, tears just starting to form.

I am worried for his life. Very much
worried. You must help me to find
him. This is very much danger.
Please, you must.

The seriousness of the situation became apparent by the look in Remy's eyes. For the first time they saw that Gene really could be in trouble, this was not just the delusion of a mad Frenchman. They listened as Remy told them where he thought he might be and how the gangsters he was with were armed and dangerous. The boys said they would do what they could and assured him that Gene would make his way out of whatever he was in. They had seen him do it many times before. Chapman told Remy there was a wildness in people who came from desolate places and that there was no cure for it, but it often did need attention. Their words were reassuring. He offered them a place to stay at his crash house. Earle told him that he had stayed there before and that his amplifier was in his back closet. For the first time Remy recognized Earle.

> Blow me away! I did not recognize you! The mustache. You worked here with Gene before. I was so busy then, I took little notice.
>
> I only was here for a week.
>
> So, now I must tell you the story of Gene and your amplificator.
>
> Amplifier.
>
> Yes, yes. So, last week Gene makes plans to go to Texas with his new bad friends. And on the way they are seduced to Las Vegas for the nightlife.

You can only imagine Gene in this savage place. This is where his raging begins. Well, something happens and all of the men become in jail. And this is where your ampli—amplif ...

Amplifier.

Yes, your ampli-flyer becomes involved. They had to take all items of value to the pawn devil in exchange for passage from jail. They do not travel to Texas. They travel to Venice and disappear in the drug alley. I am very sorry to tell you this.

Well, kiss my ass.

Excuse me?

No, no, that's just an expression. He's done this to me once before. A little closer to home. Damn ... *damn*. My luck keeps goin' downhill. Thank you for the telegram, anyway.

I am sorry.

Do you have any idea of how to find Gene?

There is a great and fearful apartment close to Speedway by Grand Canal. This is where I drove him before his journey to madness.

That's close enough. I'll find the son-
of-a-bitch if he can be found. Maybe
you can show us the place tomorrow.
Right now we are very tired and if
you are serious about us staying at
your place—

But of course. I'm closing as soon as
I will.

They followed Remy to the crash house and brought
in pillows and blankets from the back of the
Chevy. They slept on the floor in the back room
where two other dark shapes lay in the darkness. Their dreams tossed uneasy and restless. At one time in the night Kyle sat up in his
sleep and spoke the name of Judas, over and
over, as if in warning. The next morning as he
was gyrating between states of consciousness,
he swore he could see a glowing figure in the
room. Earle said that he had dreamed a Biblical
dream as well. He dreamed that Moses offered
him his staff of knowledge and told him he understood his present dilemma. Moses reached
in his pocket and pulled out a stick of gum that
had written on the wrapper: *The Wrapper Don't
Matter.* He told him not to hide, wrapped in Un-
truths, but instead live in the openness of the
Here and Now. When he stirred into wakeful-
ness he remembered his dream and thought
about how his dreams had been changing since
he had begun his new journey. Even his way
of thinking had changed. He had transformed
from a wayfarer to an explorer trying to separate the essence from the pretense. On the

way he had discovered new worlds that had opened windows in his everyday perspective. The works of visionaries had become portals through which he could let fly their revelations in solving the matters that now weighed upon him. At least it was a place to begin.

They walked the boardwalk in the cool sea breeze and stopped at the market to get coffee. Harlon, his Okie amigo, was tending the register. Earle pulled out an old Depression-era quote he had heard from his uncle Gus.

> Hey Okie, if you see Arkie, tell him Tex got the job.
>
> Well kiss my ass, I didn't 'xpect you back so quick.
>
> This is my friend Kyle. We just drove 'cross the desert in Kyle's old Chevy.
>
> Pleased to meet 'cha.
>
> Same here.

Earle thanked him again for the bottle of Night Train that had warmed up his first cold night in the Arizona desert. Harlon responded.

> Them ol' rails get cold in the moonlight.
>
> They liked to rattled me to death.

Plus someone had give me a spiked
brownie and I thought for sure that
ol' train was gonna spit my ass out
the boxcar door and leave me for the
buzzards. I jumped ship in Flagstaff.
Had to learn to walk all over again.

Harlon told them that some new guys had just arrived in Venice who had jumped the trains from
Lubbock and asked if they knew who he was
talking about. Kyle said if they were from Lubbock, sooner or later they would run into each
other. As they were leaving the market, Harlon
told them about the Peace Rally in the park on
Saturday. Cassius Clay, that is Mohammed Ali,
was scheduled to speak among others.

This bit of news elated Earle's spirit as they walked
back down the boardwalk. Musicians were beginning to gather on the sand and the winos
were cracking their first bottle of the day under the gazebo. The beach was beckoning the
village to rehearse for the upcoming spectacle.
Earle saw his friend Snowflake with a group of
Hell's Angels and was shocked at how she had
changed. In a mere three weeks she had gone
from an untainted, angelic blonde earth child,
to a tattooed, black-haired, silver-and-leather-
draped, tobacco-spitting motorcycle mama. In
all of his life he had never seen someone change
their personality so quickly and thoroughly. He
wondered if she still called herself Snowflake.
He caught her eye and was going to say hello,
but she shook her head and motioned with her
eyes to a huge hulk of a biker who seemed to

be the object of her apprehension. Sure enough, the fat Angel waddled over to her, picked her up like a toy and carried her over his shoulder and set her beside his chrome apparition. She waited while he cranked it alive and then mounted the suicide seat and rumbled stoically off into the distance.

As they rounded the corner by the incense shop, the three boys practically ran into a quintet of Lubbock refugees that the Okie had talked about earlier. Jesse Tanner and Sam Fox had ridden the trains a few days earlier and had run into Rick Fields and Steve Roe and Charlie Lennox the Younger who had just arrived after hitchhiking for days across the desert. They walked down Speedway toward Lance's place describing to each other the details of their journeys. No one had seen Gene but they had all heard the same stories about his new gangster friends and everyone shared the same concern for his safety.

Lance and Vickie came to the door in their underwear and invited everyone into their small living room where they all sat on the floor. He brought a six-pack from the kitchen and commented that the last time he had seen this group together was at Betty and Bill's house. They all laughed a nostalgic kind of laugh and the room became quiet again. There were sounds of movement coming from another room and as the disturbance reached the door they heard a familiar voice ring out.

I bet them crazy sons-a-bitches are

listening to Cryin' Time, drinkin' hot
Coors and fallin' over on each other
as we speak.

Everyone was surprised to see Gene in a bathrobe in
the doorway. Lance spoke first.

I wanted y'all to be surprised.

Gene Holiday, we heard you had died
and gone to Vegas!

Gene twirled, mocking a showgirl.

Let me ... entertain you....

The room laughed as Gene popped the top off of a
bottle of Coors. His face was puffy and still had
sheet marks pressed into one side of it, verify-
ing he had just risen from a long sleep. Surprisingly, he didn't look as bad as everyone had expected. There was a Chaplinesque side of Gene
that couldn't be concealed. Just when everyone
thought he was about to lose it, he would bounce
back with a one-man comic ballet that ridiculed
his previous condition.

Gene had not yet seen Earle who was sitting in a
chair on the other side of the room, leaning on
his guitar. In the middle of describing his wild
ride to Las Vegas, Gene saw Earle and swallowed a pair of words, stopping in mid-sentence.

Your amp is a hero. It saved our sorry
asses. I'd still be in the slammer if

not for that amp.

That's just real hunky dory.

I'll get it out. You know I'll get it out.

Every time you hear jail keys, you
hock my amplifier.

Earle had never seen Gene uncomfortable in front of
an audience, but Gene was clearly feeling guilty
for his latest round of roaring. Earle would have
been furious had he not known Gene so well.
He knew Gene would make good on his word,
so long as he stayed on the upwind side of the
jailhouse and on the topside of the graveyard.
He was truly relieved to see Gene alive.

We're all glad to see your ass. Don't
take us on that trip again. O.K.?

I was right on the edge of making
more money than everyone here put
together had ever seen before.

You can't spend it from a casket.

No, but you can buy a real nice casket!

The room cheered and slugged from their beers in
harmony like a pack of hyenas honoring one
of their own in a land far from their familiar
hunting grounds. They were the modern day
dust bowl refugees, not seeking work in the

fruit fields, but—as the offspring of those who had survived—now seeking refuge from a different form of hunger. A movement had arisen to define a society of freedom, unbound by the roadblocks that had detoured the generations before them. Unfortunately, the pursuit of freedom is accompanied by the availability of pleasure which leads in a spiral to confinement and constraint. Their ambassador to freedom had lost his way on a reckless roll through Babylon.

The day of the Peace Rally arrived. Earle popped up earlier than normal and tried to wake the scattered sleepers around him. Only Kyle and Chapman shared his enthusiasm. A nude couple meditating in the front room didn't even flinch as the three skipped out of Remy's house and on to Pacific Avenue with their thumbs in the wind. They were picked up within minutes by two girls in an old tan Renault Dauphine who were also on their way to the park. They could barely squeeze into the tiny back seat, holding on to the panic straps for extra support. The little engine choked and coughed and putted through the Los Angeles streets. All along the way they joined other vehicles stuffed with hippies on their way to the rally. A school bus covered in comets and meteors honked as it passed and a daisy came sailing by the sunroof of the Dauphine. As they neared the event the streets became carnival-like with an assortment of people from all walks of life. Students, teachers, old and young, hippies, freaks, runaways and trippers came with signs and banners and baskets of flowers all relating to the war in some way or the other.

On the other side, positioning themselves in the most obvious of places, were the L.A. Police and the National Guard. The presence of so many police created a feeling of dissonance and an uneasiness began to descend upon the crowd. Activists, one after another, filed onstage, making points and chanting chants. People were weaving in and around, getting to know one another and feeling out the situation. Few were listening to those onstage as the first speakers were too preachy for the majority who were there only to have a good time. When Country Joe and the Fish began singing a song about Viet Nam the mood changed and attention was focused back to the stage.

Between the short sets of music, other underground luminaries presented their views and impressions. The Diggers offered a view of communal living. Organizers for the North Oakland Poverty Program gave a plan to help the poor. This led to an introduction of Bobby Seale and Huey Newton, two of the Black Panthers who had started the program. They exposed harsh scrutiny of racial tensions that were flaring up again in Watts, still smoldering in the coals of the previous summer. They proposed a militant approach for the Civil Rights movement. Their purpose was to demonstrate that Martin Luther King's pacifism was not working. This rubbed much of the crowd the wrong way since the purpose of this gathering was to promote peace. Dick Gregory broke the tension with a bit of dark comedy while still remaining in the camp of the more serious, radical Panthers.

Another wave of music came to the rescue of the crowd, which had begun to polarize on the violence issues. The Jefferson Airplane turned the gathering into a sea of whirling dervishes. Earle and Chapman worked their way close to the front of the stage as Grace Slick spun in a wispy orange scarf to the impromptu refrain of her band. The music spun in a giant circle like a Ferris wheel with the added dimension of time. The smell of marijuana drifted freely over the audience as the smoke eddied in the changing spaces between the swaying bodies, then vanished into those same mysterious places where music vanishes. The riffs from the stage were hypnotic, spreading outward in all directions like a wave, creating a trance-like veil that enveloped the gathering.

The real meat of the anti-war speeches began with activist Tom Hayden painting an informative history of Southeast Asia. He walked the crowd through its civil war and involvement with France and told how the United States had become involved. The audience zoomed in on what he had to say, especially the draft-age boys and men. Earle listened intently as Mr. Hayden's speech went into the economic side of the war, how American corporations were profiting from the extension of the war. Companies like Dow Chemical, who were making huge profits selling the government deadly chemicals like Agent Orange, chemicals that were being used in a barbaric way to defoliate the jungles and kill

the crops of poor farmers. Other products like
Napalm were being dropped on villages, frying
the inhabitants with the jelly-like incendiary
substance that was impossible to extinguish.
Earle wondered why none of this information
had ever been available to the press back home.
Or, if it had been available, why was it not public knowledge?

When Mohammed Ali arrived onstage he was met
with a huge ovation. He was perhaps the most
visible person in America to take a hard stance
against the war. His recent fights had captivated the country and he not only represented the
anti-war movement but he had received much
attention recently by changing his birth name
of Cassius Clay to his new name of Mohammed
Ali. He was at the center of every controversy,
from race to religion. He spoke in short blasts,
much like he fought, and punctuated his jabs
with irony and rhyme. He was both fearless
and sensitive, an odd mixture for such a powerful fighter. He used his sense of humor as a
decoy, to keep the listener at bay until the time
came to strike the issue. He spoke in ideas and
inspirations, not in facts and figures, and his
motives against the war were moral, not political. He spoke from his heart, not his mind. His
concern was not for himself, but for the good
of humanity, and he believed, deep inside, that
the Viet Nam war was inherently evil and must
be stopped for the good of the world.

By the end of Ali's soliloquy, Earle and his friends
were captivated by the power of his commit-
ment. The long journey that had led them to

the summit now brought them fulfillment and, judging from the sound of the congregation, had inspired the masses as well. That their souls had been moved caused their feet to do the same and they soon found themselves beside the stage face-to- face with the mighty Mohammed Ali. Earle put his hand in the enormous hand of Ali and felt like he was shaking hands with a baseball glove made of flesh. He told Ali that he had crossed the desert just to hear his words and thanked him for the gift. Ali said that God had asked him to go into the world and to share His message with those who were being faced with conscientious decisions unlike any they had ever had to make before.

The fact that Ali had recently been indicted on felony draft evasion charges caused security to be especially tight and Ali's bodyguards led him away through a zigzag of chainlink fences. As he was scurried off he turned once and gave Earle a knowing wink, which was like a seal on a letter that might be the difference between his life and his death.

Earle, with his guitar over his back, staggered to the steps and leaned on the security barricade and closed his eyes and thanked God for giving him the sign he asked for. He asked for strength in the trials that might await him. And for good measure he asked if the Infinite One might just throw in a tiny bit of dinner tonight....

When he opened his eyes the world looked new and fresh and the aroma of pot was all around. When he turned towards the stage he met eyes with the bird sisters, Amethyst and Emerald.

They smiled and waved and motioned for him to join them. He scrambled through the crowd, ducking and dodging and sidestepping those on the ground wrapped in blankets in various states of nakedness and consciousness.

When they came together they kissed in a triangle, which almost buckled Earle's knees. He commented on the mynah bird on Amethyst's shoulder. She replied in a fake Italian accent.

> Thees eeza 'Marco Polo, Conqueroo
> di Venizia'.

Emerald wore a Carmen Miranda-style hat that was a hummingbird cage, with a tiny feeder in the center from which a live bird was feeding, suspended in midair, giving a surreal slant to an otherwise unreal piece of getup. They danced around each other, Hungarian style, while the Hari Krishnas chanted onstage an ode to world peace.

> Why don't you come over to our house later for tofu and bean sprouts? Emerald has a whole suitcase full of fortune cookies. You can ride with us.

Earle accepted their kind offer, although he had hoped for something more substantial than bean products. He remembered his prayer from a few minutes ago. He had been offered the very thing that he had asked for. After his last trip of riding a freight train across the desert, just about anything sounded good.

He looked for Kyle and Chapman and found them
in the company of two large Canadian women,
their heads nestled lazy-like between the breasts
of their newly found heavens. When they introduced the girls to Earle they called them their
'Moose Mama Mounties,' which, instead of in-
sulting the girls, seemed to humor them immensely. Earle told them that at one time he had
considered fleeing to Canada and wondered if it
was as cold as it was made out to be. They said
that cold was a relative thing and that Eskimos
sometimes came south to vacation in the Canada Yukon. Earle asked if there was any Mexican food where they lived and they replied that
they didn't know anything about Mexican food,
so they imagined that there was probably none.
He said that he didn't think he could live in a
land where there was no Mexican food. He told
Kyle and Chapman he would see them back in
Venice sometime. They sighed a small moan and
fell back into the pleasure of the fleshy moment.

As they drove down Sunset Boulevard at sunset in
Amethyst's Karmann Ghia convertible, their
minds drifted between the lights, the palm
trees and the radio. A trio of songs in succession
made the night electric: All You Need is Love,
Light My Fire and Good Vibrations. The cool
evening wind blew through their hair and the
smell of incense from the shops wafted through
the convertible and into the street. They parked
on La Cienega and walked down Sunset, past
the Whiskey, where a huge crowd had assembled on the street hoping to catch a refrain from
The Byrds who were playing inside. It seemed

like all of history was represented on the sidewalk as the hippies came down from the foothills and poured out of the canyons. They emulated the ones who gave them inspiration, be they Jesus, Tolstoy or Alice in a twisted Looking Glass—like looking at history reflected in a carnival mirror with a modern soundtrack added. The image became distorted as psychedelic essences were sprinkled into the mix, splaying the image of the culture into a crazy mosaic that appeared to have no rationale, no reason nor rhyme.

A sliver of a moon hung low at the ocean end of Sunset as the trio weaved south through the lights of Hollywood and west to the canals of Venice, enraptured in the moment, calling to the wild. Earle strummed his guitar, anticipating a blissful night of pleasure, full with promise and inspiration, barely aware of the pain and blood, bright in the sun, spilling into the tropical mud only an ocean away.

Betty called out for Bill but there was no reply. She called out again. Still nothing. She flailed away at the shrub she had fallen into but could not free herself. The branches were cutting into her body and the more she struggled the more she entangled herself. How could this have happened? How could she have fallen into that damned shrub? Just a second ago she was standing on the porch, smoking a cigarette and minding her own business. Where in the hell was Bill? Where is that bastard? Can't he hear?

The dumb son-of-a-bitch must be passed out somewhere? Can't he tell that she is in trouble? Somebody's got to come by. Why didn't Bill cut that damn shrub down when she told him to? It's his fault, the stupid asshole—

Bill stirred from the couch and called out for Betty to change the record. He had listened to the same Nat King Cole album three times in a row. When she didn't answer, he looked in the bedroom and the kitchen and out in the back yard. The car was in the garage, so she must be in the house. He scoured every room and when he found nothing he began to panic. He called the police, reported a missing person and popped another beer.

Sgt. Baylock received a call from dispatch reporting a missing person and—knowing it was coming from Betty and Bill's—hoped that it was true. He had been separating them for so long, he was a little surprised to be getting a report that they were separated.

When he got to the house the first thing he saw was Betty's head sticking out of the overgrown decorative bush that hid the porch. She had ceased to wiggle and had simply passed out, her head sticking out of one side and her houseshoes out the other. He knocked on the door and Bill, so drunk he could hardly stand, opened the door.

What're you doin' here Shargent?

You called me here.

Oh yesh, I remember, Betty'sh mish-
ing. Somebody shtoled her.

Baylock could hardly keep a straight face. He pulled
Bill out on the porch and pointed down to Bet-
ty's feet, still covered in pink shag houseshoes.
Bill's eyes widened.

Oh my god, she's been eaten by the bush. We
better call the poleesh.

Baylock told Bill to lift her feet while he lifted her
head, freeing her inch by inch. She came awake
in the middle of the ordeal.

What're you doing? Let me go. Help,
I'm being manhandled!

Betty, it's Sgt. Baylock. You've fallen
in a bush.

Bush, bullshit, where am I? Let me
the hell loose or I'll call my attorney!

Baylock dropped her, letting her fall back in the same
spot she was in before.

Don't trouble yourself, Mrs. Medlock,
I'll call your attorney for you and see
if *he* can help you out of this man-
eating shrub you've got yourself into.
Have a nice night.

Baylock drove away chuckling to himself. He heard
Betty screaming at him, calling him seven

kinds of son-of-a-bitches, and watched the neighbors' porch lights come on one by one in his rear view mirror.

Maggie opened the back door and walked out into the dark backyard. The cicadas, millions of them, were hissing all at once at a feverish pitch and the wind was blowing like mad from the empty West. Lightning was lighting up the sky in the north. The burst of light triggered a memory of her childhood in Dalhart during the Great Dust Bowl.

Her father had come home early from work to gather up the family and drive them to shelter at the old train depot. She remembered a wall of blackness approaching from the north. A gust of wind came up suddenly and blew a flock of English sparrows off their course and into the side of a grain elevator. She watched in horror as the birds tumbled helplessly down the side of the concrete structure. Seconds later another gust blew their car off the road into a ditch where they became stuck up to their axles in deep sand. When the rain arrived it mixed with kicked-up dust and formed chocolate-colored sheets of waving mud. The Morgan family held on for dear life in their old sedan as they watched the water rise in the furrow in which they were stranded. Her father calmly said a prayer and her mother held the kids tightly. Within a few minutes the storm passed and they climbed out the windows of the car and waded through the ditch to the road. As they walked downtown to the train depot a rainbow filled the sky with heavenly wonder and the sun broke through, warming their wet backs.

Back in the present, Maggie wondered out loud, as the lightning came closer, why couldn't the sweet part of the past repeat itself just one more time?

On the south side of Lubbock, out by The Strip, Scotty Chanteaux was hosting a poker game. All the players were there: John Silo, Glen Forest, Phil Nicks, Johnny Hill, Pedro, Charlie Dern, Chicken Box Jimmy and Ringo Tom. Even the east-siders like Schoolboy, Black Charlie, Neal, and TV were sniffing around to see if this was a payday or just a poker party. It was soon apparent that the game was worthwhile when the big-hitters arrived: Charles Ferris, Big Tommy and Johnny Rue. The gamblers fed off of each other's energy and the promise of a big pot loomed omnipresent in the humid, smoke-filled room.

The game started off cautiously, a dollar ante with a progressive limit. Don Wylie dealt to a table of eight players.

Up and Down.

Dollar.

Three dollars.

You don't realize who you're playin'.

Don, Don Wylie.

Five...

Kick ya.

One... two... three...

Eights, a pair.

Larry Shears came in from The Strip holding a bottle
of Wild Turkey.

Gimmie some'a that shit.

What is it?

Just medicine.

Check.

Three nines bet five dollars.

Not tryin' to fuck ya, know what I
mean?

Uh huh.

Four dollars.

Five dollars.

The tempo quickened around the table. Those on the
outside wanted in.

Come on, deal.

Can't come close.

All up.

Last card up?

Thought it was all up.

Last down.

Down and dirty.

John Silo introduced a new subject.

We're all movie stars, know what I mean?

Whose—

Your bet.

Wait a minute.

You owe nine out of twenty.

He tried again.

You know we ain't no different than them bastards in the movies.

Check.

I check.

Ferris reminded him.

A few million poorer.

Check.

I check.

Ferris filled up an empty space.

Why don't you pack up and go to Hollywood, fuck face?

What would I do in Hollywood?

Whaddaya have?

Kings and Queens.

Hearts.

Fuck you.

Fuck you, asshole.

Who dealt that shit?

As the hubbub increased, sentences became short bursts of barbs. At some point the limit was lifted and the small-timers dropped out. As the pot grew huge, the room became quiet and each new bet was met with flashing eyes and the snap of poker chips popping on the table. Johnny Rue was the solitary exception. There were several people in the room upon whom he would lean to throw off their game. He waited for the most inopportune moment to spout off unsolicited insults, hoping his less than perfect timing would separate the inexperienced fools from their money.

Charles Ferris said out loud what everyone else was thinking.

> You know, Johnny, if we needed a fuckin' announcer, we'd hire Howard Cosell.

To which Johnny replied,

> If I needed a worthy opponent I'd dump all you pussy-assed dupes and call Red Ferris and Titanic.

Charles defended his father.

> My dad would detour through Decatur just to bypass your braggin' ass.

Johnny stood.

> You guys go fuck yourselves, I got better ways to waste my time.

Johnny got up and kicked over the table. Drinks, ashtrays and poker chips smashed into a briny slop on the floor. A herd of players used Johnny's clothes for handles and escorted him out the door and tossed him into the cotton field. He screamed at everyone nonstop as they went back to the house laughing with each other, pretending Johnny was nowhere around.

Johnny got in his car and drove back down the dirt road toward Lubbock, cussing the whole rotten lot of no-count players. As he turned on 82nd Street, Sgt. Baylock was heading down the road to Scotty's poker den. A huge smile filled Johnny's face as he waved smugly and saluted the Sarge....

As the morning sun lit the Venice rooftops, Gene sat on the pier in a housecoat contemplating his state of affairs. He knew things were about to change. The last few weeks had set off alarms in his body. His chemical makeup had a need to escape daily drudgery but the uppers and downers he had been taking were not working in harmony with his constitution. He missed his family and friends and wanted to see them again. He had called his mother the night before and she had told him about the letter that had arrived from the Selective Service. He was to report to Amarillo to take a physical to see if he was fit for duty. His mother asked him to come back home and take care of his patriotic business. She wanted him to go back to school and, since she was a teacher and his father was the superintendent of Lubbock schools, said that she would help him plow through the necessary bureaucracy. Every person in his family was a responsible citizen except for Gene. He was not going to participate in the Viet Nam war, and he studied every angle possible to find a way to avoid it. He had some friends who had fled to Mexico, but it was only a temporary escape. He was determined to find his own creative solution.

Earle woke in a huge feather bed with memories of ecstasy so near that he could still feel them. There
were birds everywhere but they were rearranged
since the last time he was here. He lay wondering
about the nature of pleasure and how, in Eastern thought, it is so closely related to pain. He
had recently read how the search for pleasure is
all-consuming and unattainable. But in the end
it is only a transition through which each must
pass on the path to wisdom. Still, Earle thought,
he was glad that he was lucky enough to have
made his current transition.

He made himself a cup of tea while reading a note
from the sisters saying they'd gone into town
with a car full of birds to welcome a famous Indian mystic to their fair city. Earle chuckled as
he read the note. A bizarre world was before
him that unfolded like a Henry Miller novel.
Where was he? How did he get here? When he
put the note down, he stared out the window in
bewilderment of his current coordinates.

He walked down to the beach and sat at the circular park bench strumming his guitar, watching the boardwalk lazily come to life. He was
haphazardly connecting phrases together when,
out of the blue, a certain combination of chords
he played reminded him of Patricia. He saw her
dreamy eyes and could hear her whisper as he
played a kind of upside down A minor chord. He
could practically feel her breath and smell her
perfume as he went to the F chord. He had been
repressing all thoughts of her for so long he was
surprised they had resurfaced on such a random
morning. In fact, thoughts of her bubbled to the

surface many times during the day. They were often accompanied by a sharp pain that seemed to come from the back of his skull where the memory was hidden of the night when he heard her professing her love to someone else.

He heard his name being called and looked up to see his pale Lubbock friends walking down the boardwalk, hands in front pockets, looking like lost dogs trying to fit into the landscape, but not having much luck. Earle answered with a question.

> You guys lost? You look like a pack of ghosts lookin' for the Hi-D-Ho.

One of the refugees replied.

> We ain't lost but we sure as hell don't know where we are.
>
> Seen Kyle and Chapman? Wonder if they're in Canada yet.
>
> Canada?
>
> They got kidnapped by some Yukon mamas.
>
> Nah. They're face down over at Remy's. Looked like they been through it and back.

He joined them for a walk down the beach to the Pacific Ocean Pier. On a marquee in front of the Cheetah they saw where the Doors were play-

ing the following weekend. They walked back
toward the Sea View, past the Jewish quarter
where refugees from World War II had ended
up in a community on the north side of Venice.
They sat in outdoor cafes by old hotels, the tattooed numbers still visible on their hands and
arms from the concentration camps. They talked of the Six Day War and questioned the use of
force in the Holy Land. Earle read the carvings
on their faces that seemed to speak volumes of
how difficult it was for peace to grow from the
ruins of war. As they walked, the Yiddish chat-
ter faded into the sound of carefree children
playing nearby.

The group walked on to the Sea View where Gene
was whistling away, obviously glad to have his
old job back. Remy was repainting the window
trim on the outside of the building and singing in French. The boys sat around the bench
and whiled away an hour or so just watching
the seagulls and feeling the cool ocean wind on
their skin.

Later that afternoon the boys pitched in on a gallon
of Red Mountain Vin Rose. They laughed and
sang at the park bench and swapped stories
about the place they had come from. West Texas was becoming, through the veil of time, more
like a mythical dream in some dusty corner of
their collective memory. The perfect day melted
into the perfect dusk. The sun laid its drunken
head into the soft gray clouds far away over
the sea and gradually gave way to the waxing
thumbnail moon that blindly followed it into
the dark, deep, drink....

The following days were the kind of lazy, uneventful spaces in time that everyone secretly wishes for. They were the kind of days that someone might use to define a worldly utopia. The bunch's leisurely routine emerged: combing the beaches in the mornings, trying to make a few cents in the afternoons, going for dinner at the Faith City Mission at sundown, and—hopefully—lucking into a communal reefer pool to pass the long sweet evenings.

Most days were variations thereof, going back and forth between various crash houses and the beach. As the day of the Doors show approached, more and more action was required. No one had five dollars to buy a ticket, so a creative process was born of necessity. Sam and Jesse had heard the surfers talk about a way to climb around the outside edge of the pier to the back and somehow get in from there. Everyone who heard this harebrained scheme regarded it as a pure surfer fable, born of the sea and destined to return there. But those who knew Sam and Jesse knew that they were regarded as daredevils of sorts, knowing how to do things most mortals never even considered; things like jumping freight trains, climbing radio towers, and riding live Brahma bulls.

The plan forked off into two separate camps. The first bunch decided to take their chances of either sneaking in the front door or, worst-case scenario, at least hearing the band through the many cracks and crevices on the side of the broken down old pier. The second bunch would follow the surfers' plan. Lance, Flash, the Okie

and Earle were in this camp along with the local surfers and sand drummers. Sam and Jesse
led a handpicked group of winos who proudly
held up the rear of the fellowship.

They had a day to prepare. They gathered dark
clothes so to attract less attention. They borrowed, from anyone they could, tennis shoes
and gloves to protect their extremities from
the splintering pylons. And, over several more
bottles of wine, they went over the procedure
with the experienced surfers about how to ma-
neuver around the tricky spots of the dubious
wooden structure. Earle borrowed shoes from
Gene and gloves that were used to carry out
the grease pot from the kitchen at the Sea
View. Gene—of all people—warned Earle of
the danger of this ordeal, but, in the light of
his recent brush with doom, realized he had
suffered considerable damage to his credibility.
When Earle asked why he was not going to the
concert, Gene changed the subject and hurried
back into the kitchen.

They met on the Venice side of the rickety pier at dark,
a ragtag crew who might have been mistaken
for escapees from the mental prison. The head
surfer, Pipeline, had long dreadlocks and a Van
Gogh mustache and spoke with quiet authority
in between drags from a Jamaican-sized spliff.
He pointed out the 2x12 creosote rail that ran
on the outside of the massive pylons that made
up the foundation of the pier. He warned of two
places where the rail was gone, and at these
places one had to climb to the inside of the pylons in order to make the crossover. He assured

everyone that the farther out over the ocean one climbed, the darker it became. The only light was coming from the street lamps that lit up the boardwalk. Close to the end of the first rail was another rail that turned ninety degrees and went underneath the Cheetah to a hole in the floor and came up inside the building. He pointed to Lunar, a stocky, wild-eyed surfer, and said that he would be there to mark this last turn.

Groups of three made their exits every five minutes, in order to keep a steady flow as well as to draw the least amount of attention from the beach. Earle took out with Harlon the Okie and a very stoned Flash. The first part went without a hitch and the first crossover was just a matter of zigzagging down one pylon and following the rail. The view from the side of the pier was outstanding; the lights along the coast to the south were visible until they dissolved into the mist on the far side of the airport. A sea of lights spread inland, looking like a river of cheap rhinestones left behind by careless pioneers who had struck it rich in Kingdom Come, only to leave it all behind when temptation had turned paradise into property tax. He could have stayed all night had it not been for the music starting up. He could feel it vibrating through the old wood, giving an urgency to the mission at hand.

When they got to the second crossing, Flash, who had not uttered a peep until now, began to express his anxiety. First it was with a babble of words that no one could decipher and then with total convulsion, hanging onto the pylon like it was

his mother on the first day of school. He began
screaming 'I need a helicopter!' at the top of his
lungs. As Earle looked down, a rush of fear entered his being as well. The angry ocean lapped
at the pylons a hundred feet down and in between them, and in the sea were dozens of black
creosote crossties, sharp and severe. Earle saw
that Flash, who was between him and Harlon,
had to let go of the pylon and follow the rail
into the darkness. But every time they tried to
reason with him, Flash would yell, 'I need a helicopter!' Two more groups had now stacked up
behind them and the stall in the line had made
everyone nervous. Some had taken acid before
the climb, thinking it would come on about the
time they got inside. Earle had the feeling like
he might be in exactly the wrong place at exactly the wrong time. He began to sing.

> Songbird over the Ocean
> Sparrow over the Sea
> Songbird over the Ocean
> Bring my Love to Me

Flash was silent for a few seconds, then relapsed.

> Bring me a helicopter!
> I need a helicopter!

Lunar, the so-called usher-in-chief, came down the
rail to where Flash was frozen in fear. He made
a short but convincing speech.

> Look, fuckhead, you ain't gettin' a
> fuckin' helicopter! Just listen up.

You're gonna let go of this pole on
your own and follow this flashlight or
I'm gonna pry your ass off and toss
you to the sharks! You got it? You got
five seconds. One... two....

Perhaps it was the mention of the sharks or maybe
his better judgment kicked in, but Flash let go
of the pylon and inched along the rail, following Lunar to the hole in the window behind the
dance hall. The rest of the party followed close
behind and soon Lunar lifted everyone up to the
inside of a seven-foot-tall box that was deafen-
ingly loud and dark but for bright shafts of colored light that punched through the roof of the
structure they were inside of. When the song
was over it was apparent that they were under
the stage. Lunar led them to a hole by the wall
where, by taking one step forward, they were in
the front row looking up at the Doors only a few
feet away!

The contrast between the two environments was
enough to undo the hinges of any lunatic. Flash
was spinning like a dervish, arms up high and
hands horizontal. Earle shook his head and
smiled when he realized that Flash had become
his own helicopter, fueled by the music, and
therefore rising above his fears and anxieties.
As the organ swirled the endless solo part on
Light My Fire, everyone was pulled upwards in
a spiral and released all at once. The crowd felt
like they were expanding beyond the pettiness
of their tiny lives while rising on the wings of
harmonies to places never before imagined.

Everyone, that is, except for Lance, who was being dragged out by the hair for calling the bluff of a herd of security goons and threatening to whip the ass of the head bouncer.

The Chinese call it the law of yin and yang or the law of opposites. The symbol is a circle, half black and half white, in which the two opposite colors chase each other in constant, circular motion. It represents the law of natural opposite forces such as summer and winter, life and death, sickness and health, war and peace, and so on. It goes on to say that the most perfect of times are followed by the most trying. Within the next few weeks, as the war raged out of control, thousands of young men were called to face the draft. All of the Lubbock boys who were now out West were affected by the escalation. The crisis that had been building for the last few years came to a peak, ironically, during what was now being called The Summer of Love.

Earle received his telegram at the Sea View Cafe to be on notice to report to Amarillo for induction into the Army. Kyle got his letter to take his physical. They discussed plans to return to Texas at once. They made the rounds, said their goodbyes and stopped by the Western Union to pick up money that Kyle's mother had wired from home. They bought a small brick of pot in anticipation of the dark days ahead. They set out in the late afternoon, taking one last look in the rearview mirror at the sun falling into the sea. After fighting traffic across L.A. they made it to the desert and broke through the invisible city wall as it gave way to a chaotic crystal sky full of flickering stars that chuckled all at once at the frivolous and futile actions of the inhabitants of a tiny blue paradise called Earth.

The Army center in Amarillo was overflowing with farm boys signing on to take the next plane out to Saigon. Because there was virtually no information available about what was really going on, the isolated rural areas relied on billboards and truck stop hearsay. The fathers of the sons, fresh from a necessary war, did not question the validity of the war at hand, and assured their sons that they were doing the right thing by signing up. The only exception being, of course, Korea, which still had opponents on both sides. No one wanted another war that was unable to be won, but Lyndon Johnson assured everyone that this was not such a war.

The sales clerk at Gibson's Discount asked him what it was he was looking for. Doctor Milner, one of Lubbock's most esteemed psychiatrists, assured her that he was trying to find just the right size panty hose for his mother and the only way he knew how was to experience them completely. The clerk told him it was highly unusual for a man to climb into the hose with his head and arms to find out the size. Why didn't he just ask his mother? He said that although he was buying them for his mother, he was not actually going to give them to her. He was only trying to find some answers to some questions that had been bothering him all his life. He then walked across the aisle to the brassiere section and, with his arms still in the panty hose, wrapped the red lacy garment around his legs with a knee in each cup. He asked the sales girl, who was by now completely flustered, about her mother and if she remembered events that happened early in her life. The girl stared coldly at him for a few seconds and twirled quickly away saying that it was time to call the manager about this....

Sister Sonya threw a frozen package of fish sticks into the hot skillet filled with grease. As the ice bubbles boiled and popped she saw a vision starting to form. It was the mouth of a river with tall grass and palm trees on each side. For a moment she thought it was a premonition of paradise, a lazy tropical scene beckoning her to escape from the Lubbock trailer house that she had lived in for the last twenty years. But there was something wrong and it was getting closer. She heard engines behind her with a powerful whopping sound approaching quickly. She could see the tops of women and children's heads, running and screaming towards the jungle wall. The helicopters roared overhead dropping a protoplasm-like gel over the tranquil scene that burst into hellish flame, swallowing everything with flesh-smelling smoke and turning the jungle into a holocaust, an inferno that roared like a rabid dragon spitting white ash skyward until the sun was blocked and night rained down in the middle of the morning. Sister Sonya jumped back from the stove, her apron strings on fire, and ran into the yard screaming as her goats scattered and her cats looked at her quizzically. She fell on her knees and prayed for the children she had just seen. Had she seen too much, or was God preparing her for the inevitable Apocalypse? She smelled the charred smell of her vision and when she turned back to her trailer house she saw smoke pouring out of the door. She flew up the stairs but not in time to save the blackened skillet full of grim, burning fish sticks.

The interior of the First Baptist Church was so immense that it overshadowed Pastor Honey's frail form praying in the front pew of the empty space. It had been a hard week for everyone in the administration department, full of legal issues with realtors and skirmishes between opposing factions of Southern Baptist Organizations. Pastor Honey took a deep breath and began his prayer with a general thanks for his family and friends and for the blessings that had been bestowed upon them. He then prayed that the realtors and lawyers and the city council would acknowledge God's plan for adding a new wing to the present building and for annexing several square blocks of new parking to accommodate the additional congregation. He prayed that everyone could see past the fact that whole blocks of houses would be torn down, and that they could see past the Physical World to the Spiritual World, where God in His Generosity would provide all who gave of their property another dwelling in Heaven in full view of God's Majestic Cotton Field. He also prayed for the realtors and lawyers so that they could see God's Plan and that they might switch churches as to guarantee their own Salvation.

There had been no decision made on any kind of travel strategy, but there was no need of it in light of the present mood inside Kyle's Chevy Wagon. The exuberance that had been their companion on their journey west was no longer in the car. Instead, a morose silence crawled around the inside of the car and across the dash. It was absorbed into every crevice of the car's interior including the radio speakers, where it transformed the voices of peddlers and preachers into a sonic mound of background static. Each time either Earle or Kyle attempted conversation it dwindled away quickly. They could almost follow each other's words blowing around the car, bouncing off the wind sheer, being sucked down into the vents, weaving through the torn seat covers and discarding themselves out the windows into oblivion in the hot, useless desert wind.

They made their way quickly out of California and smoked a bowl in Kyle's oversized hookah at the Arizona border in a failed attempt to celebrate something or other. As they sat in the dark outside an abandoned moon-baked Phillips 66 it seemed as if the world had ended at this very spot and there was nothing beyond worth trav-

eling towards. After spending the last couple of
weeks in Venice, the concept of traveling back
to Lubbock seemed an act of insanity, the most
hair-brained action that either of them could
possibly imagine. Kyle managed to release a
mouthful of words.

Well, the girls are better in Lubbock.

Earle tried to make light of Kyle's remark without
hurting his feelings.

What about your Moose Mama?
What happened to her? How come
you ain't said nothin' about her?

She was the best I ever had.

Well, what are you doin' here? Why
ain't you in Canada?

She got another school year in L.A.
and then I'm going (he sings) North
to Alaska, north to Luscious Home.

Earle corrected him.

It's 'North to Russia's own.'

What is?

The words. That's the words.

Who said anything about Russia?

It was evident that they had crossed that line of no
return and that any attempt to save the conversation would have been futile. Before Earle
could suggest that they sleep a few hours before morning, Kyle was snoring like a volcano,
twisted in an impossible posture in the front
seat of his Chevy. Earle retreated to the back
of the wagon where he alternated between
making out constellations in the southern sky
and seeing them explode on the inside of his
closed eyelids. He wondered to himself if he
would ever again have the same feeling that
he'd had when Patricia had made him feel like
a nova within a galaxy, when she had asked
him to melt with her. As he gazed through
the universe, he saw how much larger his life
had seemed when love had bestowed meaning
upon it, than now when he felt like a tiny flaw
on a huge wallpapered room.

Without so much as a pause he considered another
situation. There was the real possibility that
he might be killed in some far distant Asian
war. As he lay in the back of the station wagon
on a sandy beach towel absorbed in the over-
whelming universe, he could not imagine fighting someone with whom he shared this fragile
planet, spilling each other's blood over the clash
of the ideologies of their leaders. Even here,
alone in this vast desert, images of war were
beginning to leak into his psyche and become
twisted like a sinister roadrunner cartoon.

As a meteor flashed across the sky, he returned to the
present and told himself to stay in the moment
and not drift too far into the unknown. After

all, he had a Gibson guitar, a sky full of stars, and a cool desert wind blowing across his face....

Gene sat in an overstuffed chair wearing a pink night-gown with a feather boa with red painted lips and blue eye shadow, his legs spread vulgar-like, holding a Marine- issue machine gun in one hand and a tube-style cocaine dispenser in the other. A Bandito in a dominatrix leather outfit walked slowly toward him with a whip in his hand. He ordered Gene to turn around and hold the straps on the bedstead and lashed the whip across his ass, tearing his thin nylon panties and opening the skin to a bloody gash. Gene groaned in pain. The Bandito spoke softly to Gene.

Must you purr so loudly, my little chimney dust?

Gene winced in agony but on his next inhale he felt himself panting with excitement.

I gotta have something for the pain.

The big Bandito ignored his request and lashed him again. Gene took a snort of coke and begged the Bandito to make love to him. Flash came out of the dark corner into the red light dressed in skimpy underwear and high-heeled leather boots. He approached Gene and kissed him all over as he popped an amulet of amyl nitrate. As the blood rushed to his head, his body heat rose as if he were in a room full of steam. Before he was mauled by the two men, he had a flashing thought: If this don't get me out of the Army, nothing will.

The broiling sun forced Kyle and Earle into an early start the next morning and by afternoon they were crossing the mountains close to Flagstaff. As they sputtered over a mountain, the car coughed to a halt near the top of the pass. Earle looked over to Kyle who was behind the wheel.

What do you reckon?

Vapor lock. She's done it before when it's high and hot.

Vapor lock? I had me one of them lookin' down from the pier the other night.

Never did fill the canteens did we?

Nope. Unless you did.

They could hear the rush of wind blowing through the tall pines. They listened for a long time before Kyle shared his knowledge about vapor locks.

We only need a little bit of water to pour over the manifold.

What about the radiator?

What about it. How you gonna get it out?

We could just turn the car upside down.

They neither one laughed, but continued listening to the wind in the trees. A cloud shaded the sun and the air became cooler. Earle finally spoke.

There's always the water pipe.

They looked in the back seat and, sure enough, the glass bowl was half full of brownish water. Kyle added.

Then we wouldn't have a water pipe.
Guess we ought do a bowl first.

They lit the pipe and passed it back and forth for what seemed like an eternity. By the time they finished the bowl, they had no desire to deal with mechanical problems of any kind. When Earle got out to take a leak, Kyle followed. As they wove their way among the pines they were overwhelmed at the majesty of the mighty trees. They continued walking over the aromatic needle bed to a place where giant granite rocks lay sleeping, covered in iridescent green moss and orange lichens, overlooking a vast valley stretching to the curved horizon. They lay on the rocks feeling the wind, watching an eagle soar from peak to lonesome peak. The thin mountain air soon made their eyelids heavy and the wind rocked them to sleep. If not for the sound of distant thunder, they might have spent the afternoon on the rock. When they woke they laughed about how little it took to sidetrack their trip back to Lubbock. When they began walking back to the car they realized they were lost and it took another hour to find it. When they did, they discovered that Earle had left the passenger door ajar, which had caused the dome light to stay on, which had caused the battery to run down. They laughed about their new dilemma.

Kyle popped the hood while Earle got the pipe and they made a kind of ceremony out of pouring the pipe-water slowly over the manifold. They jumped in the car and Kyle put in the clutch, put the Chevy in reverse, and they started rolling backwards down the mountain. When he popped the clutch nothing happened but for a screech of tires and the whirring of the dead engine.

Turn on the key!

Oh, shit! Here comes a truck!

When he twisted the key the engine came to life and Kyle crunched it down into first and floored it across the gravel and pine needles to the top of the crest. The trucker blew a blast from his air horn and they could smell his hot brakes wafting in the wind. Kyle pulled over to let him go by and the both of them sighed a sigh of relief. They poked along for the next few hours, taking in the scenery, refusing to keep pace with the hurried world. By sundown they entered the strange empty streets of Gallup, New Mexico. They had enough money to split a bowl of green chili stew, and the waitress, a drop-dead gorgeous Navajo girl, brought them mounds of extra crackers. They had both decided to move to Gallup when the front door opened and a large Indian cowboy strolled in and gave the girl something in a brown paper sack. She looked in the bag and squealed with glee and jumped into his arms. Those two drove off in a beat-up Volkswagen as Kyle and Earle looked at each other with eyebrows raised. They shook their heads and then finished the crackers.

After a few cups of coffee they were back to the road with Earle behind the wheel. He drove all night across New Mexico, stopping only for coffee and gasoline in Santa Rosa. He took his canteen into the truck stop to see if the waitress from a couple of weeks ago was there, but another waitress told him that she had taken her baby to California with a truck driver and was going to start all over, fresh. When Earle didn't reply, she grudgingly filled his canteen and looked him over suspiciously.

Kyle was snoring in the back of the wagon, so Earle hunkered down over the wheel and locked onto the highway, backtracking the same bumpy road from less than a moon ago, only richer now with knowledge and conviction than before. When he crossed the state line at Texico he did not even honk—rather, he aimed the hood ornaments as if they were gun sights set straight to face whatever it was that might challenge his life and freedom. At 5 a.m. they entered Fort Lubbock, dead to the world, and Earle drove the last few miles to Kyle's driveway, in his sleep.

CHAPTER 6

The first couple of days back home were the happiest that Earle had seen in years. Friends and family descended upon their house in droves. His grandfather had come in from Houston and his mother was in a cheery mood. Bob the Turk was fixing the grape trellis in the back yard and his uncle J.B. was spinning yarns in the living room. Bob had installed new cedar cushions in the swamp cooler, which gave it a rich, heavenly smell like a spring morning rain. His brother Mark and his friend had a gigantic model train track up and running and it stretched between the two back bedrooms. Maggie was baking a roast in the oven and a freshly shelled pot of black-eyed peas was simmering on the stove. A green bean casserole topped with canned onion rings was covered in tinfoil on the table.

Earle fired up the old Allstate 125 with a little priming and coaxing. He drove around the neighborhood comparing memories with reality and came to the conclusion that not that much had changed except, of course, himself. He felt like he saw more now, like he saw the inside of things more than the outside. He used to assume that the facade was the truth, but now he was beginning to see to the core of both the object and the observer. He drove by Phil's house and Tiny's house and by the Hagoods' and in a big circle by the Athens's where he heard the Velveteens's rehearsal leaking out into the street. He did not stop as the wind felt too good blowing in his hair and, most of all, dinner would be ready soon.

The smell of the dinner conjured up a forest of memories. It reminded Earle of those Sunday kind of meals when his father was still alive where everyone gathered in the kitchen talking and stirring and clanking and laughing.

When the table was ready they all sat down and Granddad Morgan said the prayer. He gave thanks that this gathering could all be here and gave thanks for the food they were about to eat and may it nourish their bodies that they may be strong to do the Lord's will. He asked for the Lord's help in finding and recovering his grandson, Burk, from the jungles of Viet Nam where his plane had been shot down and that he may be safe from harm from the Communists and protected by the Lord Almighty. In Jesus' name, Amen.

Earle kept his head down longer than the rest, shocked by this bit of news. Why had no one told him? He heard the shuffle of plates and raised his head but kept his eyes down that his tears might not show. When his uncle J. B. passed him the mashed potatoes he noticed that he had tears in his eyes as well. His sons, Butch and Barry, with whom he used to play as a kid, were to enter the service any day now. There had not been a word spoken since the prayer, just some clearing of throats, when Bob the Turk blurted out.

You know, LBJ don't give a flyin'
damn about our boys. All that son-of-
a-bitch thinks about is them spoiled-
ass Beagle dogs of his.

Only Maggie laughed, followed by more silence. Everyone reached for something, anything, on the
table whether they wanted it or not. J.B. opened
up the conversation and everyone followed.

Sure been hot. Cotton bolls'r no
bigger'n
Q-tips.

It has been hot.

I think it's hotter this year than it
was last.

I think so, too.

I know so.

Some rain'd be good.

We could sure use it.

Yeah it'd sure be good.

Talk of the weather brought a sense of ease to the
room among everyone but Earle. He was still
reeling from the news of his cousin. He was not
capable of doing anything but twirl his potatoes
in a spiral. Bob the Turk spoke again.

Hey everybody, it's sure good to have
Earle back. He's been out in Hollywood elbowin' with the movie stars.

Everyone nodded and glanced quickly to Earle then
back to their plates. No one was comfortable
with the fact that Earle's hair was now down
to the middle of his back, or the fact that he
wore a leather necklace holding a peace symbol.
They considered it a symbol of dissent. They
were also uncomfortable with the fact that
Earle wore only sandals and had several rings
on his toes. Although the family members were
uneasy they were not surprised. Maggie had a
long history of mental illness and it was beginning to surface in her offspring.

There was more talk about the weather and then
some talk about the church. Granddad Morgan
said that his church was heavily involved in
missionary work in Africa. He said that some
representatives from his church had brought
some newly converted African Negroes to a
dinner at the pastor's house in Amarillo. Fried
chicken was served and after the meal they noticed there weren't any bones on their plates.
Not a splinter. They had eaten every single
bone! There was a stunned gasp of disbelief in
the room and then another long silence except
for Bob the Turk who died laughing and said
he couldn't believe that no one else thought the
story was funny. Somebody murmured.

I'll swan.

Bob the Turk commented.

> Hell, I've been that hungry before.
> I've eat lots of grasshoppers. We used
> to eat locusts at the XIT. Fried 'em up
> like onion rings. When you're hungry,
> hell, pillowcases start tastin' good.

Another silence followed, broken by J.B. questioning
Earle.

> So, Earle, what's your take on this
> war?

Maggie interrupted.

> He's not going to any war. Our fam-
> ily's paid more than most.

Earle took a drink of iced tea and went back to his
plate. Granddad Morgan commented on recent
events.

> Hear 'bout them hippie fellers
> dropped all them dollar bills on the
> Stock Market? No one even looked
> up. Too busy sellin' pieces of paper
> to pick up actual greenbacks a lyin'
> on the floor. I don't know 'bout this
> world no more.

Maggie brought out a lemon meringue pie and started
a pot of coffee. Mark took Earle in the bedroom
to play with his train. Earle watched the train,
especially the boxcars, go round and round and

wished it was all that simple. He thought about the morning sun on the Arizona mountains from the vantage point of a boxcar door. He started to tell Mark, but Mark was so absorbed in the toy train that Earle didn't want to break the magic spell with his own story of misery and dust. It was then that Earle realized that no one except himself could ever experience his own experiences and even if he told them a thousand times they would be nothing more than just another story between the bookends of great silences....

The morning sun shone on the immaculate desk of Pastor Honey's secretary. She was filing her nails while reading the new Baptist Quarterly that had just arrived. She was at first surprised and then startled as she looked up to find a man standing at her desk with hair as long as the disciples' on the cover of her magazine. She tried to ask how she could help him but she could only stutter a nonsensical string of syllables.

Did you... Can I... Where in— ?

Earle helped her out.

I'm here to see Pastor Honey. He's not expecting me. At least I don't think so.

She happened to glance down at his bare feet wearing sandals, and by the time she had pulled her eyes

up to his she heard the familiar shuffle of Pastor
Honey walking out of his office toward her desk.
When he saw Earle, he too was taken aback.

Are you looking for something,
young... man?

Yes, sir. I was hoping to talk to you.

Pastor Honey, upon seeing the peace symbol around
Earle's neck, realized that Earle was not a disciple risen from the dead but rather a dissident
hiding behind an evil insignia.

I'm busy.

As a member of this church, I didn't
know where else to turn.

Those words gave the Pastor confidence that a mis-
guided soul might be nudged back on the path.

In my office. Over here. It's been a
busy day.

He shut the door, slightly too hard.

Now, my son, what's on your mind?

Earle looked for words.

I've got this voice inside me that tells
me that this war ain't right and about
two thirds of everybody is starting to
feel the same. The Army has drafted

me but my feelings tell me not to participate.

The Pastor stared firmly at Earle and held his breath for several seconds. Before he spoke he breathed out, hard.

Look, the military is a part of this government, which is, in turn, ordained by God. At least in America it is. In Asia there is no God. The people are Communists and that is why they have no misgivings about taking away every freedom that our soldiers have fought for throughout history.

Viet Nam has acknowledged a deity for thousands of years. This war is a civil war. Our forces shouldn't be there.

Look, sonny boy, if the Pentagon says we should be there, then we should be there. Our destiny is at stake.

Would Jesus have agreed with the Pentagon or made up his own mind?

How dare you defile the name of Jesus Christ? Of course he would've sided with the Pentagon. Get out of my office, apostate! Leave this church. If you do not support your country you will go to hell, simple as that. And one more thing....

Earle looked at the Pastor, stunned that he had de-
capitated the conversation.

What's that?

Get a haircut.

His secretary blushed and crossed her legs as Earle
left the Pastor's office. He walked straight to
her desk and watched as she shrunk in her
chair. He reached into his blue jeans and pulled
out a tiny seashell that he had plucked from the
beach a few days before. He laid it on her desk,
looked deep into her eyes and whispered.

Peace....

As he pushed open the heavy doors of the Church he
knew there would be many more heavy doors to
open before this episode was over. The sudden
bright sun brought water to his eyes, which, by
the time he reached his mother's turquoise Comet, had turned to tears of fury. Was he insane or
was everyone else? He started the car and floored
it, only to slam on the brakes and watch his own
dust pass him. He got out his notebook and wrote.

O Zillion Neutron
Burning Foo-tron
Einstein's Highway Patrol
Spew forth some sign
That Life is Divine
And there's no Time
For all the rigmarole

His inner tempo changed inside of his anger and he
continued.

> Let the Dead Wake Up.
> Blind Dead, and Blinder'd Dead.
> Dead Who Plastereth
> His Wall in Propaganda.
> Dead Who Believeth
> In the Parable of the Pentagon
> Dead Who Sayeth
> Not what he Knoweth
> But what he Heareth on TV
>
> Let the Dead Wake Up
> And the Dying, And the Dying And the
> Dying

He called his friend Rick Cornrich to see if he could
get him a recommendation for his psychiatrist,
Doctor Milner. He also asked if Doctor Milner
would agree to a ceiling charge of seven dollars
and fifty cents. Rick said he would see what he
could do. He called back within fifteen minutes
and told him he was on if he could make it right
after his lunch hour which was from three till
four. Earle told him he could and thanked him
for his help.

Doctor Milner's office was much different from Pastor Honey's. In fact, it did not feel at all like an
office but more like a room in someone's house.
There was no one in the room, only a TV in the
corner behind a large aquarium stuffed full
with tropical fish. Earle sat in a lounge chair,

moving his head side to side in order to make
out what was showing on the screen.

Earle heard a man's voice behind him.

> That's the way our dreams are. Con-
> trary worlds crisscrossing, while, at
> the same time, seeming to have ev-
> erything in common with each other.
> Come on back.

Earle liked him immediately. His voice, while father-
ly, had a lunatic quality about it that made it
utterly unthreatening.

Doctor Milner pulled a lawn chair from his closet and
unfolded it in the middle of the room and asked
Earle to have a seat. He then climbed up on his
desk, sitting on his haunches, monkey like, and
asked Earle if there was anything bothering
him. He reached into a bowl on his desk and
grabbed a handful of spaghetti and forced it
into his mouth while managing to keep a look
of concern on his face.

Earle tried not to laugh. As this was the first time he
had ever been to a psychiatrist, he did not know
for sure if the Doctor's behavior was strange or
not. He began by telling his situation and his
moral dilemma. He relayed what Cassius Clay
had said and told him about his conversation earlier that morning with Pastor Honey. He told him
about his father having died and his mother getting sick and about hearing his girlfriend profess
her love to another. He was about to go into more
detail when he looked again at Doctor Milner
and saw him looking down, spinning his head

in circles making the long strands of spaghetti hanging from his mouth twirl around an atlas that he had put in front of him. Earle busted out laughing. He laughed so hard that he nearly fell from the lawn chair and when he looked up again the Doctor was throwing salad around the room laughing with him, only more maniacal.

It's only the world! It's just the world! Just the little bitty world! Bitty, witty, witty-bitty world.

This was undoubtedly the most insane moment of his life, but something felt right about it. The whole bizarre scene was reassuring yet made no sense whatsoever. The Doctor had now gotten down off his desk and was lighting sparklers. He gave one to Earle and proceeded to run out of the office and down the hallway of his building. Earle watched his sparkler while he sat in front of the aquarium. He waited, but the Doctor never returned. He threw his seven dollars and fifty cents into the aquarium and went on home feeling as if a huge burden had been removed. He might be dead in a month but he, after all, was alive right now.

On his way home he stopped to see his friend, Tim Athens, to tell him of his strange day. The Baptist preacher episode did not surprise him in the least since Tim was Episcopalian. He knew of Doctor Milner and, while admitting that he was some sort of genius, wondered why Earle had wasted his money on a madman who posed as a doctor. He told Earle that if he really wanted to see the future there was only one person who could help him and that person was Sister Sonya, the famous Lubbock psychic. Many of his friends had been to see her and they had all been blown away by her insight. Earle said he might as well complete his mission with a psychic, since the first two professionals had only murkied up the waters of his misunderstanding.

The next morning Earle found himself in front of Sister Sonya's Tarot and Fortunes. Before he reached the front door she came up behind him, flowered parasol in hand, and greeted him by his first name.

I've been expecting you, Earle.

You have? I guess I should've called first.

You did. Through someone else.

Well... okay then. Well... I, uh, then I suppose you know why I'm here.

She motioned for him to join her at a wooden picnic set beside her house. She shooed a billy goat off the table and brushed the bench with her hand

You suppose right. Please, sit down. Would you like something to drink? Very well. I want you to know, I heard your thoughts last week but you should not be alarmed. The situation that will cause you the most grief is not the situation that is presently on your mind. This is usual in life. We imagine the best or the worst of the *future* and, in doing so, are careless about everyday life. The future cannot hurt you. It is only the present that can change you forever. You are not alone. Most of the world is foolish like you, putting on blinders and then forcing yourself to keep wearing them.

Earle didn't understand.

I don't know what you mean. Maybe you don't know what I mean, either. I've been drafted by the Army and I could be blown to bits in a matter of weeks.

I see no war for you. No Army, no Asia, no blood, but not to say no Trouble. Someone will come into your life and cause you much grief. Your every move will be followed, yet you will believe that you are more free than you have ever been. Every thing you do will put you in jeopardy. You will live in a metal building with stale air and not be permitted to roam from room to room.

She crossed the other leg, lit a cigarette, and continued.

Many griefs will accumulate at once and your burdens will be heavy. You

must be strong. You must have faith
in God.

Please, don't get me wrong. This will
only be temporary. After this period
will be a time of great joy. I hear music and see crowds of people covered
in steam all squinting in the same
direction. People from foreign lands
will greet you whose names you cannot pronounce. You will watch helplessly as your best friends alternate
their allegiance between life forces
and animated machines.-

On magnets you will forge a history of your triumphs and misfortunes
that will be carried by the winds in
the interest that others may not repeat your folly.

Earle was bewildered at this vision of his future. He
commented to Sister Sonya.

If things turned out half that good I'd
be thrilled.

They might turn out better. But first
you must make an effort. Even if your
life events happen like this, it is only
temporary and vain. Ultimately we
all must die. At least from this world.
There are many worlds.

So it is said.

Earle stood and looked around.

Where did you get your goats?

They are messengers from middle earth.

Is that down around Odessa?

Sister Sonya did not crack a smile. Earle told her that he had to be running along now and thanked her for her time. He asked her how much he owed, and she said he didn't owe a thing. She told him that she sensed a bit of skepticism and that she only charged when people took her advice to heart. He thanked her again and bid her farewell and gave her the last sea shell from his pocket. Sister Sophia said one more thing.

When you lose your present fear of dying, come back to see me. There will be a cake waiting for you....

Very few things were capable of intimidating Sgt. Baylock, but a souped-up Harley Davidson was at the top of the list. He approached it as if it were a part of himself. A dark dangerous part, yet exciting to the point of being sexual. He circled it like a wild animal circles when encaged. He looked at it from all sides and then circled again to see if somehow it had changed. Though he was weak with fear, he couldn't wait to touch it. He had secretly yearned for this day but never believed he would actually go through with it. A voice broke his trance.

She's a beauty, ain't she?

Baylock said nothing.

I'll may cue a deal.

Baylock turned and coldly stared at the crippled dealer, remaining dead silent.

You get the po-leece discount.

Baylock laughed sarcastically. He finally spoke.

Gas it up, fuckhead.

The dealer brought out a five-gallon can and emptied the contents into the tank of the new Harley Davidson. Baylock straddled the seat, kicked the crank three times and goosed the throttle when it came to life. A different kind of animal gushed inside of him as he looked over the handlebars to the opening in the chain link fence. The dealer was yelling at him over the roar of the engine.

You can pay it out over forty-eight months.

Baylock clanked the shifter into first and popped the clutch, spewing dust and gravel in a cloud behind him. He swung onto Buffalo Lakes Road and disappeared behind a cotton gin, roaring off into the distance. The dealer hobbled down the drive, yelling to the roar.

Wait, I need to get some information—

A pitiful-looking handful of friends gathered at the Greyhound station to see Earle off. Maggie had been crying since she woke up this morning. Bob the Turk was comforting her and cussing the draft board at the same time. Chicken Box Jimmy and Ringo Tom had arrived in the same car, no less. They were apart from everyone else, placing bets with each other on how late the bus was going to be. Noticeably absent were Earle's old close friends who disagreed with him about the politics of the times. Kyle drove up in his Chevy wagon just as the Sweetwater bus pulled in. Earle came walking out of the Bus Station Cafe with Mark, each of them eating a Nutty Buddy. Bob the Turk asked him where his suitcase was and Earle told him he didn't bring one. He said he'd tried to pack but he had no sense of what he was packing *for*. The induction notice had specified that only a small bag of necessary items was allowed. Leaving his guitar behind was almost as hard as leaving his friends and family. He figured the only thing necessary for the Army was maybe a toothbrush. Bob then asked where his shoes were and Earle said he didn't think he was going to need them where he was going.

He hugged his mother and his brother and told everyone good-bye while holding back the dammed-up tears. As he was about to get on the bus, Kyle handed him a book of Khalil Gibran's writings that his mother had asked him to pass on. Earle thanked him and told everyone that he'd write when they paid him enough to buy a ballpoint pen. He climbed aboard and sat at the window where he could see everyone. They were all waving as the bus crept forward. The tears that had been dammed up all morning began to fall like rain onto the front of his shirt. Before they rounded the corner his tears combined with laughter when he saw Chicken Box Jimmy counting out a stack of bills for Ringo Tom.

The Army Sergeant at the Induction Center straightened his tie and practiced his badass look in the mirror. He stuck out his jaw, furled his brow and squinted his eyes until his ego was satisfied with the predator image. His objective in life was to scare the daylights out of every greenhorn that walked in the door. He'd been a student of Western movie stars and had studied Bogart as well. He looked once again in the mirror. He grabbed his balls, clicked his heels and saluted himself. Satisfied, he returned to the front desk where the first person he saw was Earle.

Where you goin', civilian?

I got this notice in the mail and I....

The Sergeant saw the length of Earle's hair for the first time.

You in the wrong place. The WACs Center is around the corner.

What's a wax?

Women's Army.

Come on, man.

Don't man me, you little chickenshit,
I'll court martial your ass before you
ever enlist.

Earle looked down. His expectations had been exceeded.

Where in the hell did you come from?

Lubbock.

We processed a lot of Lubbock boys
and none of 'em looked like you.
Where's your shoes, boy?

Didn't think I'd need 'em. I'm trav-
elin' light.

You're gonna think light when your
ass is on the front lines, shot full of
holes. Here, fill out this form and
then follow the white line.

The whole office chuckled when the Sergeant turned
around shaking his head. Earle sat and filled
out the form which included several pages
of questions about his medical history and
his involvement with political organizations.
He filled it out, then took it to the next desk
where an officer scanned it and told Earle to
take a seat.

A long time passed as he watched dozens of boys breeze in and out with barely a pause. An officer approached Earle and informed him of an interview that had been arranged with an Army doctor. He led him down the hall to an official-looking door that said 'Staff Psychiatrist'. A quiet- spoken man invited him in and introduced himself as Doctor Levin. He told Earle that, a few years back, he had treated his mother for depression after his father had died. He had arranged for her to be committed to the sanitarium at Big Spring after the treatment failed. He asked how she was doing.

> Other than cryin' day and night, OK
> I guess....

> If I remember correctly, you have a
> brother?

> That's right—Mark.

> And Mark came, after the breakup,
> to stay in Amarillo with his uncle, re-
> tired Colonel Morgan, is that correct?

> Well, yeah, but....

> But what does it have to do with you?

Earle nodded.

> The fact that you are a close family
> member of a retired war hero com-
> bined with the fact that you are as-

sociating with antiwar representatives causes the Army to have some concern.

I've been on a mission to find out the truth behind this war.

The Army doesn't want the truth to be made public.

Is that so?

That is so.

Earle gulped when he understood the connotations of what the doctor was saying. He continued.

When you filled out a form in the front office, you implied that you had connections with many organizations and individuals who are considered enemies of the state: Mohammed Ali, Tom Hayden, Allen Ginsburg, Dick Gregory, Bob Dylan, Country Joe and the Fish....

Not exactly connections. I have heard them speak and I know their songs and....

And they have misled and confused you to the point of dropping out of society.

They haven't *misled* me, they have

informed me of what the hell is *really* going on. It's the Pentagon who has misled me.

You have taken a rebel stance. You against the rest of the world. How long do you think you could make it? First you go up against society, then you go up against its very government. Civilization tends to crush its rebels.

Look doctor, I'm perfectly fine. It's the oblivious herd, the walking dead, who buy all the bullshit. They're the ones who are out of their minds.

Growing your hair to your waist is fine? If you live on a desert island, maybe. Our actions are weighed against the rest of society. Not to say whether it's right or wrong. Only if it's within society's boundaries or not.

My appearance is just a symbol of what I believe in. It may look crazy to you guys. Y'all live in Amarillo, Texas, for God's sake. I've been livin' in the bohemian capitol of the world lately. They'd think you were a spaceman!

Knowing the history of your family, it's understandable why you would want to be conspicuous. With your father gone and your mother unstable, she has not been able to give you the affection that you need. You have made up for it by finding ways to attract attention to yourself. Long hair, rings on your toes....

Look Doctor, I appreciate your clinical assessment of my appearance, but you keep missing the point. This country is in danger of tearing itself apart over someone else's civil war. This is not a time for the public to sit on their dead asses and agree with everything they hear on the news.

Do you feel responsible for the world?

It's hard not to, given the shape we're in.

You are not responsible for everyone else, only yourself.

I don't want to see a nuclear war.

Do you think about it a lot?

Every day. I love this world. I don't want to see a bunch of power-mad assholes destroy it.

Do you think you have the power to stop it?

I'm going to try.

I think it would be in your best interest to see a therapist.

You mean a shrink?

If you want to call it that.

I'd be better off with a brain trans-
plant.

You need to talk to someone on a regular basis.

How will I do that in Viet Nam?

I am going to recommend against
your induction into the Army.

Earle froze, dumbfounded. This was the last thing
he expected. It offended him that the doctor
thought he was an unstable individual.

Look, doctor, I'm not crazy.

Are you on drugs?

I do a few mind-altering substances.
I don't consider them drugs.

Like what?

Pot, mushrooms, acid.

On a regular basis?

The only thing I do on a regular basis is smoke Old Golds. Now there's
a drug that ought to be illegal. It's
highly addictive and unhealthy, but
sponsored by government lobby
groups who bribe candidates with
millions in campaign dollars—yet
the drug itself costs the government
millions more once the addicts get
sick. Go figure.

Your opinion, once again, contradicts
that of the public. How about alcohol?

Another drug. Alcohol and tobacco
kill more people than all wars combined. That's who the Pentagon
should be going after, not some Third
World country trying to grow enough
rice to feed itself.

Very well, then.

The doctor wrote on some papers on his desk. He
then returned to Earle, stoic as ever, told him
again of his recommendation to seek counsel-
ing at once. Earle asked if there was another
way out of the building so he wouldn't have to
go through the reception room. The doctor let
him exit through the side door and asked him
to give his regards to his mother.

Suddenly Earle was in the bright sunshine. He stood
looking out into the parking lot in a state of
disbelief. He couldn't believe what had just tak-

en place. He felt as if he had entered another realm. The world looked liquid and shiny as if it had been given a new paint job. The air tasted sweet and entered his lungs in a silent rush. In celebration of his reprieve he wanted to scream and dance like a whirling dervish. Upon hearing the blast of a train whistle, he walked to the train yards and sat in a patch of dandelions watching a new train being put together. Recollections of childhood feelings spun inside him as he blew the parachutes off of a thistle plant.

Earle followed the tracks to where two sets veered off to the south. There, another new train was being put together and he found an empty boxcar to jump into. He waited patiently for the train to roll and felt a rush of excitement as the train left Amarillo and dropped through the rolling hills at Canyon. At sundown the air cooled and he sat cross-legged like Buddha, looking over the vast green and blooming cotton fields to the sunset that filled the sky with a fire so pure that its remnants glowed long after the fire fell over the edge of the earth.

CHAPTER 7

The giant cactus in front of the pawn shop had seen
    better days. So many people had carved their
    names into it that it was starting to look like
    a mummified chunk of rotten okra. The gravel
    in the bed around it was stabbed with cigarette
    butts and the whole compound glowed orange
    in the late afternoon sun. Gene loaded Earle's
    Super Reverb amp into the back of the old Plym-
    outh station wagon that he had bought the day
    before in Venice. Lance was still inside admir-
    ing the pistols in the glass case at the back of
    the store. When Gene came back into the store
    to retrieve him, Lance asked if he would like to
    go fifty-fifty on the chrome .45 Police Special
    that he twirled in his hand.

> You cain't go fifty-fifty on a gun.
> What if we both wanted to shoot it at
> the same time?
>
> I guess I'd have to whip your ass first.
>
> I guess you'd have to play hell first,
> turd head.

Gene pulled out a wad of bills and asked the store-
    keeper what he wanted for the gun. They bick-
    ered back and forth until they agreed on a price.

He showed his fake ID at the same time he threw a few more bills at the sales clerk for a box of bullets.

They stopped at a place on the way out of town that had all the supplies they needed to cross the desert. While Lance played the slots and teased the counter girls, Gene bought two fifths of Southern Comfort and a carton of Old Golds. He dumped out a heap of Dexedrine tabs in a bowl on the dash. Lance returned to the car excited about the trip. He felt prepared for the inevitable, whatever that might be, but just to be sure, he loaded the gun and cracked the seal on one of the fifths. Lubbock was a thousand miles in the distance and there were a lot of road signs between here and there.

John Silo had gotten word that Gene and Lance and Earle were on their way back to Lubbock. He had notified Betty and Bill who jumped at the excuse to have a big blowout celebrating their return. He arranged for a poker party in the back room and invited the hot-rodders just in case a late-night race might evolve out of the madness. If nothing else, the mystique that had grown from the disappearance of these three speculators was enough to guarantee a packed house at Betty and Bill's.

When Earle came through the screen door into the kitchen, Maggie thought she was seeing a ghost. His hair and clothes, dusty from sleeping in the

train yards the previous night, added to the illusion. The fear turned to joy when he told his
mother that the Army had deemed him unfit for
military service. Maggie was suddenly reverent.

Thank you God, for answering my
prayers.

She opened her eyes and questioned Earle.

How on earth....

They sent me to the staff shrink, Dr.
Levin, and he told me I needed help.
You might remember him. He said to
give you his regards.

You mean Amarillo Dr. Levin? That
son-of-a-bitch that sent me to Big
Spring. He liked to have killed me.
That Dr. Levin?

Same one.

Well, damn. Now I'd like to kiss him.
What did he say?

Said it ran in the family. Said I was
a rebel and was gonna get crushed
for caring about this crazy ol' world.
Said the government didn't want the
people to know the truth. I really
don't know what he said.

Thank God you're safe.

I don't know about safe but I do know
one thing. I'm just beginnin' to see.
My eyes are just startin' to open.
There's a lot of people lined up to get
themselves hurt for nothin'.

I just made some cornbread. Would
you like some?

Mmm, yeah.

After lunch Earle curled up in his pile of blankets in
front of the swamp cooler and escaped back to
the womb, silently saying prayer after prayer
to show gratitude for his newfound life. He
thanked every saint, disciple, apostle and angel that had ever lived or was yet to be born.
Since music had played a part in his search for
knowledge, he thanked every musician he could
think of from Pan to Zappa. He thanked Jimmy
Reed for passing out drunk outside the KoKo,
thereby causing a chain of events that led him
out into the world to acquire answers first-hand
and not to rely on the usual sources. He also
gave thanks for his old guitar from which he
would no longer be separated. He prayed for the
safe return of the soldiers from across the sea.
For the next couple of days he hardly left the
house, so grateful he was to be at home.

He rode his Allstate 125 up and down the empty
streets of his neighborhood. Unlike other cities
he had been in lately, people in Lubbock seemed
to have an aversion against walking outside.
They went from their house doors to their car

doors and on to the doors of their destinations. The long straight sidewalks in the neighborhoods were completely empty! He parked his scooter by the school and walked around the neighborhood by the park. He did not encounter one other person walking. This had never bothered him before, but now it did. When he returned to his motorbike, he saw Kyle and his mother come out of their house across the street. When they saw each other they waved and asked him to come over that evening.

Earle cranked his engine and puttered up Elgin Avenue, following the big power lines past the backside of his old school. He then circled the Chicken Box, Ringo Tom's and Pete's Pool Hall. He backtracked to the pool hall to knock a few balls around. When he walked in, Scotty Chanteaux was playing some ringer on the back table and spoke to Earle in a mock old man's voice.

> Howdy stranger, what brings you around these parts?

Earle played along.

> Heard word they was gamblers givin' away money by the wheelbarrow.

Scotty brought it home.

> Way I'm givin' it away today, I'd believe it. Hadn't seen you in a while. Thought you'd become a beach bum out in movie land.

I tried but they kept jerkin' the leash.

Scotty drilled the nine ball into the side pocket. The ringer put up his stick, paid Scotty and walked out the back mumbling to himself. Scotty thanked him and waited till he left then looked around to see if anyone was listening.

> Heard Gene and Lance got back last night. Big shindig at Betty and Bill's tonight.

> Wonder if Gene brought my Super Reverb back from Vegas.

> Your what?

> Amplifier. He hocked it in Vegas.

> Don't know about any amplifier, but he might have picked up something else.

> What d'ya mean?

> Word is he's gone queer.

> He's what?

> You know, changed lanes.

Earle couldn't imagine Gene being homosexual but the news didn't shock him at all. The only way that Gene could shock him would be if he were predictable. He had heard Gene say that if

nothing else worked he would show up at the
draft board in a dress. He asked Scotty if he
had talked to either Gene or Lance since they
had gotten back and Scotty said that he had not.
Earle thanked him for the gossip and said he
might see him at Betty and Bill's tonight.

There were cars parked up and down the block and
the sound of Ray Charles singing Crying Time
could be heard several houses away. He approached the house cautiously, unlike the times
before when he was brimming with abandon.
He was met at the door by Betty who was already so drunk that she could not find the handle to the screen, nor did she recognize him or
even say hello. All his old friends were there
and they greeted him politely but at a distance.
John Silo handed him a beer and incited the
conversation.

> Your ol' hair gits much longer you'll
> have to get fender skirts for your
> scooter t' keep it outta th' spokes.

> Guess I been occupied with other
> things. Haven't thought much about
> hair. You doin' O.K.?

> Still cookin' chicken. Took over
> Gene's shift when he flew the coop.
> Speakin' of Gene, he's s'posed to
> come over tonight.

> How about Lance?

He's in the bedroom playin' poker
with all the losers.

Sounds like you might'a just come
from there.

Boring game.

Lance jumped up when he saw Earle and slugged him
on the shoulder as hard as he could. Earle accepted it as an affectionate form of West Texas
greeting. He asked how his draft board meeting went.

They cut me loose. Army doctor said
I didn't have good sense. How 'bout
you?

Mine comes up next week.

Good luck.

Lance took a long swig from a bottle of Cuervo that
still had a Mexican tax stamp on the seal.

Hey, guess what? You're not gonna
believe this.

Earle shrugged his sore shoulder.

Remember that old Super Reverb
amp of yours.

Earle motioned with his hands for more information.

Well, we got it out of the pawn shop
in Vegas....

Yeah, O.K. Where is it?

We got pulled over in Clovis. We had
to hock it again.

Earle looked down, vacant.

No—don't tell me.

Lance doubled over with laughter and admitted his
fib. He dragged Earle down the hall where the
amplifier sat in the middle of the room looking
straight at him like a dream, like some beat up
sage who had weathered the elements to return
home to be with his master. He went on.

We did get pulled over. Gene gave the
cop a roll of twenties.

Where's Gene now?

He was supposed to be here a couple
of hours ago. Guess he got diverted.
John, help Earle here.

John helped him carry the amplifier and put it in
the car. Earle told him the story of how they
had carried it for miles out in Venice and how
he had used it for a pillow and how Gene had
hocked it twice and how—

Guess y'all had a pretty good time.

Ain't shit happenin' around here. I
need to get out of this cotton town
before I turn to stone.

You gotta give up somethin'. Looks
like you been eatin' pretty good.

Chicken Box Jimmy might not always pay ya' but he damn well makes
sure you're fed.

They walked back to the rowdy house but before they
could cut in the keg line a murmur started to
shuffle its way around the house. Everyone was
making their way toward the front door in anticipation of Gene's arrival. It was only then that Earle realized how much Gene had become a legendary figure around town. The story of his escape
was equaled only by the story of his return. In fact,
all of the stories, past and present, had taken on
greater proportions than ever before. Everyone
saw Gene as being larger than life and was prepared to bestow a hero's welcome upon him.

Everyone's expectations crumbled to dust when Gene
entered the front door propped up by Tiny on
one arm and Scotty Chanteaux on the other. He
was as pale as porcelain and his eyes darted
wildly, not meeting anyone's eyes. It was apparent that there was something going on with
Gene beyond a normal Saturday night overin-
dulgence episode.

They forded the crowd and took Gene into the back
room. Lance, Earle and John followed behind
and locked the door. John asked,

What's goin' on?

Tiny told his side.

> We drove from Levelland out to the airport. We both saw something we can't explain.

John agreed.

> I don't know how those damn things fly either, but....
>
> No, not that. Something came *in*.
>
> What do you mean, came in?
>
> I don't know. Gene started scream-ing. I saw it, too. We tried to get away. Something was banging on the roof of the car. We pulled under a gas station awning. We lost track of time. We thought five minutes had gone by—it was really more like an hour and a half.

Gene shivered and looked around. His eyes went to each person in the room and gazed into their eyes in a way that no one had ever seen Gene look before.

After a long uneasy silence, Earle tried to lighten the room by a short testimony.

> I, for one, have been witness to su-pernatural occurrences, but I usually

had a little help from something I in-
gested....

Lance pitched in.

There's a lotta weird stuff out at that
ol' airport.

Gene started to cry. Tiny reiterated.

I don't know what it was, but it came *in*.

John shook his head in disgust, said he needed a beer
and left the room. Lance asked Gene where he
had stashed the gun at the same time as Scotty
was telling him where he could find some killer
mushrooms. Gene said not a word but kept his
eye on a gas jet in the corner of the room, as if
it might be a portal, either into the room from
some other place or a way out of the room to
another dimension, not yet realized....

The party raged on in the rest of the house, getting
louder and louder as the kegs got lighter. Lance
had taken the opportunity to position himself
as the emissary from the West and had a large
audience lapping up his every word. Earle listened for a minute until he realized that Lance's
perception of the counterculture was the total
opposite of his own. Lance spoke of the danger, of drug wars, of alleys and police, not even
mentioning the ocean, the music or the quest
for truth and freedom that was Earle's idea of it
all. In fact, for the first time, Earle found himself not enjoying one of Betty and Bill's parties

in the least. Everyone was talking at once, yet there was nothing being said and the ones who had taken control were the ones who were in the least control. Even though he was concerned about Gene and Tiny's ordeal, he felt powerless to do anything about it.

Earle walked outside into the cool night air and saw the Scorpion raise its stinger in the western sky. The Great Summer Triangle tugged at his sleeve and he allowed himself to be pulled away in the direction of Kyle's house. The lights were on and he tapped lightly at the door and was invited in by Kyle. His mother, Lortha, sat at the piano playing Bach in candlelight and he breathed deeply as Kyle poured him a glass of wine. Maybe it was the contrast between the two extremes, but he found himself savoring this moment like a desert straggler at an oasis and he continued to savor it until it poured into a dream of a steep green hillside falling down into a blue-black sea.

Gene woke in Betty and Bill's front bedroom with the previous night playing over and over in his head. He wrapped his arms around his shoulders and shivered, still feeling as if a stranger was inside his body. He played the scene at the airport over and over and relived the encounter at the gas station. He had little recollection after that and was not quite sure how he got to wherever he was now. He walked to the dresser mirror and did not recognize the person being reflected. Splotches of redness smeared randomly about

his body and his face was contorted beyond recognition. He peeked out the door into a quiet
house wrecked with paper cups and beer cans.
He tiptoed out the door past the elm tree and
took the first turn into the alley. He followed
the alleys until he found his parents' house and
was crying on the front step when his mother
came home and let him in. She bathed him
with hot towels, plastered his whelps with cala-
mine lotion, put him in bed and fed him chicken
soup. She was relieved when he slowly returned.
They began to talk in simple sentences and she
could see that he had been through something
quite terrifying.

On Monday morning she reminded him about the
Army physical and offered to drive him to Amarillo. She waited at the bottom of the stairs
in the living room until Gene came down. He
was dressed in her favorite flowery dress, lips
smeared in red lipstick, holding a straw purse
and wobbling from stair to stair in red high-
heeled shoes. He spoke in baby talk from the
last stair.

I'm ready to go to the Army, Mama.

Maggie showed Chuck around the room. She showed
him the bathroom and where he could keep his
towel. She told him about the neighborhood
and pointed out the way to the drugstore, laundry and grocery store. He told her again that
he would only be renting the room for a short

while until he finished his work in Lubbock. She told him to keep it as long as he needed as the money was tight around their house at the present time. He asked if he could take her out to dinner as a token of his appreciation and she accepted, radiantly.

When Earle came in she introduced him to Chuck and explained to him why she was forced to rent out rooms in the house. There was simply not enough money left over after her Social Security check to pay the bills. Chuck seemed to be a friendly enough person but there was something about him that raised suspicion in Earle.

He said he would find some work playing the clubs around town to help out as much as he could. He went to the phone and called Velda and asked if he could play the Hideaway Club tomorrow night and make a few bucks by passing the hat. She said he could come in and play the next couple of weekends at their little speakeasy. The customers drank more when the music was live.

Maggie was thrilled when she heard this news and whistled while she dressed for her first dinner engagement in many months.

The weeks that followed were overflowing with music. Earle spent most of his time at Kyle's house. Kyle would bring out the stash they had brought back from California and they would reverently smoke a bowl and then journey through centuries of music. Lortha, being the master of history's harmony, would play the piano at the slightest enticement and centuries of melody would come pouring out, transforming the listeners into time travelers drawing ever closer to the source.

Sergeant Pepper was always spinning on the turntable, much to the delight of Lortha. Even though she was the head of the music department and therefore steeped in every kind of music imaginable, she took a keen interest in the pop music of the day. Earle carried his Super Reverb over to her house and the nights would find them looking for a bridge to merge vastly different worlds into one. The word spread quickly and other Lubbock musicians began to meet at Lortha's studio to take in what was going down. Earle wanted to arrange a Lubbock summit with all the musicians from the bands who had inspired him in his early years, and tried to get them together to share the exciting times through which he believed they were living. He was surprised to find that many of them were suspicious of the modern culture from which the current music had come and disassociated themselves from the anti-war themes of the day. They wanted to reel back to the safe whiskey days of Fifties rock when little was at stake save the manhood of the already insecure singer.

On the opposite extreme was Kyle's mother, Lortha. She was, in a word, a rebel. She was a solitary individualist who, with impeccable taste and boundless energy, was able to communicate her every emotion with a wave of her nimble fingers over the eighty-eight black and white keys that were the object of her devotion and the center of her controlled recklessness. One evening she invited her guests down to the First Methodist church to listen to her practice the pipe organ for next Sunday's program. Kyle passed out mushrooms to those who asked and the small congregation met at the choir entrance at midnight.

Nothing could prepare anyone for what was to follow. Lortha, looking frail against the backdrop of thirty-foot-tall pipes, began with a wispy chord played on high like a cloud that just happened to be passing by. The chord broke up into smaller parts and the clouds divided and danced against the blue background, inviting flocks of white geese and doves to frolic in the foreground. The birds divided into groups and began to choreograph themselves into a geometric dance that gave birth to dozens of smaller kaleidoscopic whirlpools. As the music built, the wind rose, and swarms of locusts darkened the skies. The clouds turned thick as the wind changed and the locusts became blackbirds with diamond eyes and iridescent feathers. The sky turned purple velvet and swam in waves, shedding an ultramarine dust that swirled in the eddies of the blackbirds. As Lortha's hands spread wider apart, the crescendo darkened into a wall of thunder. The floor of the church shook as if somewhere deep down the Earth's magma was frantically looking for a fissure. The rumble of the giant pipes reverberated the ribcages of all those within the four church walls. Just at the moment it seemed intolerable, an immense space in the heavens opened, filled with sunlight, and revealed a rainbow, pastel and translucent, that peeled away in immense layers of cellophane-thin silk, spiraling away into a distant light...

If the universe is revealed in moments of great beauty, why cannot these moments be closer together? Earle was weak and covered in sweat but felt like his chest had been filled with light and was expanding with each breath. He felt as if all those who had shared the same experience were as full of the same spirit as was the volume of vast space in which they sat.

Mike Shoal passed around a bottle of wine for which everyone was truly grateful. They could barely contain the sheer joy that had filled them to the brim. Lortha played again, this time a more serene, pastoral piece that swayed everyone in a summer breeze by a lazy river by a rope swing tied to a cypress tree.

Piston rods as tall as telephone poles rammed the ceiling of the gymnasium. Green water hoses sputtered in clumsy circles and dripped down shaved wooden walls following the paths of past rusty stains....

As his dream began to unravel, Earle heard the familiar whomp of the swamp cooler spitting the moist air out the louvers while pounding its heavy frame against the rotting windowsill. His first thought was of his experience the night before. When he closed his eyes the dream returned in full glory. He wanted to stay in the dream but first he had to scribble down a verse.

Ruby-eyed Rhythm Choir
Raise our hearts even higher
Sweet-talk the Dead with song
Let melody be born
From the Angel's Golden Horn
As the Dead Wake Up
And Dance all Night Long

On his morning walk to the park, Earle followed trails of red ants bringing seeds back to their mound. He observed that when they encountered an obstacle they simply went around it or over it. The route changed with the first ant and kept evolving as each ant discovered a slightly better way. He thought about the freeways in Los Angeles packed with some people chasing their dreams while others were in a mad dash chasing each other.

Since he had gone out into the world he had met many people who followed their inspiration and were sharing their passion with the world. These people had altered his direction and had given him the inspiration to do the same. Music had always been a part of his life but after last night he saw how powerful it could be. He felt as if he were a different person from who he used to be. In contrast, the party at Betty and Bill's had left him with an empty feeling, as if everyone was chasing one oblivion after another.

Earle came upon his house from the back way and noticed Chuck putting suitcases in the trunk of his car. He asked his mother if Chuck was leaving. She said she was sure he was going to be there for quite a while.

Chuck's not going anywhere. He has
a lot of work to do. In fact he invited
me to dinner tonight for the third
time in a little over a week. I'm becoming more than a little fond of him.
I haven't met anyone in a long time
as sweet and sensitive as Chuck.

Earle was not so sure.

I just have a weird feeling....

You just miss your old room. Mark
is perfectly happy in the back room.
Since you've been gone so much, I
didn't know what else to do.

No, it's not that. I actually like sleeping in front of the swamp cooler. It's
just that I think Chuck has a lot of
things going on that he's not telling
you.

You've got it all wrong. I find him to
be very straightforward.

What does he do, anyway?

He's never quite said. But he's told
me he works with some nice people.
He is so easy to get along with.

Okay. For your sake I hope you're
right. By the way, I'm going over to

Kyle's house for a cookout this afternoon so don't fix anything for me.

You've been spending a lot of time over there.

There's a lot of music there.

I know how you love music.

See you later, mother. Enjoy your evening.

Okay, hon. You, too.

Earle walked the long way by the park and noticed what looked like Jimmy Dunn's car parked by the school yard a block away from Kyle's house. He wondered why he would park so far away. Jimmy Dunn had suddenly burst upon the scene just a couple of weeks back when Earle had returned from Amarillo and now everyone seemed to know him.

Earle stood at the back screen for a long time, watching Lortha prepare vegetables to the soundtrack of a Peer Gynt Suite. She had a restless energy that Earle could relate to. He felt as if he had met someone in his life that he was to become. When he entered the room, she stopped and smiled.

What a glorious day.

An extension of last night. I've never experienced music like that in my life.

She looked down.

> You're exaggerating. I don't play it
> that well.
>
> No, no. It was unbelievable. I can't
> really say it in words.
>
> I accept the compliment. It is more
> special coming from you. I was try-
> ing to project it toward you. Could
> you tell?

Before Earle could answer, the doorbell rang. Lortha
asked Earle if he could get it. On his way he
said hello to his friends in the living room listening to the stereo. The overture In the Hall
of the Mountain King intensified as he walked
to the door.

Upon opening the door he was confused to see Sgt.
Baylock's face. But before he could speak, the
door was shoved into his shoulder and Baylock
grabbed his shirt and knocked him to the floor,
hitting Earle's head on the bookcase. A train
of police rushed in, guns drawn, yelling loudly
and throwing everyone to the floor. Earle could
hear Lortha in the kitchen screaming for them
to take their tainted hands off her consecrated
possessions and to get out of her house, at once.
He heard a commotion in the kitchen, with her
screaming in pain, and watched with one eye
from the floor while the officer dragged her by
her hair into the living room and threw her face
down to the floor. A wall of police held riot guns

upon the defenseless group as others fanned out and began ripping through the house. They pulled all the books from the bookshelves and ripped open the cushions of the couch. Lortha screamed in panic as she helplessly witnessed her world being shredded. She could hear them ravage room after room as Baylock read them their rights in his cocky, I-told-you-so kind of way. One of the cops came into the room carrying the pot that they had brought back from California. He pulled Lance off the floor and asked.

You don't never learn, do you son?

Lance looked at him coldly.

You don't never learn, do you Baylock?

Baylock backhanded him and ordered them all into the squad cars. Lance asked what the charges were.

Didn't you read the paper today? All psychedelic drugs became illegal today. And this much marijuana became a felony. Felony possession. *Twenty years.* It's your lucky day!

At the station the group was separated into three. Lance and Earle were put in a room together, then stripped, searched and booked. They were given one phone call each but neither of them was able to get an answer. When Earle asked when he could call back, the booking cop told him not to worry, that his people would read about it in the papers. They were led, in chains, to a holding tank on the top floor of the County Jail where they were given a blanket and pushed into a cell. The door clanged shut with such finality that they listened greedily for the echo so that it might not die. They wondered what had become of the others and how they were handling it all. They could hear groans and whispers of nearby inmates and a fear of the unknown began to emerge. They whispered back and forth about their situation and decided there was nothing they could do about it. Earle heard the whistle of the freight engines and lay listening to the night. But it was not the night that he heard. He heard the organ shaking the walls of the church and the sound of his daddy's voice rocking him to sleep at the top of a giant green hill under a full moon disappearing into a dark sea....

The word spread around the small town and by sundown several people had told Maggie about the raid at Kyle and Lortha's house. Bob the Turk came over at Maggie's request and was cussing the Lubbock Police Department even as he walked in the door.

> The son-of-a-bitches can't catch a crook, but they can throw innocent kids in the pokey just for smokin' a little pot. In the old country it was the police who protected the pot farmers so the country wouldn't fall apart.

Maggie was pacing the living room floor.

I've got to get through to Earle tonight.

Bob assured her that Earle didn't have a phone in his
cell.

He probably tried to call while we
were at the drug store.

Maggie looked worried.

And where is Chuck? Why are all of
his clothes gone? He was supposed
to be here by now. Earle said he saw
him packing his suitcases. Where
could he be?

Bob put two and two together.

I don't think you'll see ol' Chuckie boy
anymore. I think he was a goddamn
government spy. I never did trust the
son-of-a-bitch. He was sent here to
track Earle. Bet you anything.

Maggie looked pale. She went to Chuck's room one
more time. Not a single thread of his belongings remained. Her denial changed to fear—
then to anger.

This can't be. I'm callin' the police.

Callin' the cops on a cop?

He couldn't....

I think he just did.

Around town the story was beginning to grow. At first it was said that three houses were raided. Lortha's, Mike Shoal's and the McClarty-Peters house. By midnight that number had expanded to a dozen or more and the story had blossomed into a prime topic at the Hi-D-Ho and Pete's Pool Hall. The next morning, when the raid made the headlines, the story had grown beyond a mere topic. It was now a full-blown scandal. Because of Lortha, Texas Tech was in the center of it.

Gene reflected on his past week in West Texas as the Arizona yuccas rolled past his open window. He knew something strange had happened to him but he couldn't recall the details. He still felt like someone else was living in his body with him. Every action that he took required permission from this other presence. Maybe in California he could find someone who could help him become free again. At least the specter of Viet Nam was off his back. He recoiled at the memory of that day. In fact, every day that he had spent in Lubbock recently had ended in a nightmare. He decided to never set foot there again.

He had seen signs for miles advertising the 'Mystery Spot?' When he reached the place he found himself turning into the parking lot and staring at the black circle on the side of the building. He opened the car door and put his foot out onto the gravel, but something told him to get out of there, *fast*. An image of Earle and Lance and Sgt. Baylock flashed across his mind. He floored the old Plymouth and fishtailed across the parking lot while tourists gawked in puzzlement at the runaway car. He lost control and skidded sideways to a halt, but then gunned it through the dust and the bar ditch and across the wrong lane of traffic. His face was a waterfall of sweat when he found the road that led him West— West into the sun, West toward the place that would, please Lord, set him free again.

The inmates were rousted at dawn. Earle woke on the steel bed with a crick in his neck the size of an axe handle. The cell doors opened into the common room and everyone was ordered to stand at attention while the cells were searched. Earle and Lance were ordered to the side door. Their vision was restricted to the ten or so men who populated the common room but they could see that they were in heavy company. Lance stopped in the middle of the room and asked the collective room what the fuck they were looking at. Earle gulped. The inmates stared, surprised that a newcomer was so defiant. Two jailers took the boys downstairs in the elevator and then into a brightly lit room. A trustee with a pair of scissors invited one of them to the chair in the middle of the room. He snickered as Earle sat down.

I ain't never seed hair this long on a man. Y'all some kind of homos?

Lance snapped.

> Shut the fuck up, hillbilly. I might
> stick them scissors up your scrawny
> ass.

The trustee tried to act brave, knowing the two jailers were in the hallway.

> You don't talk t'me 'at a way. I'm th'
> only go-between you got.

He started whacking clumps out of Earle's hair and
they fell in slow motion to the floor like memories when they fade. The ordeal didn't affect
him like he thought it would. There was nothing anyone could do to him that would make
any difference to what he believed in.

Lance began to laugh and told Earle he wished there
was a mirror in the room so that he could see
himself.

> You ain't gonna believe what you look
> like. You ever seen a dog with mange?

Earle replied smugly.

> Keep laughin', turd face, you're next.

When the trustee finished, Earle ran his hands
through his hair to try and fashion a picture
from feel. Some places had been peeled to the
scalp, while other places puffed out in wads.
The picture he formed was hugely depressing,

although Lance was now laughing hysterically. The trustee tried to cut him short.

Next.

Lance strutted to the chair. Before he turned to sit, he stopped and stared at the trustee. He gave him a warning.

If you even think about doin' that to me....

The trustee stopped him.

Look here, let's lay somethin' out on the table. I ain't no policeman, I'm in jail jus' like you are. Seven more months. I can't go nowheres on the outside just like you cain't. They given me the trust to be on the outside of the cell, not the outside of the jail. I can be the bestest friend you got or I can be the worstest. I ain't givin' haircuts 'cause I know how. I'm givin' 'em 'cause I'm the only sum-bitch they trust with scissors.

Lance flopped one hundred and eighty degrees.

What's your name?

Tatum.

Tatum, I'm Lance. Pleased to make your acquaintance.

That's better. 'Member—this ain't City, this is County. Just a horsefly away from State 'n Fed. Now sit ch'r se'f down and let's git done wit' it.

Lance switched into angel mode and didn't say a word during the proceedings. Earle could see his gears turning. His wily mind had already sniffed out the first chink in the mortar. Everything else was but a sacrifice away....

The jailers led the boys to the phone to make their one call. Lance got Betty on the phone but she was already drunk and was no help whatsoever. Earle reached his mother and she yelled for a couple of minutes, then she started crying. There was not much to say, as bail had not yet been set, so he just told her that he loved her and not to worry. The jailer said it was time to go and he left her crying on the phone.

They were taken back up to the common room where the inmates were performing their morning ritual of rolling a day's worth of cigarettes. Earle watched, fascinated by the fact they were using the plastic from a bread wrapper secured inside a Bible and a yellow #2 pencil for a roller. When they were done one of the inmates passed the boys their roller with a stack of tobacco and papers. It was a monumental act of kindness, considering it might be a couple of days before they could order any supplies from the commissary.

Lance wanted to hear news from the outside world and one of the inmates told him of a way to talk to the floor below. The process was to bang on the commode water pipe until someone banged back. After taking off the back lid of the tank you could yell down the fill pipe and be heard one floor down. Mike Shoal was two floors down; his message had to be relayed by the floor inbetween before it could be received. He said there was a hearing later that day where bail would be set. He said Lortha was the only one that had a lawyer but that they all needed one soon. Lance said needing one and being able to afford one were two different animals.

In a couple of hours the boys were led from their cell to a room downstairs where court-appointed attorneys advised them of the proceedings of the day. After lunch they were handcuffed and chained together and led to the courthouse for their hearing. They saw their friends for the first time since the bust. Fear had turned their complexions pale and made their eyes cold and lost. The backdrop of the courtroom was painted in fluorescent light that grated against the tan walls and reeked of hopelessness. The judge spoke coldly, with nothing personal in his voice whatsoever. He spoke in packets, laced with a heavy drawl that was unintelligible to everyone but the lawyers who responded mechanically, as if they were bad actors in a worn-out drama.

The judge set everyone's bail at fifty thousand dollars, a figure that seemed to surprise even the lawyers. When they inquired about the severity of the bail, the judge said the new laws required stiff penalties and sealed his decree with a smack of the gavel.

They returned to their cells in time for supper, which was a bowl of thin potato soup. Their cellmates

were impressed that their bail had been set
so high and wanted to know more about their
charges. One of the inmates was in for killing
his mother and his bail was half that of Lance
and Earle's. Two others were charged with
armed robbery and had bail set at ten thousand
dollars. After this conversation it was, for some
unknown reason, the appropriate time for the
murderer to introduce everyone.

> Name's Strapper. This here's Bandy,
> Jones, Brewster and Fly Boy.

Lance did the honors.

> Lance. And this is Earle.

At sundown, when the jailer arrived, everyone left the
common room and went silently to be locked in
the smaller bunk rooms. The jailer left and in
a few minutes Tatum, the trustee, showed up
to do the nightly duty of turning out the lights.
Strapper engaged Tatum in a barter proposition.

> Tatum, could I swap you somethin' for
> that burned out light bulb, yonder?

> I was jus' fixin' to change that one
> out. I could use a flat of Bugler.

> Ain't a even swap. I need a utensil
> and some wire.

> Can't get nothin' sharp. Got a old
> spoon you could use tonight. And

some waar come outta the ol' ra-did-io.
Soun's like you boilin' some nightcaps.

Tatum brought Strapper the light bulb and left the room to get the other goods. Strapper carefully worked at the lead contact on the bottom of the bulb, using the corner of his bunk to work it back and forth. When Tatum returned with the goods, he used the spoon to finish the job. He carefully shook out the filament leaving an empty glass bulb. He tied the wire around the threaded brass end and asked for chocolate donations from the cellmates. He broke a Three Musketeers Bar into small pieces and stuffed them into the light bulb. He filled the bulb to the top with tap water. He then loosely wrapped a couple of yards of toilet paper into a cone and built a small fire over which he dangled the light bulb until the mixture melted into a strange form of gypsy hot chocolate. Strapper passed the concoction around and everyone reverently did partake in the ritual. After making several more batches the unfortunate lot wound down and crawled into their hard bunks for a long, restless, uneasy sleep....

Morning hit cold-bloodedly. The rank echo of slamming steel jarred Lance's sleepless, jangled nerves. A Merle Haggard song, Branded Man, played on a radio across the cell and was barely recognizable as it ricocheted thousands of times around the iron cages looking for a soft place to fall. By the time it reached anyone's ears it had become a trashcan of sonic, metallic splinters but had retained—maybe even magnified—its meaning. The singer sang about being judged by society long after paying the price of doing his prison time.

It was a terrible way to greet the morning. In his first waking breath, Lance condensed his life to see how it had come about that he had been reduced so low, so quickly. Nothing made sense. The world had thrown him a curve ball that had hit him between the eyes. He didn't feel he had disrupted anyone's life, hurt anyone or taken anything that wasn't his. Had he broken the law? He didn't do anything. He hadn't possessed anything illegal. He was simply sitting in someone's house, partaking in plants that had been gathered from distant places. The fact that he was in jail was so baffling that it was beyond comprehension. Lance told himself that if it were not for these bars he would maim every son-of-a-bitch in the whole fuckin' unit.

Earle, on the other hand, woke in a spiral. He had been dreaming of the sounds of massive pipe organs. In his dream, the organ was a tall building with bursts of steam blowing out of its windows. Hundreds of owls circled the building looking up at it with curious eyes. At the end of the song a burst of thunder erupted and a huge net shot out of the top of the building. Before the poor owls could get away the net fluttered to the ground, leaving them hopelessly entangled.

Earle shook off the dream and hardened himself against the harsh clanging of metal. His first thought of the day was of his father and the happy days they shared before he died. The old used clothing store where he worked was only a few blocks away. He remembered, years ago, walking past the jail, holding his father's hand and looking up at the barred windows and wondering what was going on inside. On hot days when the windows were open, the yelling of the inmates and the ring of slamming metal could be heard clearly on the street below. Now, it was he who was on the inside, unable to conceive of a way out. He didn't feel he had committed a crime. In fact, the last few months had awakened something in him that had been dormant in his previous life. Only yesterday he was listening to Lortha spin incantations from the grand piano in her front room. The rapture had become despair so quickly that it all seemed like a bad dream. Yet, unlike a bad dream, there was no end in sight.

The cells were opened again to the common room and coffee and hard biscuits were served by a different trustee. After breakfast the tobacco-rolling process started over again with great enthusiasm, as if time would boycott those who lagged behind. When each had made himself an ample stack of smokes the routine turned to writing letters. Some wrote to their loved ones in a lonely attempt to stay connected while others wrote to maintain power from a distance. Some wrote in a struggle for justice while others just needed money. Some never sent their letters, hindered by shame or pride or the price of postage—or simply by the feeling they had been deserted and forsaken by those once close to their hearts.

Next came a visit from the jailer to deliver mail and take orders for goods from the commissary.

Consumables like toothpaste, candy bars and tobacco were deducted from each person's cash account, which led to all sorts of deals and schemes. As each man's balance waxed and waned, so did his sense of privilege. Having to borrow from other inmates was akin to indebted servitude. It was not a healthy place to be.

By 9 a.m. most of the mental duties of the day were behind them and the men began to prowl like caged lions, roaring at each other in a dim-witted game of jailhouse supremacy. Most of the time it was a game of cleverness, with the winner being the one who reduced the others, without their ability to defend themselves, to a subservient state. Lance—much to everyone's dismay—was a master of these kinds of sports and a more dangerous contest began to emerge in which most of the men did not want to compete. Like a high-stakes poker game, the cards were played close to the vest and the bluff was as important as the play. Resources were limited, so the only weapons available existed in the realm of the mind. Of course, each person's physical strength was a force to be considered, but it too could be played like a bluff if the actor was convincing enough. The objective had no real meaning since, unlike the extravagances afforded to a king, the top dog in a jail cell had only an aurora of fear seeping from his shadow to show for all his trouble.

The jailer called Earle downstairs to see a visitor. A distinguished-looking man sat in a chair in the room that had earlier been the barbershop. He introduced himself as Travis Shamblin and said he had been secured by Earle's grandfather to counsel him in his case.

I suppose you are aware of the seriousness of your case.

Yessir, I suppose I am. The other inmates were impressed by the size of the bail. Even the guy that killed his mother got less.

My first order is to convince the judge of that point. It may take awhile. The newspapers are eating this story up. The arrest was timed to coincide with a new law. You and your friends are being made an example of this new law. That is the substance with which I have to convince the judge.

What do you mean by 'awhile'.

I wish I could say. Maybe a few days, maybe even weeks.

A weakness fell through Earle's chest.

I'm not very good at being locked up.

I understand. I'll do the best I can to expedite the process. By the way, visiting day is Saturday. You'll have to wait till then to see your family.

Is everyone all right? I mean, considerin'.

Your family is fine. Your grandfather is quite a man.

A railroad man. I lived with him when my daddy died. Mother couldn't handle the whole deal.

Your mother is a sweet woman. Now tell me, how well did you know this 'Chuck' fellow?

Didn't know him much. He was just renting a room in our house.

More than *just* a tenant. I have reason to believe he plays a major role in this case. He might have been watching you for quite some time.

He was dating my mother.

This is new to me. How long had this been going on?

He ask'd her to dinner the day he moved in.

Mr. Shamblin pondered the thought.

Hmm, strange.

Earle agreed wholeheartedly.

The whole mess is strange. He showed up a few days after I was rejected from the Army. You think there's any connection?

This was a major operation. Several places around town were raided at once. I've never seen anything like it for as long as I've been in this town. The orders seemed to be coming from some place higher.

Like the government?

We'll see. I'll be talking to you on a regular basis as questions come up. Meanwhile, don't talk to anyone about this. Jailers, trustees, inmates, no one. Inside the walls of this jailhouse, little pieces of information can become get-out-of-jail-free cards.

I understand.

Take care. Oh by the way, your guardian angel left you twenty dollars in your commissary account. I'll be in touch.

Thanks. Tell my family that I love them.

A tumbleweed blew across the Idalou highway and into the wall at the Seven Acres Lodge. Sgt.

Baylock sat, stiff as a board, feeling invincible, rumbling down the road on his new Harley. When he got to the Palm Room he hit the throttle till he reached a hundred miles an hour. An ancient essence gushed inside him. A sound came out of his head.

G'YAAAAAAD aaaEEEE....

As he throttled it back down he thought about the poor bastards he had arrested a few days before who were still sealed in the county jail. A smug sense of pride welled up in him and he chuckled to himself haughtily. The only thing *not* perfect about it all was that Gene wasn't at the house where he had led the raid. He'd gotten word that Gene had slipped into town with Lance a few days before. He had been dead certain that the two would have been together at the music lady's house. Damn! Why can't he catch the wily son-of-a-bitch? In his frustration, he hit the throttle again and by the time he saw the flashing lights of the Highway Patrol in his rear view mirror he was going a hundred and fifteen in a sixty....

Lance wanted to know about Earle's conversation with his lawyer and Earle told him. For several minutes they both stared in silence at the stained concrete floor. There was not a soul they knew who could put up that kind of money. There was nothing they could do from the inside and there was no way to freely talk to the outside. Uncertainty was worming its way under their skin.

Never in their lives had they been forced to deal with a predicament like this. Besides not having the faintest idea of a solution to their problems, they had no notion of even where to *begin*. The one thing they *did* have was time to reflect on the events leading up to the bust. Lance started in on the suspected informers.

I hope I never see them motherfuckers again.

You won't. They're long gone.

What about that Chuck guy?

Looks like he was the one that done us in. Him and maybe one other.

Who's that?

The morning of the bust, I saw Jimmy Dunn's car by the park, around the corner from Lortha's house. No one was at the park. I figured he was at Lortha's. When Baylock drove us away, I noticed his car being gone. Can't prove it, but somethin' ain't right.

Where did he come from, anyway?

He just showed up about the time I got back from the draft office. I think there's somethin' goin' on here.

Lance broke the flow of the conversation to redirect
the emphasis.

> Whose shit was that. I ain't goin' up
> the river for someone else's shit.

Earle assured him he would not.

> Yep, here you are. Picture of inno-
> cence.

> I guess there's one good thing.

> What's that?

> I don't think they're gonna come 'n
> drag me outta these bars and send
> me off to Viet Nam.

> What made you think that?

> I was s'ppos'd to go for my physical
> today.

Earle looked at Lance, then over toward the window.
He could only see a small piece of the dusty sky.
If he craned his neck a foot he could see the
tip top of an elm tree being flailed by the hot,
sharp wind. But mostly what he could see was
bars. Bars around everything that opened or
closed. Gray-black bars. Between himself and
the window were three sets of such bars.

With each passing second there was nothing to reason as to why they were locked away. If anyone

should be locked up, it should be the madmen who were perpetrating the mad war. How many kids were being locked away each day as a result of the upheaval brought about by unnecessary discontent? Everywhere, scenes were unfolding much like this, provoked by the changes that were brought about by the unpopular war. Kids were rebelling and the government was reacting. Earle thought maybe a cruel irony was taking place in this *very* cell. Perhaps being contained was the one thing that could have saved Lance's life. Maybe their containment dilemma was part of a larger plan that had not yet been revealed to them, or maybe, more likely, it was the sleep before a hangover.

The day was heating up and the cell was starting to feel like a firebox grate. By late afternoon the heat was so sweltering that there was nothing to do but pant like chained yard dogs. The room had a constant soundtrack of country radio ricocheting off of endless steel. A snore, a fart or a snort would erupt from the din now and then. The cicadas in the outside elm trees were screaming a single note, pausing for a response, pausing more, then pursuing their desperate quest all over again. The incessant screech of the insects began to sound like audience applause reacting to the degenerate jailhouse symphony. A pair of vagrant cockroaches slalomed between the bars and wiggled their antennas arrogantly, then sashayed fearlessly between cells. The day ground to a halt in a swampy bog of noise and sweat. Flies buzzed freely, having the distinction of being the only

movement in the steamy room. Finally Bandy
lit a smoke, which prompted Fly Boy and Brewster to light one as well. A misspent shaft of light
sliced through the bars and made the cigarette
smoke into blue ghosts, which slithered about
the room trying to vanish before being drawn
into the dark places between the shadows...

Gene dove through the glass window of a Tijuana
motel room. A volley of bullets followed him as
he scampered down the trash-lined street. He
heard a sharp explosion and jerked his head
rearward in time to see the door blow off of the
motel room and into the patio fountain. He flew
across the side street to the parking lot where
this evening's botched episode had begun only
minutes before. Everything looked larger than
before and the change of light made the whole
set look different. He had not noticed the sput-
tering neon sign of a flying donkey at the entrance to the lot. Seeing his blue rent-a-car
sent a pang of relief through his body. Maybe
he could get out of there without getting shot.
When he opened the door to the car, the limp
body of Flash fell from the door into the parking lot. Gene recoiled in terror at the sight of
the bullet hole in his friend's forehead. He spun
a complete spiral into a clenching kind of horror filled with bleached fear. He could hear running footsteps behind him and he braced hard
as he leaped over Flash and into the car. He
peeled a half-circle from the potholed street and
raced through tears in the general direction of
the border. He parked the car a block from the

crossing. He bought a shot of Southern Comfort at the closest bar, slugged it down and washed the brine off of his face in the rest- room. The face in the mirror startled him—he did not recognize it as his own. There was blood in his hair and he washed it out in the sink. His eyes looked back into the eyes in the mirror, yet he could not be sure who he was looking at. He ordered another shot and downed it and walked out the back door into the neon alley with prostitutes calling after him, then over the bridge, through customs, and back into the United States of America, land of the pursued....

On Saturday afternoon, Maggie and Bob the Turk came to see Earle at the jail, both of them dressed in their finest Sunday clothes. Earle had never seen Bob in anything but work clothes and the sight was downright comical. Maggie laughed as well, which was the exact opposite of how Earle had imagined their reunion would be. He commented through the slot in the glass.

I bet the jailers all figured y'all mistook the jailhouse for the church house.

Bob jumped in.

Your mama's so crazy, she puts on her finest dress and tells me I got to wear a suit! I told her, the only time I'll ever wear a suit is when they stick me in the ground. Even then I'd have

it off by the time they got me covered
up. It's hot in them fluffy ol' caskets.

Earle asked.

But here you are, all dressed up.

Bob explained.

She said she'd buy me a chicken fried
steak at Chandler's.

So you were bribed.

That's the only way, ain't it?

The men laughed again. It was a relief to be able to laugh
in a place like this. At the end of the laugh there
was a pause that lasted a tiny bit too long. Maggie
started to cry. Everyone tightened up a bit.

What have they done to you, poor
baby? Who cut your hair? They can't
do this—they can't do this to my son.

Mama, the trustees are the only ones
they'll let have scissors. There ain't
no barbershop.

What do they feed you? You're so
skinny. Poor baby.

Ain't great, but don't you worry about
it. Chicken fried steak sounds pretty
damn good about now.

Bob cut in.

> When I was in the pokey they threw
> in a hotdog twice a day. Never a
> variation. I's only in for three days,
> though. Seemed like three weeks. Or
> three years.

Maggie cried harder at the mention of the passage of
time. She talked through her tears.

> We're doing everything we can to get
> you out. The lawyer thinks he might,
> thinks he might have got the judge
> talked down. Dad is going to put up
> his house for bail as soon as they
> knock it down to about half. How did
> you let this happen? I know, I know
> you were framed. That Baylock has
> been on you forever. This is his, this
> is his doing. Always coming over,
> coming over and asking how I'm do-
> ing. Stabbing me in the back without
> me even knowing it. Travis thinks
> they sent, they sent Chuck from the
> FBI to live in our house. How could
> they? How *could* they?

Maggie broke down completely and Bob had to hold
her up. He had to say good-bye for the both of
them and practically carry her out of the room.

Time trudged on and each day bled into the next.
Snippets of news would arrive from the outside

world and occasional visits from lawyers would break the dreadful daily routine. Good news seemed to always be followed by bad news and vice versa. It was not possible to have more than one packet of good news without something coming along to nullify it. There was no such thing as progress, as that would imply that the confinees had more than a crumb of control over their situation. When things of a larger nature happened, it was followed by a change in order. Usually this meant someone's trial had come up and they had been transferred to another location, never to be heard from again.

In the middle of the week following the next, one of the days was notable as the entire structure of the block changed without warning. Starting at 9 a.m. a jailer showed up every few minutes with a new request. The first surprise was that someone had made bail for Lance and within seconds he was gone, with nothing but a grumble under his breath of 'it's about damn time.' Within the hour, the trustee informed Strapper that he was to be sent to a different holding tank to await the long haul to Huntsville where he would be for the next ten years. Strapper accepted the news stoically and, while packing his meager belongings, distributed his large collection of rolling papers among his cellmates. No one said a word, out of fear that showing gratitude might be an outward sign of weakness. The next upheaval involved Bandy, who was presented with an unexpected transfer to the Seagoville Unit east of Dallas. This news thrilled him immensely as he squealed with delight and kicked his heels in midair. Someone made bail for Fly Boy and he was gone like old smoke as soon as he got the word. In his sudden good fortune, Fly Boy revealed that he had gotten his name from the way he flitted around when things were going his way. Meanwhile, Jones had complained of stomach pains when he had woken up this morning and the jailer had come to escort him to the infirmary. An hour later another jailer came for his belongings and simply said that Jones would not be back. Most of the day, communication consisted of that which was left unsaid, and it seemed normal that there was rarely an explanation when anything *was* said.

The sudden release of the inmates gave a little relief to the pressure inside the cell. Earle had instinctively kept his distance from these dangerous creatures and had gone out of his way to avoid any personal conversation. Sometimes at night when melancholy set in, some of them did offer brief reflections as tokens to their colleagues at bay. Amazing as it was, after three weeks of living in the same room he knew practically nothing about the men, not even their last names. He *did* know what each man was accused of and that was plenty enough for him. There were only two others that now shared the large cell: Brewster, a total introvert who was prone to seizures; and Jesus, a kind-eyed migrant worker who spoke only Spanish.

The sense of space was short-lived, however, as a new cartel of armed robbers came from out of nowhere. They not only broke the silence, they shattered it into shards. Time, once again, seemed to spiral out where it had been spiraling in.

In the context of confinement, the word 'time' had taken on a new meaning. It was no longer an infinite concept contained in the present nor was it a duration between events. Time had been reduced, cheapened, in fact, to the status of a rain gauge that would either fill or empty depending upon the situation at hand. The gauge could change in a single sentence, and the space with which the speaker surrounded his words could be distorted by his perceived advantage. With the arrival of new inmates, each one's actions had to be observed in detail. Every movement was suspect and each day that passed revealed partial clues. A tiny pause at the end of a sentence might last lifetimes and carry considerably more weight than even the vilest profanity. Less was more. The ones who wielded the most power were the ones who shrewdly appeared to be in control of the ticks of the clock. Their eyes and their actions moved like snakes in slow motion while giving the illusion that they might strike at any moment. When emotions intensified, the static conversation stood ready to explode. Then other would-be leader types would join the incoherent wash until the reverb of the iron hall turned in on itself and became a physical barrier that nothing could penetrate. Every so often some one would hurl an object through the air as a punctuation mark designed to end the conversation in progress. The hurler would then either be pummeled into nullity, or be excommunicated to sulk in his cell until another infantile domination attempt wiped away the memory of the one before.

To pass the time, Earle kept his mind occupied. He thought about the girl whom he had met a few weeks back at Charlie's Alley. He realized he had never met anyone like that before in his life. She seemed to have shafts of energy radiating from her body at all times. He breathed in, hoping that he could beckon the same spirit that was in her to appear inside him now. She had told him that they had met for a reason and that they would see each other from that point on. The way she nonchalantly delivered such an abstract prediction convinced Earle that what he had just heard might have been the largest statement he had ever heard anyone declare. Her carefree confidence made Earle agree without the slightest doubt. Maybe not in the near future, but he felt that, whatever it was, it would someday be revealed.

There was a wildness about her that defied capture, yet teased to be tamed. Even now, in the dungeon of his dreams, he could smell her wild hair and could see it play and roll in the cool night wind. He could see the sparkle of the streetlight in her playful eyes and wished she were here to hear the laugh in her voice. He tried, metaphysically, to move the both of them to another place— on the shores at Buffalo Lake or by the swing set at Mackenzie Park. But, for the time being, they would be separated by their own sutuations.

The harsh environment was beginning to affect Earle's health. His body ached from sleeping on steel straps. His neck felt like it was attached with cold steel pins to the back of his pounding head. His throat stung from the strong tobacco. The jail food made his stomach feel like it was full of nails. He felt his head again but he still didn't recognize that it was his own. He had taken up a strange habit of rubbing his eyebrow with his thumbnail and it was starting to shave a line down through one eyebrow.

His dreams had been infected by his fears and he would wake in the middle of the night on his steel bed and listen for hours for any sign of movement. Three of the gang had an obsession with giving themselves tattoos and would work on them after the lights went out. The aroma of burning Styrofoam would snake around the room, mixed with the smell of Zippo lighters. They would stir the black ashes of the Styrofoam with a few drops of water to make a kind of poison ink which they would punch into their skin with a contraband utensil of some kind. Earle would not dare try to see what was going on, but in not doing so caused the time to drag along, suspended in a vision of purgatory from which he could only imagine an escape.

His imagination had helped him retain his sanity these past few weeks and he had learned how to awaken it at will. Sometimes he could see himself flying from place to place at treetop level and he could do this for hours at a time without tiring. He would fly between trees and through the red dirt canyons at Palo Duro and Ceta. He would fly into Amarillo and dip between houses and see into peoples' fenced back yards.

At other times, music and words would come to him in a flood and he would try to put them together, much like one would put together a puzzle. Each existed in a different time plane. There would always be the frustration of where the music might be a few hundred miles to the east and a thousand feet in the air and in a time frame of two weeks from now. Words seldom had a location but they always had a sense of being in a certain time. To meld the two together took a concentration so difficult as to overpower the reality that waited, inches away. As he felt the movement in the cell die down, he flew higher—beyond the boundaries where clouds are made—and weaved between the golden billows at sunset far from the concerns of the world below. He saw the old Reverend's Oldsmobile floating on a highway below and he felt as if he was not alone any more, and so slipped back to sleep in the transient place he had made for himself....

The next day began—not unlike any one before—with a jarring echo of steel and a blast of Buck Owens singing Together Again. By habit, Earle lined up with the others to go to the common room while the cells were inspected. The daily routine followed through breakfast up until the time the jailer came to deliver goods from the commissary. After he had called out all the names, Earle realized that his order had not come. He stepped forward to get the jailer's attention.

Uh, I think you forgot my order.

Nope. Didn't forget. Your account's

closed. Ain't nothin' in it.

My amigos put another twenty in
there day before yesterday.

Look, fuckhead, it's closed. You might
read it as a good sign if you jus' stop
y'r ass-babblin' and 'hink about it.

Since there had been so many weeks of disappoint-
ing news, the idea of good tidings was not something that could easily inspire optimism in
Earle. Maybe Kyle and Chapman had had good
intentions but had not followed through with
their promise. Any number of things could have
gone wrong and probably had.

Earle went to his corner and pulled out his writing
pad. He read over the pieces he had been writing over the past few weeks and decided the majority of them were not worth keeping. They had
gone downhill with each day of diminished hope.
In the first days of being locked up there was
a defiance in his voice that was full of fire and
courage. He sang to himself the staccato verse.

O Fool Masqueraded,
Seven Times Jaded
Bullrider's Illegitimate Son
Yell down to the devil,
That if he's on the Level
He Better Urge the Dead to Run

Corner the winds
Drink from the Suns

Shout to the Skies
For the dead to come

Let the Dead Wake Up
And Break from Jail
Let the Dead Wake Up
And Make their Bail

O Chickenshit Lawman
Impostor of Straw-man
Don't Squander your Honor for Pay
When Poets dream Rapture
It's not for you to Capture
Their Souls to Lock them Away

A song not Sung
Will cost you your Tongue
Just when you Needed to Vamp
The Blood on your Hands
Is from the Holy Land
From When your Confederates arrested
The Tramp.

But as time wore on his blade began to dull and his
words began to whine. This, obviously, had to go.

As he wadded up the pages he felt someone behind him.
Before he could turn around he was grabbed
around his forehead and he saw a kitchen fork
flash in front of his eyes. He felt a cold sharp-
ness push under his chin and heard the menacing voice of the leader of the newly incarcerated
gang, whispering in his ear.

What'cha writin' there, kingpin. You
bein' keepin' kinda secret, ain't'cha?

I was just readin'....

You wouldn't be writin' no report on
your compadres in crime, would 'ya
now, honcho?

He pressed the fork deeper into Earle's neck. Another
of the men put his face inches away from Earle's
and grabbed his ear and twisted it in a full circle.

We jus' the neighborly type and was
wonderin' what you waddin' up there?
Nothin' 'bout us, I s'pose?

The fork felt like it was going to come up through
his tongue on the inside of his mouth. The pain
poured out his eyes but he couldn't speak. The
sound of jangling keys changed everything in
an instant. The men released Earle and appeared to be intensely interested in something
over by the sink. The fork vanished in a blink,
backhandedly into the desperado's front pocket.
Earle saw the jailer eye the men for a second
but then turn his attention to the piece of paper
in his hand.

Earle. Is they an Earle in here?

Earle jumped up holding his neck. He raised his other hand and spoke.

You damn right there is.

You made bail.

Earle looked at the two men who had just threatened
him.

Did you boys hear that? Now I can
read 'em the novel I been writin' 'bout
you two low lifes...

They scowled threateningly at Earle.

...if I didn't think you could write it better
yourselves. Better, more tragic ending.

He picked up his writings, including the wadded up
ones, and announced that the rest of his belongings would go to Brewster and Jesus. Brewster
stood as Earle walked out and he noticed tears
in his eyes. He spoke the only words Earle had
heard him say since he had been locked up.

Bless you.

Jesus spoke as well, a funny kind of slang.

Que la Madre Maria iluminará para
siempre su viaje...

Earle replied, hoping he understood the meaning.

No hay cárcel que puede contener el
corazón humano...

Jesus smiled and gave the sign of the cross. Earle smiled back. The door clanged shut with such a finality that he knew he would never see this particular group again and wondered if *anyone* would ever hear Brewster's voice again. He turned to tell him goodbye, but he had already retreated to his corner and assumed his cloistered position.

Travis Shamblin, Earle's lawyer, waited in the conference room to greet Earle and tell him about the judge finally agreeing to halve the bail. He also told him his grandfather had offered his house to secure the bail and warned him of the consequences if he decided to run. Earle assured him he was grateful that his family still cared for him and he had no intention of splitting. Travis said the judge was being a hard ass and was shooting for twenty years in Huntsville. Travis added that he was doing all he could but, considering all the publicity that had been given this case, he could not guarantee anything at this point.

He gave Earle a ride to his house and told him he could change clothes and then go meet his family for a nice lunch at Furr's Cafeteria. They were waiting out front when he arrived. Maggie, Mark, Bob the Turk and his grandfather, J.N. Maggie began to cry the minute they arrived but Bob the Turk timed his greeting just right to make everybody laugh.

> You're too late. Ain't nothin' left. We ate 'em outta everything and they had'ta padlock the doors and weld

shut the vents!

As he went through the cafeteria line, Earle's eyes were swimming at all the possibilities and combinations. He decided on baked whitefish, corn, green beans, fried okra, a sourdough roll and a piece of pumpkin pie with whipped cream on top. Travis joined them at a spacious round table, where a lively conversation kept everyone at an even pace. Earle said little, but kept his attention focused on what was said. He prayed no one would ask him about his experiences in jail and his prayers were almost answered until Bob the Turk felt compelled to ask one solitary question.

Well, Earle, did you whip any of thems' sorry asses in that rotten ol' jail house?

Bob's bad timing for his ill-conceived question caused everyone to pretend they did not hear anything. At once everyone's fork went for their least favorite dish as if to drag attention away from the present and into another place. J.N. remarked on how hot it had been and how there seemed to be more grasshoppers than usual this year. Mark said he had one in a jar and that it liked icebox lettuce better than the leaves from their backyard. Bob the Turk said that grasshoppers were little cannibals and ate each other whenever they got the chance. Travis proposed a toast to a wonderful family reunion and everyone nodded their heads, raised their glasses and said, rather awkwardly, 'amen.'

CHAPTER 8

Gene turned down a Houston alley and flipped off his
lights and waited. The inside of his body felt as
if it had been hollowed out, scraped with a sharp
dipper all the way to the boundaries of his skin.
He felt strong winds blowing inside him: hot,
dry winds left over from a long drought. What
was happening to him? He thought about his
mother and wished he was with her back in
Lubbock. She's probably worried sick about her
crazy son. Why did he ever leave? What was he
looking for? Would he ever find it? He probed
this question and he could only go back as far
as that night at the Lubbock airport. Whatever
it was that happened that night had emptied
his very being, yet given him great promise.
Whatever it was would be revealed to him at a
later date, when he was able to handle it. What
concerned him now was trying to make out
the reason he was being followed. They would
surely let him know when it was time for him
to stop running. He closed his eyes and nearly
dozed off to sleep, and when he awoke there
were car headlights coming at him from both
ends of the alley. There was nowhere else to go.
This must be what he was waiting for. He was
ready, his body tensed. Time slowed down to a
crawl. His attention did not. He braced....

To Earle, it felt like years had gone by instead of twenty-four days. There were clues that were obvious. The grass around his home had grown tall and large patches had turned brown from lack of watering. The thistle had long since bloomed and turned spiky, and the deadly nightshade had born its fruit and the fruit had dried and turned black and poison. The grapes had fallen from the vines and been set upon by herds of Japanese beetles. The space between the concrete driveway strips had filled with goat-heads, large as a quarter, with thorns deep enough to ravage a motorcycle tire. To make things worse, the drought and the south wind had conspired to fill the atmosphere with dust, making the daily air dingy and stifling.

Other clues were not so obvious but became so upon contact with the outside world. Whatever friends Earle still had made themselves hard to find. They avoided contact with him as if he were diseased and in quarantine. With each passing day he became more of a recluse, only going out at night to drive his motor scooter around the moonlit cotton fields or to follow the dirt trails under the cottonwoods at the old elephant graveyard.

His lawyer had advised him to look for a job so as to enhance his image when the trial came up. He talked to Chicken Box Jimmy, but Jimmy said Sgt. Baylock had been leaning hard on their poker games and for him to hire Earle would be the opportunity he needed to break them up for good. Across the street, Ringo Tom basically said the same thing. Even Pete at the pool hall told Earle he would attract too much negative attention to his place of business. The newspaper offered a few jobs but they were mostly without substance and promoted notions he could not support. Every day Travis pressured him to take anything he could find and not worry about what it was that he did.

The advertisement looking for Burger Chef 'interns' made it sound as if they were giving away a college education. In reality, they were merely teaching new recruits the world of hamburgers. Earle was hired in a heartbeat, and after a ten-minute training course was put on the assembly line and made a productive member of society.

The boss, Captain Mikey from San Diego, had just retired from the Navy at a ripe old age of 36. He ran the Burger Chef as if it were a nuclear submarine on high alert. He would stand, ridiculously, in the middle of the 'Prep Room' and give a pep talk before every so-called rush hour. He would remind everyone of their duty and, if they were good soldiers, he would dangle the carrot of becoming a 'future manager' in front of their eyes.

The patties of meat and the buns were put on a sprocket grill that moved slowly for about six feet through an open- flame broiler. At the end of that journey they plopped down into a catch tray filled with other patties. The buns followed a similar path on a separate sprocket and slid down a chute onto a stainless steel table right above the meat. Sitting next to the meat tray was a strange electronic machine that, with one press upward, splatted out a perfectly measured portion of mustard and ketchup on the freshly toasted bun in the palm of your hand. The pickle pan was next on the assembly line but was too small and difficult to remove and refill in the heat of the rush hour.

It did not take Earle long to tire of this highly efficient cooking scheme and by the end of the day he had learned everything about being a Burger Chef 'intern'—from the giant electric potato peeler and slicer to freezer management and soft drink canister replacement. By the second day he was promoted to 'assembler.' Within minutes he had his role down pat, everything except dealing with the faulty pickle pan.

During rush hour the pickle pan would be empty within fifteen minutes and he would have to stop assembling, pry out the pan with the quick of his fingernails and go to the 'Prep Room' and refill it from the five-gallon container. Prying out the pan with greasy hands proved impossible, so the extra step of washing his hands was involved in the process. By the time he returned to 'assembly duty' the meat and buns had stacked up to such a point they were overflowing all over the counter and often spilling onto the floor, making it greasy and difficult to stand without slipping. At this point, Capt. Mikey would bustle in, giving orders as if the ship were sinking, while shouting insults that the crew were a bunch of morons who could not bail water fast enough to save a toy rowboat. Earle would stand aside and watch while Capt. Mikey saved the day and then would come back when the rush had slowed a bit.

If it were not for the faulty pickle pan the job would
have been tolerable, but after the same scenario played out day after day Earle began having
the feeling he was stuck in a nightmare-loop
over which he had no control.

One day, during an exceptionally big rush, Earle
found himself at the five-gallon pickle can every
few minutes while the meat and buns stacked
up. Capt. Mikey, as usual, screamed his sinking
ship speech into Earle's ear as he was filling the
pickle pan. Earle pulled one slice of pickle slowly
out of the can between his thumb and forefinger
and, pretending it was a bird, let it fly up to the
ceiling. Capt. Mikey could not believe what he
had just seen and backed into the center of the
room screaming at the top of his lungs. The customers out front were peering into the kitchen
to see what the commotion was all about. The
next time his hand dove into the pickle can,
Earle had a handful which he tossed into the air,
gracefully, like a whole flock of birds. His tempo
accelerated until he was flinging pickles like
they were Mardi Gras beads into every corner,
onto every wall, and even over the rampart that
separated the customers from the kitchen. All of
the employees were dumbstruck, watching this
surreal scene as if it were a dream, with pickles
slowly sliding down every wall in the building.
Some of the customers were actually enjoying
this command performance, laughing as pickles
carelessly flew about the room, and so gave the
kitchen an ovation for the encore.

Earle calmly took off his apron and saluted the Captain, telling him 'Sir, Private Earle, sir, not

reporting for duty, sir.' He then tap-danced out the back door singing Penny Lane in a mock Broadway musical kind of way and walked three miles across town to his uncertain future, probably not as a 'future manager.'

He saw John Silo's DeSoto parked in front of his house. Inside the living room John and Lance sat looking serious and glum. Earle greeted them with a question.

Hey, Lance, haven't seen you without bars all around you in some time. Howdy, John. What's the deal? Somethin' wrong with y'all?

A silence descended that was much too long.

Gene's been killed. They found him shot in Houston.

Earle stumbled backwards, feeling for a chair.

What? Who's *they*?

Po-leece. Looked like a set-up.

God... no....

Nope. It's real all right.

A stunned orb of silence surrounded them. John spoke again.

Guess you heard 'bout Baylock?

Earle took a minute and shook his head, looking down.

Killed Hernando. Thought he was someone else. Captain give him a leave, though. Ironic, ain't it?

The three of them sat speechless, listening to cars go by on Boston Avenue. Then a bus went by, roaring through the gears. The cicadas were screeching in the low afternoon light. Maggie came in from the grocery store and when she heard the news they all cried for several minutes, still in disbelief that someone as vibrant as Gene could be stilled in death. John and Lance excused themselves, saying they had the difficult task of bringing the news to Betty and Bill.

The phone rang and it was Chicken Box Jimmy asking if Earle had heard the news. Earle could hear the tears choking his voice as he told him how much he loved Gene and how, if he could have kept him working at the Chicken Box, he would still be with us. Earle told him that Gene had made his own decisions and for Jimmy not to feel responsible. Jimmy told how Gene made people laugh and how there was not enough laughter in this sad old world. Earle agreed and there came another long silence, this one broken by a click and the dial tone of the telephone.

Earle went to his mother and combed the graying hair at her temples. He told her how Gene always asked about her in California and how he used to come over just to enjoy an afternoon conversation with her. She said she knew that Gene was in trouble and wished she could have done something about it. He told her there was nothing she could have done.

The phone rang again and Earle didn't want to answer it but he did. It was Patricia calling collect from Ohio.

Earle... Earle?

Earle choked back the ball in his throat.

Yeah.

I just wanted you to know that I'm having a baby. They said they'll find it a good home. I'm so sorry about everything. I didn't mean to hurt you. Everything got so screwed up. I've got to go now. I'm not supposed to call anyone. I'll always love you.

Pa... Patricia, wait a minute, wait—!

She was gone. Everything was gone. There was nothing left. He looked down through the grate of the black floor furnace for a long time and saw many dark things deep within the crevasses. He managed to force a different thought upon himself and pulled up his eyes as if they were on a leash.

In the middle room where the air conditioner was, Earle's old Gibson guitar waited for him. He picked it up for the first time in a month, tuned it and strummed a soft A minor chord. The swamp cooler rattled a primitive rhythm as it beat against the wall. Earle tried to find its inner beat. The chords changed with each new cycle and Earle closed his eyes and listened. The guitar found the beginning of the circle and rode it, Earle holding on as long as he could. For a moment it sounded like a wave, building in the distance, then getting closer as the roar increased and shattered. He could see Gene on the shore in Venice, looking out across the ocean into the golden clouds, looking for a place that he never found, a place unburdened by the troubles of this world. The guitar took him away from his own troubles as well, and he played it long into the night and saw a glimpse of a place only visible through music and harmony. The old cooler clacked and clattered while the cicadas screeched in the trees and the west wind scratched the lilac bush up against the window screen in the dusty, wild night.

• • • • • • •

ALSO BY

LETTERSAT3AMPRESS

Slap Noir—James BigBoy Medlin
This Music—Karen Holden

LettersAt3amPress

CPSIA information can be obtained at www.ICGtesting.com
Printed in the USA
BVOW03s0818240914

368150BV00003B/40/P